Delirious praise for *New York Times* bestseller

TERRY PRATCHETT

and

DISCWORLD®

"Any similarity between mad, chaotic Discworld and our own supposedly intelligent planet is purely— and hilariously—intentional."
Baltimore Sun

"Terry Pratchett seems constitutionally unable to write a page without at least a twitch of the grin muscles. . . . [But] the notions Pratchett plays with are nae so narrow or nae so silly as your ordinary British farce. Seriously."
San Diego Union-Tribune

"The preeminent comic fantasist of our time."
Washington Post

"Pratchett is a master storyteller. He is endlessly inventive. . . . He is a master of complex jokes, good bad jokes, good dreadful jokes, and a kind of insidious wisdom about human nature (and other forms of alien nature). . . . I read his books at a gallop and then reread them every time I am ill or exhausted."
A. S. Byatt

"[Pratchett is] always clever, always funny, and always surprisingly timely. . . . His world is more than just an alternate universe—it's a delirious roller-coaster ride that never allows the reader to even consider getting off."
Philadelphia Inquirer

"A top-notch satirist."
Denver Post

"Pratchett's writing is hilarious."
Cleveland Plain Dealer

Terry Pratchett

THE LiGHt FƏNtASTIC

A Novel of Discworld®

HARPER

An Imprint of HarperCollinsPublishers

HARPER

An Imprint of HarperCollins*Publishers*
195 Broadway,
New York, NY 10007.

Copyright © 1986 by Terry Pratchett
Cover illustration by Ben Perrini
Terry Pratchett® and Discworld® are registered trademarks.
ISBN 978-0-06-222568-9

First Harper premium printing: February 2013
First Harper mass market printing: March 2008
First HarperTorch mass market printing: April 2001
First HarperPaperbacks printing: February 2000

HarperCollins ® and Harper ® are registered trademarks of HarperCollins Publishers.

Printed in the United States of America

Visit Harper paperbacks on the World Wide Web at
www.harpercollins.com

10

THE LiGHt FaNtASTIC

The sun rose slowly, as if it wasn't sure it was worth all the effort.

Another Disc day dawned, but very gradually, and this is why.

When light encounters a strong magical field it loses all sense of urgency. It slows right down. And on the Discworld the magic was embarrassingly strong, which meant that the soft yellow light of dawn flowed over the sleeping landscape like the caress of a gentle lover or, as some would have it, like golden syrup. It paused to fill up valleys. It piled up against mountain ranges. When it reached Cori Celesti, the ten-mile spire of gray stone and green ice that marked the hub of the Disc and was the home of its gods, it built up in heaps until it finally crashed in great lazy tsunami as silent as velvet, across the dark landscape beyond.

It was a sight to be seen on no other world.

Of course, no other world was carried through the starry infinity on the backs of four giant elephants, who were themselves perched on the shell of a giant turtle. His name—or Her name, according to another school of thought—was Great A'Tuin; he—or, as it might be, she—will not take a central role in what follows but it is vital to an understanding of the Disc that he—or she—is there, down below the mines and sea ooze and fake fossil bones put there by a Creator with nothing better to do than upset archaeologists and give them silly ideas.

Great A'Tuin the star turtle, shell frosted with frozen methane, pitted with meteor craters, and scoured with asteroidal dust. Great A'Tuin, with eyes like ancient seas and a brain the size of a continent through which thoughts moved like little glittering glaciers. Great A'Tuin of the great slow sad flippers and star-polished carapace, laboring through the galactic night under the weight of the Disc. As large as worlds. As old as Time. As patient as a brick.

Actually, the philosophers have got it all wrong. Great A'Tuin is in fact having a great time.

Great A'Tuin is the only creature in the entire universe that knows exactly where it is going.

Of course, philosophers have debated for years about where Great A'Tuin might be going, and have often said how worried they are that they might never find out.

They're due to find out in about two months. And then they're really going to worry . . .

Something else that has long worried the more imaginative philosophers on the Disc is the question of Great A'Tuin's sex, and quite a lot of time and trouble has been spent in trying to establish it once and for all.

In fact, as the great dark shape drifts past like an endless tortoiseshell hairbrush, the results of the latest effort are just coming into view.

Tumbling past, totally out of control, is the bronze shell of the *Potent Voyager*, a sort of neolithic spaceship built and pushed over the edge by the astronomer-priests of Krull, which is conveniently situated on the very rim of the world and proves, whatever people say, that there is such a thing as a free launch.

Inside the ship is Twoflower, the Disc's first tourist. He had recently spent some months exploring it and is now rapidly leaving it for reasons that are rather complicated but have to do with an attempt to escape from Krull.

This attempt has been one thousand percent successful.

But despite all the evidence that he may be the Disc's last tourist as well, he is enjoying the view.

Plunging along some two miles above him is Rincewind the wizard, in what on the Disc passes for a spacesuit. Picture it as a diving suit designed by men who have never seen the sea. Six months ago he was a perfectly ordinary failed wizard. Then he met Twoflower, was employed at an outrageous salary as his guide, and has spent most of the intervening time being shot at, terrorized, chased and hanging from high places with no hope of salvation or, as is now the case, dropping from high places.

He isn't looking at the view because his past life keeps flashing in front of his eyes and getting in the way. He is learning why it is that when you put on a spacesuit it is vitally important not to forget the helmet.

A lot more could be included now to explain why these two are dropping out of the world, and why Twoflower's Luggage, last seen desperately trying to follow him on hundreds of little legs, is no ordinary suitcase, but such questions take time and could be more trouble than they are worth. For example, it is said that someone at a party once asked the famous philosopher Ly Tin Weedle "Why are you here?" and the reply took three years.

What is far more important is an event happening way overhead, far above A'Tuin, the elephants and the rapidly expiring wizard. The very fabric of time and space is about to be put through the wringer.

The air was greasy with the distinctive feel of magic, and acrid with the smoke of candles made of a black wax whose precise origin a wise man wouldn't inquire about.

There was something very strange about this room deep in the cellars of Unseen University, the Disc's premier college of magic. For one thing it seemed to have too many dimensions, not exactly visible, just hovering out of eyeshot. The walls were covered with occult symbols, and most of the floor was taken up by the Eightfold Seal of Stasis, generally agreed in magical circles to have all the stopping power of a well-aimed halfbrick.

The only furnishing in the room was a lectern of dark wood, carved into the shape of a bird—well, to be frank, into the shape of a winged thing it is probably best not to examine too closely—and on the lectern, fastened to it by a heavy chain covered in padlocks, was a book.

A large, but not particularly impressive, book. Other books in the University's libraries had covers inlaid with rare jewels and fascinating wood, or bound with dragon skin. This one was just a rather tatty leather. It looked the sort of book described in library catalogues as "slightly foxed," although it would be more honest to admit that it looked as though it had been badgered, wolved and possibly beared as well.

Metal clasps held it shut. They weren't decorated, they were just very heavy—like the chain, which didn't so much attach the book to the lectern as tether it.

They looked like the work of someone who had a pretty definite aim in mind, and who had spent most of his life making training harness for elephants.

The air thickened and swirled. The pages of the book began to crinkle in a quite horrible, deliberate way, and blue light spilled out from between them. The silence of the room crowded in like a fist, slowly being clenched.

Half a dozen wizards in their nightshirts were taking turns to peer in through the little grille in the door. No wizard could sleep with this sort of thing going on—the build-up of raw magic was rising through the University like a tide.

"Right," said a voice. "What's going on? And why wasn't I summoned?"

Galder Weatherwax, Supreme Grand Conjuror of the Order of the Silver Star, Lord Imperial of the Sacred Staff, Eighth Level Ipsissimus and 304th Chancellor of Unseen University, wasn't simply an impressive sight even in his red nightshirt with the hand-embroidered mystic runes, even in his long cap with the bobble on, even with the Wee Willie Winkie candlestick in his hand. He even managed to very nearly pull it off in fluffy pompom slippers as well.

Six frightened faces turned toward him.

"Um, you were summoned, lord," said one of the underwizards.

"That's why you're here," he added helpfully.

"I mean why wasn't I summoned *before*?" snapped Galder, pushing his way to the grille.

"Um, before who, lord?" said the wizard.

Galder glared at him, and ventured a quick glance through the grille.

The air in the room was now sparkling with tiny flashes as dust motes incinerated in the flow of raw magic. The Seal of Stasis was beginning to blister and curl up at the edges.

The book in question was called the Octavo and, quite obviously, it was no ordinary book.

There are of course many famous books of magic. Some may talk of the Necrotelicomnicon, with its pages made of ancient lizard skin; some may point to the Book of Going Forth Around Elevenish, written by a mysterious and rather lazy Llamaic sect; some may recall that the Bumper Fun Grimoire reputedly contains the one original joke left in the universe. But they are all mere pamphlets when compared with the Octavo, which the Creator of the Universe reputedly left behind—with characteristic absentmindedness—shortly after completing his major work.

The eight spells imprisoned in its pages led a secret and complex life of their own, and it was generally believed that—

Galder's brow furrowed as he stared into the troubled room. Of course, there were only seven spells now. Some young idiot of a student wizard had stolen a look at the book one day and one of the spells had escaped and lodged in his mind. No one had ever managed to get to the bottom of how it had happened. What was his name, now? Winswand?

Octarine and purple sparks glittered on the spine of the book. A thin curl of smoke was beginning to rise from the lectern, and the heavy metal clasps that held the book shut were definitely beginning to look strained.

"Why are the spells so restless?" said one of the younger wizards.

Galder shrugged. He couldn't show it, of course, but he was beginning to be really worried. As a skilled eighth-level wizard he could see the half-imaginary shapes that appeared momentarily in the vibrating air, wheedling and beckoning. In much the same way that gnats appear before a thunderstorm, really heavy build-ups of magic always attracted things from the chaotic Dungeon Dimensions—nasty Things, all misplaced organs and spittle, forever searching for any gap through which they might sidle into the world of men.*

This had to be stopped.

"I shall need a volunteer," he said firmly.

There was a sudden silence. The only sound came from behind the door. It was the nasty little noise of metal parting under stress.

"Very well, then," he said. "In that case I shall need some silver tweezers, about two pints of cat's blood, a small whip and a chair—"

It is said that the opposite of noise is silence. This isn't true. Silence is only the absence of noise. Silence would have been a terrible din compared to the sudden soft implosion of noiselessness that hit the wizards with the force of an exploding dandelion clock.

A thick column of spitting light sprang up from the book, hit the ceiling in a splash of flame, and disappeared.

Galder stared up at the hole, ignoring the smoldering patches in his beard. He pointed dramatically.

"To the upper cellars!" he cried, and bounded up the stone stairs. Slippers flapping and nightshirts billowing the other wizards followed him, falling over one another in their eagerness to be last.

Nevertheless, they were all in time to see the fireball of occult potentiality disappear into the ceiling of the room above.

---

* They won't be described, since even the pretty ones looked like the offspring of an octopus and a bicycle. It is well known that things from undesirable universes are always seeking an entrance into this one, which is the psychic equivalent of handy for the buses and closer to the shops.

"Urgh," said the youngest wizard, and pointed to the floor.

The room had been part of the library until the magic had drifted through, violently reassembling the possibility particles of everything in its path. So it was reasonable to assume that the small purple newts had been part of the floor and the pineapple custard may once have been some books. And several of the wizards later swore that the small sad orangutan sitting in the middle of it all looked very much like the head librarian.

Galder stared upward. "To the kitchen!" he bellowed, wading through the custard to the next flight of stairs.

No one ever found out what the great cast-iron cooking range had been turned into, because it had broken down a wall and made good its escape before the disheveled party of wild-eyed mages burst into the room. The vegetable chef was found much later hiding in the soup cauldron, gibbering unhelpful things like "The knuckles! The horrible knuckles!"

The last wisps of magic, now somewhat slowed, were disappearing into the ceiling.

"To the Great Hall!"

The stairs were much wider here, and better lit. Panting and pineapple-flavored, the fitter wizards got to the top by the time the fireball had reached the middle of the huge drafty chamber that was the University's main hall. It hung motionless, except for the occasional small prominence that arched and spluttered across its surface.

Wizards smoke, as everyone knows. That probably explained the chorus of coffin coughs and sawtooth wheezes that erupted behind Galder as he stood appraising the situation and wondering if he dare look for somewhere to hide. He grabbed a frightened student.

"Get me seers, farseers, scryers and withinlookmen!" he barked. "I want this studied!"

Something was taking shape inside the fireball. Galder shielded his eyes and peered at the shape forming in front of him. There was no mistaking it. It was the universe.

He was quite sure of this, because he had a model of it in his study and it was generally agreed to be far more impressive than the real thing. Faced with the possibilities offered by seed pearls and silver filigree, the Creator had been at a complete loss.

But the tiny universe inside the fireball was uncannily—well, real. The only thing missing was color. It was all in translucent misty white.

There was Great A'Tuin, and the four elephants, and the Disc itself. From this angle Galder couldn't see the surface very well, but he knew with cold certainty that it would be absolutely accurately modeled. He could, though, just make out a miniature replica of Cori Celesti, upon whose utter peak the world's quarrelsome and somewhat bourgeois gods lived in a palace of marble, alabaster and uncut moquette three-piece suites they had chosen to call Dunmanifestin. It was always a considerable annoyance to any Disc citizen with pretensions to culture that they were ruled by gods whose idea of an uplifting artistic experience was a musical doorbell.

The little embryo universe began to move slowly, tilting . . .

Galder tried to shout, but his voice refused to come out.

Gently, but with the unstoppable force of an explosion, the shape expanded.

He watched in horror, and then in astonishment, as it passed through him as lightly as a thought. He held out a hand and watched the pale ghosts of rock strata stream through his fingers in busy silence.

Great A'Tuin had already sunk peacefully below floor level, larger than a house.

The wizards behind Galder were waist deep in seas. A boat smaller than a thimble caught Galder's eye for a moment before the rush carried it through the walls and away.

"To the roof!" he managed, pointing a shaking finger skyward.

Those wizards with enough marbles left to think with and enough breath to run followed him, running through continents that sleeted smoothly through the solid stone.

It was a still night, tinted with the promise of dawn. A crescent moon was just setting. Ankh-Morpork, largest city in the lands around the Circle Sea, slept.

That statement is not really true.

On the one hand, those parts of the city which normally concerned themselves with, for example, selling vegetables, shoeing horses, carving exquisite small jade ornaments, changing money and making tables, on the whole, slept. Unless they had insomnia. Or had got up in the night, as it might be, to go to the lavatory. On the other hand, many of the less law-abiding citizens were wide awake and, for instance, climbing through windows that didn't belong to them, slitting throats, mugging one another, listening to loud music in smoky cellars and generally having a lot more fun. But most of the animals were asleep, except for the rats. And the bats, too, of course. As far as the insects were concerned . . .

The point is that descriptive writing is very rarely entirely accurate and during the reign of Olaf Quimby II as Patrician of Ankh some legislation was passed in a determined attempt to put a stop to this sort of thing and introduce some honesty into reporting. Thus, if a legend said of a notable hero that "all men spoke of his prowess" any bard who valued his life would add hastily "except for a couple of people in his home village who thought he was a liar, and quite a lot of other people who had never really heard of him." Poetic simile was strictly limited to statements like "his mighty steed was as fleet as the wind on a fairly calm day, say about Force Three," and any loose talk about a beloved having a face that launched a thousand ships would have to be backed by evidence that the object of desire did indeed look like a bottle of champagne.

Quimby was eventually killed by a disgruntled poet during an experiment conducted in the palace grounds to prove the disputed accuracy of the proverb "The pen is mightier than the sword," and in his memory it was amended to include the phrase "only if the sword is very small and the pen is very sharp."

So. Approximately sixty-seven, maybe sixty-eight percent, of the city slept. Not that the other citizens creeping about on their generally unlawful occasions noticed the pale tide streaming through the streets. Only the wizards, used to seeing the invisible, watched it foam across the distant fields.

The Disc, being flat, has no real horizon. Any adventurous sailors who got funny ideas from staring at eggs and oranges for too long and set out for the antipodes soon learned that the reason why distant ships sometimes looked as though they were disappearing over the edge of the world was that they *were* disappearing over the edge of the world.

But there was still a limit even to Galder's vision in the mist-swirled, dust-filled air. He looked up. Looming high over the University was the grim and ancient Tower of Art, said to be the oldest building on the Disc, with its famous spiral staircase of eight thousand, eight hundred and eighty-eight steps. From its crenellated roof, the haunt of ravens and disconcertingly alert gargoyles, a wizard might see to the very edge of the Disc. After spending ten minutes or so coughing horribly, of course.

"Sod that," he muttered. "What's the good of being a wizard, after all? Avyento, thessalous! I would fly! To me, spirits of air and darkness!"

He spread a gnarled hand and pointed to a piece of crumbling parapet. Octarine fire sprouted from under his nicotine-stained nails and burst against the rotting stone far above.

It fell. By a finely calculated exchange of velocities Galder rose, nightshirt flapping around his bony legs. Higher and higher he soared, hurtling through the pale light like a, like a—all right, like an elderly but powerful wizard being propelled upward by an expertly judged thumb on the scales of the universe.

He landed in a litter of old nests, caught his balance, and stared down at the vertiginous view of a Disc dawn.

At this time of the long year the Circle Sea was almost on the sunset side of Cori Celesti, and as the daylight sloshed down into the lands around Ankh-Morpork the shadow of the mountain scythed across the landscape like the gnomon of God's sundial. But nightward, racing the slow light toward the edge of the world, a line of white mist surged on.

There was a crackling of dry twigs behind him. He turned to see Ymper Trymon, second in command of the Order, who had been the only other wizard able to keep up.

Galder ignored him for the moment, taking care only to keep a firm grip on the stonework and strengthen his personal spells of protection. Promotion was slow in a profession that traditionally bestowed long life, and it was accepted that younger wizards would frequently seek advancement via dead men's curly shoes, having previously emptied them of their occupants. Besides, there was something disquieting about young Trymon. He didn't smoke, only drank boiled water, and Galder had the nasty suspicion that he was clever. He didn't smile often enough, and he liked figures and the sort of organization charts that show lots of squares with arrows pointing to other squares. In short, he was the sort of man who could use the word "personnel" and mean it.

The whole of the visible Disc was now covered with a shimmering white skin that fitted it perfectly.

Galder looked down at his own hands and saw them covered with a pale network of shining threads that followed every movement.

He recognized this kind of spell. He'd used them himself. But his had been smaller—much smaller.

"It's a Change spell," said Trymon. "The whole world is being changed."

Some people, thought Galder grimly, would have had the decency to put an exclamation mark on the end of a statement like that.

There was the faintest of pure sounds, high and sharp, like the breaking of a mouse's heart.

"What was that?" he said.

Trymon cocked his head.

"C-sharp, I think," he said.

Galder said nothing. The white shimmer had vanished, and the first sounds of the waking city began to filter up to the two wizards. Everything seemed exactly the same as it had before. All that, just to make things stay the same?

He patted his nightshirt pockets distractedly and finally found what he was looking for lodged behind his ear. He put the soggy dogend in his mouth, called up mystical fire from between his fingers, and dragged hard on the wretched rollup until little blue lights flashed in front of his eyes. He coughed once or twice.

He was thinking very hard indeed.

He was trying to remember if any gods owed him any favors.

In fact the Gods were as puzzled by all this as the wizards were, but they were powerless to do anything and in any case were engaged in an eons-old battle with the Ice Giants, who had refused to return the lawnmower.

But some clue as to what actually had happened might be found in the fact that Rincewind, whose past life had just got up to a quite interesting bit when he was fifteen, suddenly found himself not dying after all but hanging upside down in a pine tree.

He got down easily by dropping uncontrollably from branch to branch until he landed on his head in a pile of pine needles, where he lay gasping for breath and wishing he'd been a better person.

Somewhere, he knew, there had to be a perfectly logical connection. One minute one happens to be dying, having dropped off the rim of the world, and the next one is upside down in a tree.

As always happened at times like this, the Spell rose up in his mind.

Rincewind had been generally reckoned by his tutors to be a natural wizard in the same way that fish are natural mountaineers. He probably would have been thrown out of Unseen University anyway—he couldn't remember spells and smoking made him feel ill—but what had really caused trouble was all that stupid business about sneaking into the room where the Octavo was chained and opening it.

And what made the trouble even *worse* was that no one could figure out why all the locks had temporarily become unlocked.

The spell wasn't a demanding lodger. It just sat there like an old toad at the bottom of a pond. But whenever Rincewind was feeling really tired or very afraid it tried to get itself said. No one knew what would happen if one of the Eight Great Spells was said by itself, but the general agreement was that the best place from which to watch the effects would be the next universe.

It was a weird thought to have, lying on a heap of pine needles after just falling off the edge of the world, but Rincewind had a feeling that the spell wanted to keep him alive.

"Suits me," he thought.

He sat up and looked at the trees. Rincewind was a city wizard and, although he was aware that there were various differences among types of tree by which their nearest and dearest could tell them apart, the only thing he knew for certain was that the end without the leaves on fitted into the ground. There were far too many of them, arranged with absolutely no sense of order. The place hadn't been swept for ages.

He remembered something about being able to tell where you were by looking at which side of a tree the moss grew on. These trees had moss everywhere, and wooden warts, and scrabbly old branches; if trees were people, these trees would be sitting in rocking chairs.

Rincewind gave the nearest one a kick. With unerring aim it dropped an acorn on him. He said "Ow." The tree, in a voice like a very old door swinging open, said, "Serves you right."

There was a long silence.

Then Rincewind said, "Did you say that?"

"Yes."

"And that too?"

"Yes."

"Oh." He thought for a bit. Then he tried, "I suppose you wouldn't happen to know the way out of the forest, possibly, by any chance?"

"No. I don't get about much," said the tree.

"Fairly boring life, I imagine," said Rincewind.

"I wouldn't know. I've never been anything else," said the tree.

Rincewind looked at it closely. It seemed pretty much like every other tree he'd seen.

"Are you magical?" he said.

"No one's ever said," said the tree, "I suppose so."

Rincewind thought: I can't be talking to a tree. If I was talking to a tree I'd be mad, and I'm not mad, so trees can't talk.

"Goodbye," he said firmly.

"Hey, don't go," the tree began, and then realized the hopelessness of it all. It watched him stagger off through the bushes, and settled down to feeling the sun on its leaves, the slurp and gurgle of the water in its roots, and the very ebb and flow of its sap in response to the natural tug of the sun and moon. Boring, it thought. What a strange thing to say. Trees can be bored, of course, beetles do it all the time, but I don't think that was what he was trying to mean. And: can you actually be anything else?

In fact Rincewind never spoke to this particular tree again, but from that brief conversation it spun the basis of the first tree religion which, in time, swept the forests of the world. Its tenet of faith was this: a tree that was a good tree, and led a clean, decent and upstanding life, could be assured of a future life after death. If it was very good indeed it would eventually be reincarnated as five thousand rolls of lavatory paper.

A few miles away Twoflower was also getting over his surprise at finding himself back on the Disc. He was sitting on the hull of the *Potent Voyager* as it gurgled gradually under the dark waters of a large lake, surrounded by trees.

Strangely enough, he was not particularly worried. Twoflower was a tourist, the first of the species to evolve on the Disc, and fundamental to his very existence was the rock-hard belief that nothing bad could really happen to him because he was *not involved*; he also believed that anyone could understand anything he said provided he spoke loudly and slowly, that people were basically trustworthy, and that anything could be sorted out among men of goodwill if they just acted sensibly.

On the face of it this gave him a survival value

marginally less than, say, a soap herring, but to Rincewind's amazement it all seemed to work and the little man's total obliviousness to all forms of danger somehow made danger so discouraged that it gave up and went away.

Merely being faced with drowning stood no chance. Twoflower was quite certain that in a well-organized society people would not be allowed to go around getting drowned.

He was a little bothered, though, about where his Luggage had got to. But he comforted himself with the knowledge that it was made of sapient pear-wood, and ought to be intelligent enough to look after itself . . .

In yet another part of the forest a young shaman was undergoing a very essential part of his training. He had eaten of the sacred toadstool, he had smoked the holy rhizome, he had carefully powdered up and inserted into various orifices the mystic mushroom and now, sitting cross-legged under a pine tree, he was concentrating firstly on making contact with the strange and wonderful secrets at the heart of Being but mainly on stopping the top of his head from unscrewing and floating away.

Blue four-sided triangles pinwheeled across his vision. Occasionally he smiled knowingly at nothing very much and said things like "Wow" and "Urgh."

There was a movement in the air and what he later described as "like, a sort of explosion only backward, you know?," and suddenly where there had only been nothing there was a large, battered, wooden chest.

It landed heavily on the leafmold, extended dozens of little legs, and turned around ponderously to look at the shaman. That is to say, it had no face, but even through the mycological haze he was horribly aware that it was looking at him. And not a nice look, either. It was amazing how baleful a keyhole and a couple of knotholes could be.

To his intense relief it gave a sort of wooden shrug, and set off through the trees at a canter.

With superhuman effort the shaman recalled the correct sequence of movements for standing up and even managed a couple of steps before he looked down and gave up, having run out of legs.

Rincewind, meanwhile, had found a path. It wound about a good deal, and he would have been happier if it had been cobbled, but following it gave him something to do.

Several trees tried to strike up a conversation, but Rincewind was nearly certain that this was not normal behavior for trees and ignored them.

The day lengthened. There was no sound but the murmur of nasty little stinging insects, the occasional crack of a falling branch, and the whispering of the trees discussing religion and the trouble with squirrels. Rincewind began to feel very lonely. He imagined himself living in the woods forever, sleeping on leaves and eating . . . and eating . . . whatever there was to eat in woods. Trees, he supposed, and nuts and berries. He would have to . . .

"Rincewind!"

There, coming up the path, was Twoflower—dripping wet, but beaming with delight. The Luggage trotted along behind him (anything made of the wood would follow its owner anywhere and it was often used to make luggage for the grave goods of very rich dead kings who wanted to be sure of starting a new life in the next world with clean underwear).

Rincewind sighed. Up to now, he'd thought the day couldn't possibly get worse.

It began to rain a particularly wet and cold rain. Rincewind and Twoflower sat under a tree and watched it.

"Rincewind?"

"Um?"

"Why are we here?"

"Well, some say that the Creator of the Universe made the Disc and everything on it, others say that its all a very complicated story involving the testicles of the Sky God and the milk of the Celestial Cow, and some even hold that we're all just due to the total random accretion of probability particles. But if you mean why are we here as opposed to falling off the Disc, I haven't the faintest idea. It's probably all some ghastly mistake."

"Oh. Do you think there's anything to eat in this forest?"

"Yes," said the wizard bitterly, "us."

"I've got some acorns, if you like," said the tree helpfully.

They sat in damp silence for some moments.

"Rincewind, the tree said—"

"Trees can't talk," snapped Rincewind. "It's very important to remember that."

"But you just heard—"

Rincewind sighed. "Look," he said. "It's all down to simple biology, isn't it? If you're going to talk you need the right equipment, like lungs and lips and, and—"

"Vocal cords," said the tree.

"Yeah, them," said Rincewind. He shut up and stared gloomily at the rain.

"*I* thought wizards knew all about trees and wild food and things," said Twoflower reproachfully. It was very seldom that anything in his voice suggested that he thought of Rincewind as anything other than a magnificent enchanter, and the wizard was stung into action.

"I do, I do," he snapped.

"Well, what kind of tree is this?" said the tourist. Rincewind looked up.

"Beech," he said firmly.

"Actually—" began the tree, and shut up quickly. It had caught Rincewind's look.

"Those things up there look like acorns," said Twoflower.

"Yes, well, this is the sessile or heptocarpic variety," said Rincewind. "The nuts look very much like acorns, in fact. They can fool practically anybody."

"Gosh," said Twoflower, and, "What's that bush over there, then?"

"Mistletoe."

"But it's got thorns and red berries!"

"Well?" said Rincewind sternly, and stared hard at him. Twoflower broke first.

"Nothing," he said meekly. "I must have been misinformed."

"Right."

"But there's some big mushrooms under it. Can you eat them?"

Rincewind looked at them cautiously. They were, indeed, very big, and had red and white spotted caps. They were in fact a variety that the local shaman (who at this point was some miles away, making friends with a rock) would only eat after first attaching one leg to a large stone with a rope. There was nothing for it but to go out in the rain and look at them.

He knelt down in the leafmold and peered under the cap. After a while he said weakly, "No, no good to eat at all."

"Why?" called Twoflower. "Are the gills the wrong shade of yellow?"

"No, not really . . ."

"I expect the stems haven't got the right kind of fluting, then."

"They look okay, actually."

"The cap, then, I expect the cap is the wrong color," said Twoflower.

"Not sure about that."

"Well then, why can't you eat them?"

Rincewind coughed. "It's the little doors and windows," he said wretchedly, "it's a dead giveaway." Thunder rolled across Unseen University.

Rain poured over its roofs and gurgled out of its gargoyles, although one or two of the more cunning ones had scuttled off to shelter among the maze of tiles.

Far below, in the Great Hall, the eight most powerful wizards on the Discworld gathered at the angles of a ceremonial octogram. Actually they probably weren't the most powerful, if the truth were known, but they certainly had great powers of survival which, in the highly competitive world of magic, was pretty much the same thing. Behind every wizard of the eighth rank were half a dozen seventh rank wizards trying to bump him off, and senior wizards had to develop an inquiring attitude to, for example, scorpions in their bed. An ancient proverb summed it up: When a wizard is tired of looking for broken glass in his dinner, it ran, he is tired of life.

The oldest wizard, Greyhald Spold of the Ancient and Truly Original Sages of the Unbroken Circle, leaned heavily on his carven staff and spake thusly:

"Get on with it, Weatherwax, my feet are giving me gyp."

Galder, who had merely paused for effect, glared at him.

"Very well, then, I will be brief—"

"Jolly good."

"We all sought guidance as to the events of this morning. Can anyone among us say he received it?"

The wizards looked sidelong at one another. Nowhere outside a trades union conference fraternal benefit night can so much mutual distrust and suspicion be found as among a gathering of senior enchanters. But the plain fact was that the day had gone very badly. Normally informative demons, summoned abruptly from the Dungeon Dimensions, had looked sheepish and sidled away when questioned. Magic mirrors had cracked. Tarot cards had mysteriously become blank. Crystal balls had gone all cloudy. Even tea leaves, normally scorned by wizards as frivolous and unworthy of contemplation, had clustered together at the bottom of cups and refused to move.

In short, the assembled wizards were at a loss. There was a general murmur of agreement.

"And therefore I propose that we perform the Rite of AshkEnte," said Galder dramatically.

He had to admit that he had hoped for a better response, something on the lines of, well, "No, not the Rite of AshkEnte! Man was not meant to meddle with such things!"

In fact there was a general mutter of approval.

"Good idea."

"Seems reasonable."

"Get on with it, then."

Slightly put out, he summoned a procession of lesser wizards who carried various magical implements into the hall.

It has already been hinted that around this time there was some disagreement among the fraternity of wizards about how to practice magic.

Younger wizards in particular went about saying that it was time that magic started to update its image and that they should all stop mucking about with bits of wax and bone and put the whole thing on a properly organized basis, with research programs and three-day conventions in good hotels where they could read papers with titles like "Whither Geomancy?" and "The Role of Seven-League Boots in a Caring Society."

Trymon, for example, hardly ever did any magic these days but ran the Order with hourglass efficiency and wrote lots of memos and had a big chart on his office wall, covered with colored blobs and flags and lines that no one else really understood but which looked very impressive.

The other type of wizard thought all this was so much marsh gas and wouldn't have anything to do with an image unless it was made of wax and had pins stuck in it.

The heads of the eight orders were all of this persuasion, traditionalists to a mage, and the utensils that were heaped around the octogram had a definite, no-nonsense occult look about them. Rams horns, skulls, baroque metalwork and heavy candles were much in evidence, despite the discovery by younger wizards that the Rite of AshkEnte could perfectly well be performed with three small bits of wood and 4 cc of mouse blood.

The preparations normally took several hours, but the combined powers of the senior wizards shortened it considerably and, after a mere forty minutes, Galder chanted the final words of the spell. They hung in front of him for a moment before dissolving.

The air in the center of the octogram shimmered and thickened, and suddenly contained a tall, dark figure. Most of it was hidden by a black robe and hood and this was probably just as well. It held a long scythe in one hand and one couldn't help noticing that what should have been fingers were simply white bone.

The other skeletal hand held small cubes of cheese and pineapple on a stick.

"WELL?" said Death, in a voice with all the warmth and color of an iceberg. He caught the wizards' gaze, and glanced down at the stick.

I WAS AT A PARTY, he added, a shade reproachfully.

"O Creature of Earth and Darkness, we do charge thee to abjure from—" began Galder in a firm, commanding voice. Death nodded.

YES, YES, I KNOW ALL THAT, he said. WHY HAVE YOU SUMMONED ME?

"It is said that you can see both the past and future," said Galder a little sulkily, because the big speech of binding and conjuration was one he rather liked and people had said he was very good at it.

THAT IS ABSOLUTELY CORRECT.

"Then perhaps you can tell us what exactly it was that happened this morning?" said Galder. He pulled himself together, and added loudly, "I command this by Azimrothe, by T'chikel, by—"

ALL RIGHT, YOU'VE MADE YOUR POINT, said Death. WHAT PRECISELY WAS IT YOU WISHED TO KNOW? QUITE A LOT OF THINGS HAPPENED THIS MORNING, PEOPLE WERE BORN, PEOPLE DIED, ALL THE TREES

GREW A BIT TALLER, RIPPLES MADE INTERESTING PATTERNS ON THE SEA—

"I mean about the Octavo," said Galder coldly.

THAT? OH, THAT WAS JUST A READJUSTMENT OF REALITY. I UNDERSTAND THE OCTAVO WAS ANXIOUS NOT TO LOSE THE EIGHTH SPELL. IT WAS DROPPING OFF THE DISC, APPARENTLY.

"Hold on, hold on," said Galder. He scratched his chin. "Are we talking about the one inside the head of Rincewind? Tall thin man, bit scraggy? The one—"

—THAT HE HAS BEEN CARRYING AROUND ALL THESE YEARS, YES.

Galder frowned. It seemed a lot of trouble to go to. Everyone knew that when a wizard died all the spells in his head would go free, so why bother to save Rincewind? The spell would just float back eventually.

"Any idea why?" he said without thinking and then, remembering himself in time, added hastily, "By Yrriph and Kcharla I do abjure thee and—"

I WISH YOU WOULDN'T KEEP DOING THAT, said Death, ALL THAT I KNOW IS THAT ALL THE SPELLS HAVE TO BE SAID TOGETHER NEXT HOGSWATCH-NIGHT OR THE DISC WILL BE DESTROYED.

"Speak up there!" demanded Greyhald Spold.

"Shut up!" said Galder.

ME?

"No, him. Daft old—"

"I heard that!" snapped Spold, "You young people—" He stopped. Death was looking at him thoughtfully, as if he was trying to remember his face.

"Look," said Galder, "just repeat that bit again, will you? The Disc will be what?"

DESTROYED, said Death. CAN I GO NOW? I LEFT MY DRINK.

"Hang on," said Galder hurriedly. "By Cheliliki and Orizone and so forth, what do you mean, destroyed?"

IT'S AN ANCIENT PROPHECY WRITTEN ON THE INNER WALLS OF THE GREAT PYRAMID OF TSORT. THE WORD "DESTROYED" SEEMS QUITE SELF-EXPLANATORY TO ME.

"That's all you can tell us?"

YES.

"But Hogswatchnight is only two months away!"

YES.

"At least you can tell us where Rincewind is now!"

Death shrugged. It was a gesture he was particularly well built for.

THE FOREST OF SKUND, RIMWARD OF THE RAMTOP MOUNTAINS.

"What is he doing there?"

FEELING VERY SORRY FOR HIMSELF.

"Oh."

NOW MAY I GO?

Galder nodded distractedly. He had been thinking wistfully of the banishment ritual, which started "Begone, foul shade" and had some rather impressive passages which he had been practicing, but somehow he couldn't work up any enthusiasm.

"Oh, yes," he said. "Thank you, yes." And then, because it's as well not to make enemies even among the creatures of night, he added politely, "I hope it is a good party."

Death didn't answer. He was looking at Spold in the same way that a dog looks at a bone, only in this case things were more or less the other way around.

"I said I hope it is a good party," said Galder, loudly.

AT THE MOMENT IT IS, said Death levelly. I THINK IT MIGHT GO DOWNHILL VERY QUICKLY AT MIDNIGHT.

"Why?"

THAT'S WHEN THEY THINK I'LL BE TAKING MY MASK OFF.

He vanished, leaving only a cocktail stick and a short paper streamer behind.

There had been an unseen observer of all this. It was of course entirely against the rules, but Trymon knew all about rules and had always considered they were for making, not obeying.

Long before the eight mages had got down to some serious arguing about what the apparition had meant he was down in the main levels of the University library.

It was an awe-inspiring place. Many of the books were magical, and the important thing to remember about grimoires is that they are deadly in the hands of any librarian who cares about order, because he's bound to stick them all on the same shelf. This is not a good idea with books that tend to leak

magic, because more than one or two of them together form a critical Black Mass. On top of that,
many of the lesser spells are quite particular about
the company they keep, and tend to express any
objections by hurling their books viciously across
the room. And, of course, there is always the half-
felt presence of the Things from the Dungeon Dimensions, clustering around the magical leakage
and constantly probing the walls of reality.

The job of magical librarian, who has to spend
his working days in this sort of highly charged atmosphere, is a high-risk occupation.

The Head Librarian was sitting on top of his
desk, quietly peeling an orange, and was well aware
of that.

He glanced up when Trymon entered.

"I'm looking for anything we've got on the Pyramid of Tshut," said Trymon. He had come prepared: he took a banana out of his pocket.

The librarian looked at it mournfully, and then
flopped down heavily on the floor. Trymon found a
soft hand poked gently into his and the librarian led
the way, waddling sadly between the bookshelves.
It was like holding a little leather glove.

Around them the books sizzled and sparked, with
the occasional discharge of undirected magic flashing over to the carefully placed earthing rods nailed
to the shelves. There was a tinny, blue smell and,
just at the very limit of hearing, the horrible chittering of the dungeon creatures.

Like many other parts of Unseen University the
library occupied rather more space than its outside

dimensions would suggest, because magic distorts space in strange ways, and it was probably the only library in the universe with Mobius shelves. But the librarian's mental catalogue was ticking over perfectly. He stopped by a soaring stack of musty books and swung himself up into the darkness. There was the sound of rustling paper, and a cloud of dust floated down to Trymon. Then the librarian was back, a slim volume in his hands.

"Oook," he said.

Trymon took it gingerly.

The cover was scratched and very dog-eared, the gold of its lettering had long ago curled off, but he could just make out, in the old magic tongue of the Tsort Valley, the words: *lyt Gryet Teymple hyte Tsort, Y Hiystory Myistical.*

"Oook?" said the librarian, anxiously.

Trymon turned the pages cautiously. He wasn't very good at languages, he'd always found them highly inefficient things which by rights ought to be replaced by some sort of easily understood numerical system, but this seemed exactly what he was looking for. There were whole pages covered with meaningful hieroglyphs.

"Is this the only book you've got about the Pyramid of Tsort?" he said slowly.

"Oook."

"You're quite sure?"

"Oook."

Trymon listened. He could hear, a long way off, the sound of approaching feet and arguing voices. But he had been prepared for that, too.

He reached into a pocket.

"Would you like another banana?" he said.

The Forest of Skund was indeed enchanted, which was nothing unusual on the Disc, and was also the only forest in the whole universe to be called—in the local language—Your Finger You Fool, which was the literal meaning of the word Skund.

The reason for this is regrettably all too common. When the first explorers from the warm lands around the Circle Sea traveled into the chilly hinterland they filled in the blank spaces on their maps by grabbing the nearest native, pointing at some distant landmark, speaking very clearly in a loud voice, and writing down whatever the bemused man told them. Thus were immortalized in generations of atlases such geographical oddities as Just a Mountain, I Don't Know, What? and, of course, Your Finger You Fool.

Rainclouds clustered around the bald heights of Mt. Oolskunrahod ("Who Is This Fool Who Does Not Know What a Mountain Is") and the Luggage settled itself more comfortably under a dripping tree, which tried unsuccessfully to strike up a conversation.

Twoflower and Rincewind were arguing. The person they were arguing about sat on his mushroom and watched them with interest. He looked like someone who smelled like someone who lived in a mushroom, and that bothered Twoflower.

"Well, why hasn't he got a red hat?"

Rincewind hesitated, desperately trying to imagine what Twoflower was getting at.

"What?" he said, giving in.

"He should have a red hat," said Twoflower. "And he certainly ought to be cleaner and more, more sort of jolly. He doesn't look like any sort of gnome to me."

"What are you going on about?"

"Look at that beard," said Twoflower sternly. "I've seen better beards on a piece of cheese."

"Look, he's six inches high and lives in a mushroom," snarled Rincewind. "Of course he's a bloody gnome."

"We've only got his word for it."

Rincewind looked down at the gnome.

"Excuse me," he said. He took Twoflower to the other side of the clearing.

"Listen," he said between his teeth. "If he was fifteen feet tall and said he was a giant we'd only have his word for that too, wouldn't we?"

"He could be a goblin," said Twoflower defiantly.

Rincewind looked back at the tiny figure, which was industriously picking its nose.

"Well?" he said. "So what? Gnome, goblin, pixie—so what?"

"Not a pixie," said Twoflower firmly. "Pixies, they wear these sort of green combinations and they have pointy caps and little knobbly antenna thingies sticking out of their heads. I've seen pictures."

"Where?"

Twoflower hesitated, and looked at his feet. "I think it was called the 'mutter, mutter, mutter.'"

"The what? Called the what?"

The little man took a sudden interest in the backs of his hands.

"The Little Folks' Book of Flower Fairies," he muttered.

Rincewind looked blank.

"It's a book on how to avoid them?" he said.

"Oh no," said Twoflower hurriedly. "It tells you where to look for them. I can remember the pictures now." A dreamy look came over his face, and Rincewind groaned inwardly. "There was even a special fairy that came and took your teeth away."

"What, came and pulled out your actual teeth—?"

"No, no, you're wrong, I mean after they'd fallen out, what you did was, you put the tooth under your pillow and the fairy came and took it away and left a *rhinu* piece."

"Why?"

"Why what?"

"Why did it collect teeth?"

"It just did."

Rincewind formed a mental picture of some strange entity living in a castle made of teeth. It was the kind of mental picture you tried to forget. Unsuccessfully.

"Urgh," he said.

Red hats! He wondered whether to enlighten the tourist about what life was really like when a frog was a good meal, a rabbit hole a useful place to shelter out of the rain, and an owl a drifting, silent terror in the night. Moleskin trousers sounded quaint unless you personally had to remove them from their original owner when the vicious little sod was cornered in his burrow. As for red hats, anyone who went around a forest looking bright and conspicuous would only do so very, very briefly.

He wanted to say: Look, the life of gnomes and goblins is nasty, brutish and short. So are they.

He wanted to say all this, and couldn't. For a man with an itch to see the whole of infinity, Twoflower never actually moved outside his own head. Telling him the truth would be like kicking a spaniel.

"Swee whee weedle wheet," said a voice by his foot. He looked down. The gnome, who had introduced himself as Swires, looked up. Rincewind had a very good ear for languages. The gnome had just said, "I've got some newt sorbet left over from yesterday."

"Sounds wonderful," said Rincewind.

Swires gave him another prod in the ankle.

"The other bigger, is he all right?" he said solicitously.

"He's just suffering from reality shock," said Rincewind. "You haven't got a red hat, by any chance?"

"Wheet?"

"Just a thought."

"I know where there's some food for biggers," said the gnome, "and shelter, too. It's not far."

Rincewind looked at the lowering sky. The

daylight was draining out of the landscape and the clouds looked as if they had heard about snow and were considering the idea. Of course, people who lived in mushrooms couldn't necessarily be trusted, but right now a trap baited with a hot meal and clean sheets would have had the wizard hammering to get in.

They set off. After a few seconds the Luggage got carefully to its feet and started to follow.

"Psst!"

It turned carefully, little legs moving in a complicated pattern, and appeared to look up.

"Is it good, being joinery?" said the tree, anxiously. "Did it hurt?"

The Luggage seemed to think about this. Every brass handle, every knothole, radiated extreme concentration.

Then it shrugged its lid and waddled away.

The tree sighed, and shook a few dead leaves out of its twigs.

The cottage was small, tumbledown and as ornate as a doily. Some mad whittler had got to work on it, Rincewind decided, and had created terrible havoc before he could be dragged away. Every door, every shutter had its clusters of wooden grapes and half-moon cutouts, and there were massed outbreaks of fretwork pinecones all over the walls. He half expected a giant cuckoo to come hurtling out of an upper window.

What he also noticed was the characteristic

greasy feel in the air. Tiny green and purple sparks flashed from his fingernails.

"Strong magical field," he muttered. "A hundred millithaums* at least."

"There's magic all over the place," said Swires. "An old witch used to live around here. She went a long time ago but the magic still keeps the house going."

"Here, there's something odd about that door," said Twoflower.

"Why should a house need magic to keep it going?" said Rincewind. Twoflower touched a wall gingerly.

"It's all sticky!"

"Nougat," said Swires.

"Good grief! A real gingerbread cottage! Rincewind, a real—"

Rincewind nodded glumly. "Yeah, the Confectionary School of Architecture," he said. "It never caught on."

He looked suspiciously at the licorice doorknocker.

"It sort of regenerates," said Swires. "Marvelous, really. You just don't get this sort of place nowadays, you just can't get the gingerbread."

"Really?" said Rincewind, gloomily.

"Come on in," said the gnome, "but mind the doormat."

---

* A Thaum is the basic unit of magical strength. It has been universally established as the amount of magic needed to create one small white pigeon or three normal-sized billiard balls.

"Why?"

"Candyfloss."

The great Disc spun slowly under its toiling sun, and daylight pooled in hollows and finally drained away as night fell.

In his chilly room in Unseen University Trymon pored over the book, his lips moving as his finger traced the unfamiliar, ancient script. He read that the Great Pyramid of Tsort, now long vanished, was made of one million, three thousand and ten limestone blocks. He read that ten thousand slaves had been worked to death in its building. He learned that it was a maze of secret passages, their walls reputedly decorated with the distilled wisdom of ancient Tsort. He read that its height plus its length divided by half its width equaled exactly 1.67563, or precisely 1,237.98712567 times the difference between the distance to the sun and the weight of a small orange. He learned that sixty years had been devoted entirely to its construction.

It all seemed, he thought, to be rather a lot of trouble to go to just to sharpen a razor blade.

And in the Forest of Skund Twoflower and Rincewind settled down to a meal of gingerbread mantelpiece and thought longingly of pickled onions.

And far away, but set as it were on a collision course, the greatest hero the Disc ever produced rolled himself a cigarette, entirely unaware of the role that lay in store for him.

It was quite an interesting tailormade that he

twirled expertly between his fingers because, like many of the wandering wizards from whom he had picked up the art, he was in the habit of saving dogends in a leather bag and rolling them into fresh smokes. The implacable law of averages therefore dictated that some of that tobacco had been smoked almost continuously for many years now. The thing he was trying unsuccessfully to light was, well, you could have coated roads with it.

So great was the reputation of this person that a group of nomadic barbarian horsemen had respectfully invited him to join them as they sat around a horseturd fire. The nomads of the Hub regions usually migrated rimward for the winter, and these were part of a tribe who had pitched their felt tents in the sweltering heat wave of a mere −3 degrees and were going around with peeling noses and complaining about heatstroke.

The barbarian chieftain said: "What then are the greatest things that a man may find in life?" This is the sort of thing you're supposed to say to maintain steppecred in barbarian circles.

The man on his right thoughtfully drank his cocktail of mare's milk and snowcat blood, and spoke thus: "The crisp horizon of the steppe, the wind in your hair, a fresh horse under you."

The man on his left said: "The cry of the white eagle in the heights, the fall of snow in the forest, a true arrow in your bow."

The chieftain nodded, and said: "Surely it is the sight of your enemy slain, the humiliation of his tribe and the lamentation of his women."

There was a general murmur of whiskery approval at this outrageous display.

Then the chieftain turned respectfully to his guest, a small figure carefully warming his chilblains by the fire, and said: "But our guest, whose name is legend, must tell us truly: What is it that a man may call the greatest things in life?"

The guest paused in the middle of another unsuccessful attempt to light up.

"What shay?" he said, toothlessly.

"I said: What is it that a man may call the greatest things in life?"

The warriors leaned closer. This should be worth hearing.

The guest thought long and hard and then said, with deliberation: "Hot water, good dentishtry and shoft lavatory paper."

Brilliant octarine light flared in the forge. Galder Weatherwax, stripped to the waist, his face hidden by a mask of smoked glass, squinted into the glow and brought a hammer down with surgical precision. The magic squealed and writhed in the tongs but still he worked it, drawing it into a line of agonized fire.

A floorboard creaked. Galder had spent many hours tuning them, always a wise precaution with an ambitious assistant who walked like a cat.

D-flat. That meant he was just to the right of the door.

"Ah, Trymon," he said, without turning, and noted with some satisfaction the faint indrawing of breath behind him. "Good of you to come. Shut the door, will you?"

Trymon pushed the heavy door, his face expressionless. On the high shelf above him various bottled impossibilities wallowed in their pickle jars and watched him with interest.

Like all wizards' workshops, the place looked as though a taxidermist had dropped his stock in a foundry and then had a fight with a maddened glass-blower, braining a passing crocodile in the process (it hung from the ceiling and smelled strongly of camphor). There were lamps and rings that Trymon itched to rub, and mirrors that looked as though they could repay a second glance. A pair of seven-league boots stirred restlessly in a cage. A whole library of grimoires, not of course as powerful as the Octavo but still heavy with spells, creaked and rattled their chains as they sensed the wizard's covetous glance on them. The naked power of it all stirred him as nothing else could, but he deplored the scruffiness and Galder's sense of theater.

For example, he happened to know that the green liquid bubbling mysteriously through a maze of contorted pipework on one of the benches was just green dye with soap in it, because he'd bribed one of the servants.

One day, he thought, it's all going to go. Starting with that bloody alligator. His knuckles whitened . . .

"Well, now," said Galder cheerfully, hanging up his apron and sitting back in his chair with the lion paw arms and duck legs, "You sent me this memmything."

Trymon shrugged. "Memo. I merely pointed out, lord, that the other Orders have all sent agents to Skund Forest to recapture the spell, while you do nothing," he said. "No doubt you will reveal your reasons in good time."

"Your faith shames me," said Galder.

"The wizard who captures the spell will bring great honor on himself and his order," said Trymon. "The others have used boots and all manner of elsewhere spells. What do you propose using, master?"

"Did I detect a hint of sarcasm there?"

"Absolutely not, master."

"Not even a smidgeon?"

"Not even the merest smidgeon, master."

"Good. Because I don't propose to go." Galder reached down and picked up an ancient book. He mumbled a command and it creaked open; a bookmark suspiciously like a tongue flicked back into the binding.

He fumbled down beside his cushion and produced a little leather bag of tobacco and a pipe the size of an incinerator. With all the skill of a terminal nicotine addict he rubbed a nut of tobacco between his hands and tamped it into the bowl. He snapped his fingers and fire flared. He sucked deep, sighed with satisfaction . . .

. . . looked up.

"Still here, Trymon?"

"You summoned me, master," said Trymon levelly. At least, that's what his voice said. Deep in his gray eyes was the faintest glitter that said he had a list of every slight, every patronizing twinkle, every gentle reproof, every knowing glance, and for every single one Galder's living brain was going to spend a year in acid.

"Oh, yes, so I did. Humor the deficiencies of an old man," said Galder pleasantly. He held up the book he had been reading.

"I don't hold with all this running about," he said. "It's all very dramatic, mucking about with magic carpets and the like, but it isn't true magic to my mind. Take seven-league boots, now. If men were meant to walk twenty-one miles at a step I am sure God would have given us longer legs . . . Where was I?"

"I am not sure," said Trymon coldly.

"Ah, yes. Strange that we could find nothing about the Pyramid of Tsort in the Library, you would have thought there'd be something, wouldn't you?"

"The librarian will be disciplined, of course."

Galder looked sideways at him. "Nothing drastic," he said. "Withold his bananas, perhaps."

They looked at each other for a moment.

Galder broke off first—looking hard at Trymon always bothered him. It had the same disconcerting effect as gazing into a mirror and seeing no one there.

"Anyway," he said, "strangely enough, I found assistance elsewhere. In my own modest bookshelves, in fact. The journal of Skrelt Changebasket, the founder of our order. You, my keen young man who would rush off so soon, do you know what happens when a wizard dies?"

"Any spells he has memorized say themselves," said Trymon. "It is one of the first things we learn."

"In fact it is not true of the original Eight Great Spells. By dint of close study Skrelt learned that a Great Spell will simply take refuge in the nearest mind open and ready to receive it. Just push the big mirror over here, will you?"

Galder got to his feet and shuffled across to the forge, which was now cold. The strand of magic still writhed, though, at once present and not present, like a slit cut into another universe full of hot blue light. He picked it up easily, took a longbow from a rack, said a word of power, and watched with satisfaction as the magic grasped the ends of the bow and then tightened until the wood creaked. Then he selected an arrow.

Trymon had tugged a heavy, full-length mirror into the middle of the floor. When I am head of the Order, he told himself, I certainly won't shuffle around in carpet slippers.

Trymon, as mentioned earlier, felt that a lot could be done by fresh blood if only the dead wood could be removed—but, just for the moment, he was genuinely interested in seeing what the old fool would do next.

He may have derived some satisfaction if he had known that Galder and Skrelt Changebasket were both absolutely wrong.

Galder made a few passes in front of the glass, which clouded over and then cleared to show an aerial view of the Forest of Skund. He looked at it intently while holding the bow with the arrow pointing vaguely at the ceiling. He muttered a few words like "allow for wind speed of, say, three knots" and "adjust for temperature" and then, with a rather disappointing movement, released the arrow.

If the laws of action and reaction had anything to do with it, it should have flopped to the ground a few feet away. But no one was listening to them.

With a sound that defies description, but which for the sake of completeness can be thought of basically as "spang!" plus three days hard work in any decently equipped radiophonic workshop, the arrow vanished.

Galder threw the bow aside and grinned.

"Of course, it'll take about an hour to get there," he said. "Then the spell will simply follow the ionized path back here. To me."

"Remarkable," said Trymon, but any passing telepath would have read in letters ten yards high: If you, then why not me? He looked down at the cluttered workbench, when a long and very sharp knife looked tailor-made for what he suddenly had in mind.

Violence was not something he liked to be involved in except at one remove. But the Pyramid of Tsort had been quite clear about the rewards for whoever brought all eight spells together at the right time, and Trymon was not about to let years of painstaking work go for nothing because some old fool had a bright idea.

"Would you like some cocoa while we're waiting?" said Galder, hobbling across the room to the servants' bell.

"Certainly," said Trymon. He picked up the knife, weighing it for balance and accuracy. "I must congratulate you, master. I can see that we must all get up very early in the morning to get the better of you."

Galder laughed. And the knife left Trymon's hand at such speed that (because of the somewhat sluggish nature of Disc light) it actually grew a bit shorter and a little more massive as it plunged, with unerring aim, toward Galder's neck.

It didn't reach it. Instead, it swerved to one side and began a fast orbit—so fast that Galder appeared suddenly to be wearing a metal collar. He turned around, and to Trymon it seemed that he had suddenly grown several feet taller and much more powerful.

The knife broke away and shuddered into the door a mere shadow's depth from Trymon's ear.

"Early in the morning?" said Galder pleasantly. "My dear lad, you will need to stay up all night."

"Have a bit more table," said Rincewind.

"No thanks, I don't like marzipan," said Two-flower. "Anyway, I'm sure it's not right to eat other people's furniture."

"Don't worry," said Swires. "The old witch hasn't been seen for years. They say she was done up good and proper by a couple of young tearaways."

"Kids of today," commented Rincewind.

"I blame the parents," said Twoflower.

Once you had made the necessary mental adjustments, the gingerbread cottage was quite a pleasant place. Residual magic kept it standing and it was shunned by such local wild animals who hadn't already died of terminal tooth decay. A bright fire of licorice logs burned rather messily in the fireplace; Rincewind had tried gathering wood outside, but had given up. It's hard to burn wood that talks to you.

He belched.

"This isn't very healthy," he said. "I mean, why sweets? Why not crispbread and cheese? Or salami, now—I could just do with a nice salami sofa."

"Search me," said Swires. "Old Granny Whitlow just did sweets. You should have seen her meringues—"

"I have," said Rincewind, "I looked at the mattresses . . ."

"Gingerbread is more traditional," said Twoflower.

"What, for mattresses?"

"Don't be silly," said Twoflower reasonably. "Whoever heard of a gingerbread mattress?"

Rincewind grunted. He was thinking of food—more accurately, of food in Ankh-Morpork. Funny how the old place seemed more attractive the farther he got from it. He only had to close his eyes to picture, in dribbling detail, the food stalls of a hundred different cultures in the market places. You could eat squishi or shark's fin soup so fresh that swimmers wouldn't go near it, and—

"Do you think I could buy this place?" said Twoflower. Rincewind hesitated. He'd found it always paid to think very carefully before answering Twoflower's more surprising questions.

"What for?" he said, cautiously.

"Well, it just reeks of ambience."

"Oh."

"What's ambience?" said Swires, sniffing cautiously and wearing the kind of expression that said that he hadn't done it, whatever it was.

"I think it's a kind of frog," said Rincewind. "Anyway, you can't buy this place because there isn't anyone to buy it *from*—"

"I think I could probably arrange that, on behalf of the forest council of course," interrupted Swires, trying to avoid Rincewind's glare.

"—and anyway you couldn't take it with you, I mean, you could hardly pack it in the Luggage, could you?" Rincewind indicated the Luggage, which was lying by the fire and managing in some quite impossible way to look like a contented but alert tiger, and then looked back at Twoflower. His face fell.

"Could you?" he repeated.

He had never quite come to terms with the fact that the inside of the Luggage didn't seem to inhabit quite the same world as the outside. Of course, this was simply a byproduct of its essential weirdness, but it was disconcerting to see Twoflower fill it full of dirty shirts and old socks and then open the lid again on a pile of nice crisp laundry, smelling faintly of lavender. Twoflower also bought a lot of quaint native artifacts or, as Rincewind would put it, junk, and even a seven-foot ceremonial pig tickling pole seemed to fit inside quite easily without sticking out anywhere.

"I don't know," said Twoflower. "You're a wizard, you know about these things."

"Yes, well, of course, but baggage magic is a highly specialized art," said Rincewind. "Anyway, I'm sure the gnomes wouldn't really want to sell it, it's, it's—" he groped through what he knew of Twoflower's mad vocabulary—"it's a tourist attraction."

"What's that?" said Swires, interestedly.

"It means that lots of people like him will come and look at it," said Rincewind.

"Why?"

"Because—" Rincewind groped for words "—it's quaint. Um, oldey worldey. Folkloresque. Er, a delightful example of a vanished folk art, steeped in the traditions of an age long gone."

"It is?" said Swires, looking at the cottage in bewilderment.

"Yes."

"All that?"

"'Fraid so."

"I'll help you pack."

And the night wears on, under a blanket of lowering clouds which covers most of the Disc—which is fortuitous, because when it clears and the astrologers get a good view of the sky they are going to get angry and upset.

And in various parts of the forest parties of wizards are getting lost, and going around in circles, and hiding from each other, and getting upset because whenever they bump into a tree it apologizes to them. But, unsteadily though it may be, many of them are getting quite close to the cottage . . .

Which is a good time to get back to the rambling

buildings of Unseen University and in particular the apartments of Greyhald Spold, currently the oldest wizard on the Disc and determined to keep it that way.

He has just been extremely surprised and upset.

For the last few hours he has been very busy. He may be deaf and a little hard of thinking, but elderly wizards have very well-trained survival instincts, and they know that when a tall figure in a black robe and the latest in agricultural hand tools starts looking thoughtfully at you it is time to act fast. The servants have been dismissed. The doorways have been sealed with a paste made from powdered may-flies, and protective octograms have been drawn on the windows. Rare and rather smelly oils have been poured in complex patterns on the floor, in designs which hurt the eyes and suggest the designer was drunk or from some other dimension or, possibly, both; in the very center of the room is the eightfold octogram of Witholding, surrounded by red and green candles. And in the center of that is a box made from wood of the curlyfern pine, which grows to a great age, and it is lined with red silk and yet more protective amulets. Because Greyhald Spold knows that Death is looking for him, and has spent many years designing an impregnable hiding place.

He has just set the complicated clockwork of the lock and shut the lid, lying back in the knowledge that here at last is the perfect defense against the most ultimate of all his enemies, although as yet he has not considered the important part that airholes must play in an enterprise of this kind.

And right beside him, very close to his ear, a voice has just said: DARK IN HERE, ISN'T IT?

It began to snow. The barleysugar windows of the cottage showed bright and cheerful against the blackness.

At one side of the clearing three tiny red points of light glowed momentarily and there was the sound of a chesty cough, abruptly silenced.

"Shut up!" hissed a third rank wizard. "They'll hear us!"

"Who will? We gave the lads from the Brotherhood of the Hoodwink the slip in the swamp, and those idiots from the Venerable Council of Seers went off the wrong way anyway."

"Yeah," said the most junior wizard, "but who keeps talking to us? They say this is a magic wood, it's full of goblins and wolves and—"

"Trees," said a voice out of the darkness, high above. It possessed what can only be described as timbre.

"Yeah," said the youngest wizard. He sucked on his dogend, and shivered.

The leader of the party peered over the rock and watched the cottage.

"Right then," he said, knocking out his pipe on the heel of his seven-league boot, who squeaked in protest. "We rush in, we grab them, we're away. Okay?"

"You sure it's just people?" said the youngest wizard nervously.

"Of course I'm sure," snarled the leader. "What do you expect, three bears?"

"There could be monsters. This is the sort of wood that has monsters."

"And trees," said a friendly voice from the branches.

"Yeah," said the leader, cautiously.

Rincewind looked carefully at the bed. It was quite a nice little bed, in a sort of hard toffee inlaid with caramel, but he'd rather eat it than sleep in it and it looked as though someone already had.

"Someone's been eating my bed," he said.

"I like toffee," said Twoflower defensively.

"If you don't watch out the fairy will come and take all your teeth away," said Rincewind.

"No, that's elves," said Swires from the dressing table. "Elves do that. Toenails, too. Very touchy at times, elves can be."

Twoflower sat down heavily on his bed.

"You've got it wrong," he said. "Elves are noble and beautiful and wise and fair; I'm sure I read that somewhere."

Swires and Rincewind's kneecap exchanged glances.

"I think you must be thinking about different elves," the gnome said slowly. "We've just got the other sort around here. Not that you could call them quick-tempered," he added hastily. "Not if you didn't want to take your teeth home in your hat, anyway."

There was the tiny, distinctive sound of a nougat door opening. At the same time, from the other side of the cottage, came the faintest of tinkles, like a rock smashing a barleysugar window as delicately as possible.

"What was that?" said Twoflower.

"Which one?" said Rincewind.

There was the clonk of a heavy branch banging against the windowsill. With a cry of "Elves!" Swires scuttled across the floor to a mouse hole and vanished.

"What shall we do?" said Twoflower.

"Panic?" said Rincewind hopefully. He always held that panic was the best means of survival; back in the olden days, his theory went, people faced with hungry saber-toothed tigers could be divided very simply into those who panicked and those who stood there saying "What a magnificent brute!" and "Here, pussy."

"There's a cupboard," said Twoflower, pointing to a narrow door that was squeezed between the wall and the chimneybreast. They scrambled into sweet, musty darkness.

There was the creak of a chocolate floorboard outside. Someone said, "I heard voices."

Someone else said, "Yeah, downstairs. I think it's the Hoodwinkers."

"I thought you said we'd given them the slip!"

"Hey, you two, you can eat this place! Here, look you can—"

"*Shut up!*"

There was a lot more creaking, and a muffled scream from downstairs where a Venerable Seer, creeping carefully through the darkness from the broken window, had trodden on the fingers of a

Hoodwinker who was hiding under the table. There was the sudden zip and zing of magic.

"Bugger!" said a voice outside. "They've got him! Let's go!"

There was more creaking, and then silence. After a while Twoflower said, "Rincewind, I think there's a broomstick in this cupboard."

"Well, what's so unusual about that?"

"This one's got handlebars."

There was a piercing shriek from below. In the darkness a wizard had tried to open the Luggage's lid. A crash from the scullery indicated the sudden arrival of a party of Illuminated Mages of the Unbroken Circle.

"What do you think they're after?" whispered Twoflower.

"I don't know, but I think it might be a good idea not to find out," said Rincewind thoughtfully.

"You could be right."

Rincewind pushed open the door gingerly. The room was empty. He tiptoed across to the window, and looked down into the upturned faces of three Brothers of the Order of Midnight.

"That's him!"

He drew back hurriedly and rushed for the stairs.

The scene below was indescribable but since that statement would earn the death penalty in the reign of Olaf Quimby II the attempt better be made. Firstly, most of the struggling wizards were trying to illuminate the scene by various flames, fireballs and magical glows, so the overall lighting gave the impression of a disco in a strobe-light factory;

each man was trying to find a position from which he could see the rest of the room without being attacked himself, and absolutely everyone was trying to keep out of the way of the Luggage, which had two Venerable Seers pinned in a corner and was snapping its lid at anyone who approached. But one wizard did happen to look up.

"It's him!"

Rincewind jerked back, and something bumped into him. He looked around hurriedly, and stared when he saw Twoflower sitting on the broomstick—which was floating in midair.

"The witch must have left it behind!" said Twoflower. "A genuine magic broomstick!"

Rincewind hesitated. Octarine sparks were spitting off the broomstick's bristles and he hated heights almost more than anything else, but what he really hated more than anything at all was a dozen very angry and bad-tempered wizards rushing up the stairs toward him, and this was happening.

"All right," he said, "but I'll drive."

He lashed out with a boot at a wizard who was halfway through a Spell of Binding and jumped onto the broomstick, which bobbed down the stairwell and then turned upside down so that Rincewind was horribly eye to eye with a Brother of Midnight.

He yelped and gave the handlebars a convulsive twist.

Several things happened at once. The broomstick shot forward and broke through the wall in a shower of crumbs; the Luggage surged forward and bit the Brother in the leg; and with a strange whistling sound an arrow appeared from nowhere, missed Rincewind by inches, and struck the Luggage's lid with a very solid thud.

The Luggage vanished.

In a little village deep in the forest an ancient shaman threw a few more twigs on his fire and stared through the smoke at his shamefaced apprentice.

"A box with legs on?" he said.

"Yes, master. It just appeared out of the sky and looked at me," said the apprentice.

"It had eyes then, this box?"

"N—" began the apprentice and stopped, puzzled. The old man frowned.

"Many have seen Topaxci, God of the Red Mushroom, and they earn the name of shaman," he said. "Some have seen Skelde, spirit of the smoke, and they are called sorcerers. A few have been privileged to see Umcherrel, the soul of the forest, and they are known as spirit masters. But none have seen a box with hundreds of legs that looked at them without eyes, and they are known as idio—"

The interruption was caused by a sudden screaming noise and a flurry of snow and sparks that blew the fire across the dark hut; there was a brief blurred vision and then the opposite wall was blasted aside and the apparition vanished.

There was a long silence. Then a slightly shorter silence. Then the old shaman said carefully, "You didn't just see two men go through upside down on a broomstick, shouting and screaming at each other, did you?"

The boy looked at him levelly. "Certainly not," he said.

The old man heaved a sigh of relief. "Thank goodness for that," he said. "Neither did I."

The cottage was in turmoil, because not only did the wizards want to follow the broomstick, they also wanted to prevent each other from doing so, and this led to several regrettable incidents. The most spectacular, and certainly the most tragic, happened when one Seer attempted to use his seven-league boots without the proper sequence of spells and preparations. Seven-league boots, as has already been intimated, are a tricksy form of magic at best, and he remembered too late that the utmost caution must be taken in using a means of transport which, when all is said and done, relies for its effectiveness on trying to put one foot twenty-one miles in front of the other.

The first snowstorms of winter were raging, and in fact there was a suspiciously heavy covering of cloud over most of the Disc. And yet, from far above and by the silver light of the Discworld's tiny moon, it presented one of the most beautiful sights in the multiverse.

Great streamers of cloud, hundreds of miles along, swirled from the waterfall at the Rim to the mountains of the Hub. In the cold crystal silence the huge white spiral glittered frostily under the stars, imperceptibly turning, very much as though God had stirred His coffee and then poured the cream in.

Nothing disturbed the glowing scene, which—

Something small and distant broke through the cloud layer, trailing shreds of vapor. In the stratospheric calm the sounds of bickering came sharp and clear.

"You said you could fly one of these things!"

"No I didn't; I just said you couldn't!"

"But I've never been on one before!"

"What a coincidence!"

"Anyway, you said—*Look at the sky!*"

"No I didn't!"

"What's happened to the stars?"

And so it was that Rincewind and Twoflower became the first two people on the Disc to see what the future held.

A thousand miles behind them the Hub mountain of Cori Celesti stabbed the sky and cast a knife-bright shadow across the broiling clouds, so that Gods ought to have noticed too—but the Gods don't normally look at the sky and in any case were engaged in litigation with the Ice Giants, who had refused to turn their radio down.

Rimward, in the direction of Great A'Tuin's travel, the sky had been swept of stars.

In that circle of blackness there was just one star, a red and baleful star, a star like the glitter in the eye socket of a rabid mink. It was small and horrible and uncompromising. And the Disc was being carried straight toward it.

Rincewind knew precisely what to do in these circumstances. He screamed and pointed the broomstick straight down.

Galder Weatherwax stood in the center of the octogram and raised his hands.

"Urshalo, dileptor, c'hula, do my bidding!"

A small mist formed over his head. He glanced sideways at Trymon, who was sulking at the edge of the magic circle.

"This next bit's quite impressive," he said. "Watch. *Kot-b'hai! Kot-sham!* To me, o spirits of small isolated rocks and worried mice not less than three inches long!"

"What?" said Trymon.

"That bit took quite a lot of research," agreed Galder, "especially the mice. Anyway, where was I? Oh, yes . . ."

He raised his arms again. Trymon watched him, and licked his lips distractedly. The old fool was really concentrating, bending his mind entirely to the Spell and hardly paying any attention to Trymon.

Words of power rolled around the room, bouncing off the walls and scuttling out of sight behind shelves and jars. Trymon hesitated.

Galder shut his eyes momentarily, his face a mask of ecstasy as he mouthed the final word.

Trymon tensed, his fingers curling around the

knife again. And Galder opened one eye, nodded at him and sent a sideways blast of power that picked the younger man up and sent him sprawling against the wall.

Galder winked at him and raised his arms again.

"To me, o spirits of—"

There was a thunderclap, an implosion of light and a moment of complete physical uncertainty during which even the walls seemed to turn in on themselves. Trymon heard a sharp intake of breath and then a dull, solid thump:

The room was suddenly silent.

After a few minutes Trymon crawled out from behind a chair and dusted himself off. He whistled a few bars of nothing much and turned toward the door with exaggerated care, looking at the ceiling as if he had never seen it before. He moved in a way that suggested he was attempting the world speed record for the nonchalant walk.

The Luggage squatted in the center of the circle and opened its lid.

Trymon stopped. He turned very, very carefully, dreading what he might see.

The Luggage seemed to contain some clean laundry, smelling slightly of lavender. Somehow it was quite the most terrifying thing the wizard had ever seen.

"Well, er," he said. "You, um, wouldn't have seen another wizard around here, by any chance?"

The Luggage contrived to look more menacing.

"Oh," said Trymon. "Well, fine. It doesn't matter."

He pulled vaguely at the hem of his robe and took

a brief interest in the detail of its stitching. When he looked up the horrible box was still there.

"Goodbye," he said, and ran. He managed to get through the door just in time.

"Rincewind?"

Rincewind opened his eyes. Not that it helped much. It just meant that instead of seeing nothing but blackness he saw nothing but whiteness which, surprisingly, was worse.

"Are you all right?"

"No."

"Ah."

Rincewind sat up. He appeared to be on a rock speckled with snow, but it didn't seem to be everything a rock ought to be. For example, it shouldn't be moving.

Snow blew around him. Twoflower was a few feet away, a look of genuine concern on his face.

Rincewind groaned. His bones were very angry at the treatment they had recently received and were queuing up to complain.

"What now?" he said.

"You know when we were flying and I was worried we might hit something in the storm and you said the only thing we could possibly hit at this height was a cloud stuffed with rocks?"

"Well?"

"How did you know?"

Rincewind looked around, but for all the variety and interest in the scene around him they might as well have been in the inside of a Ping-Pong ball.

The rock underneath was—well, rocking. He ran his hands over it, and felt the scoring of chisels. When he put an ear to the cold wet stone he fancied he could hear a dull, slow thumping, like a heartbeat. He crawled forward until he came to an edge, and peered very cautiously over it.

At that moment the rock must have been passing over a break in the clouds, because he caught a dim but horribly distant view of jagged-edged mountain peaks. They were a long way down.

He gurgled incoherently and inched his way backward.

"This is ridiculous," he told Twoflower. "Rocks don't fly. They're noted for not doing it."

"Maybe they would if they could," said Twoflower. "Perhaps this one just found out how."

"Let's just hope it doesn't forget again," said Rincewind. He huddled up in his soaking robe and looked glumly at the cloud around him. He supposed there were some people somewhere who had some control over their lives; they got up in the mornings, and went to bed at night in the reasonable certainty of not falling over the edge of the world or being attacked by lunatics or waking up on a rock with ideas above its station. He dimly remembered leading a life like that once.

Rincewind sniffed. This rock smelled of frying. The smell seemed to be coming from up ahead, and appealed straight to his stomach.

"Can you smell anything?" he said.

"I think it's bacon," said Twoflower.

"I hope it's bacon," said Rincewind, "because I'm going to eat it." He stood up on the trembling stone and tottered forward into the clouds, peering through the wet gloom.

At the front or leading edge of the rock a small druid was sitting cross-legged in front of a small fire. A square of oilskin was tied across his head and knotted under his chin. He was poking at a pan of bacon with an ornamental sickle.

"Um," said Rincewind. The druid looked up, and dropped the pan into the fire. He leapt to his feet and gripped the sickle aggressively, or at least as aggressively as anyone can look in a long wet white nightshirt and a dripping headscarf.

"I warn you, I shall deal harshly with hijackers," he said, and sneezed violently.

"We'll help," said Rincewind, looking longingly at the burning bacon. This seemed to puzzle the druid who, to Rincewind's mild surprise, was quite young; he supposed there had to be such things as young druids, theoretically, it was just that he had never imagined them.

"You're not trying to steal the rock?" said the druid, lowering the sickle a fraction.

"I didn't even know you could steal rocks," said Rincewind wearily.

"Excuse me," said Twoflower politely, "I think your breakfast is on fire."

The druid glanced down and flailed ineffectually at the flames. Rincewind hurried forward to help, there was a fair amount of smoke, ash and confusion, and the shared triumph of actually rescuing a few pieces of rather charred bacon did more good than a whole book on diplomacy.

"How did you get here, actually?" said the druid. "We're five hundred feet up, unless I've got the runes wrong again."

Rincewind tried not to think about height. "We sort of dropped in as we were passing," he said.

"On our way to the ground," Twoflower added.

"Only your rock broke our fall," said Rincewind. His back complained. "Thanks," he added.

"I thought we'd run into some turbulence a while back," said the druid, whose name turned out to be Belafon. "That must have been you." He shivered. "It must be morning by now," he said. "Sod the rules, I'm taking us up. Hang on."

"What to?" said Rincewind.

"Well, just indicate a general unwillingness to fall off," said Belafon. He took a large iron pendulum out of his robe and swung it in a series of baffling sweeps over the fire.

Clouds whipped around them, there was a horrible feeling of heaviness, and suddenly the rock burst into sunlight.

It leveled off a few feet above the clouds, in a cold but bright blue sky. The clouds that had seemed chillingly distant last night and horribly clammy this morning were now a fleecy white carpet, stretching away in all directions; a few mountain peaks stood out like islands. Behind the rock the wind of its passage sculpted the clouds into transient whirls. The rock—

It was about thirty feet long and ten feet wide, and blueish.

"What an amazing panorama," said Twoflower, his eyes shining.

"Um, what's keeping us up?" said Rincewind.

"Persuasion," said Belafon, wringing out the hem of his robe.

"Ah," said Rincewind sagely.

"Keeping them up is easy," said the druid, holding up a thumb and squinting down the length of his arm at a distant mountain, "The hard part is landing."

"You wouldn't think so, would you?" said Twoflower.

"Persuasion is what keeps the whole universe together," said Belafon. "It's no good saying it's all done by magic."

Rincewind happened to glance down through the thinning cloud to a snowy landscape a considerable distance below. He knew he was in the presence of a madman, but he was used to that; if listening to this madman meant he stayed up here, he was all ears.

Belafon sat down with his feet dangling over the edge of the rock.

"Look, don't worry," he said. "If you keep thinking the rock shouldn't be flying it might hear you and become persuaded and you will turn out to be right, okay? It's obvious you aren't up to date with modern thinking."

"So it would seem," said Rincewind weakly. He was trying not to think about rocks on the ground. He was trying to think about rocks swooping like swallows, bounding across landscapes in the sheer joy of levity, zooming skyward in a—

He was horribly aware he wasn't very good at it.

The druids of the Disc prided themselves on their forward-looking approach to the discovery of the mysteries of the universe. Of course, like druids everywhere they believed in the essential unity of all life, the healing power of plants, the natural rhythm of the seasons and the burning alive of anyone who didn't approach all this in the right frame of mind, but they had also thought long and hard about the very basis of creation and had formulated the following theory:

The universe, they said, depended for its operation on the balance of four forces which they identified as charm, persuasion, uncertainty and bloody-mindedness.

Thus it was that the sun and moon orbited the Disc because they were persuaded not to fall down, but didn't actually fly away because of uncertainty. Charm allowed trees to grow and bloody-mindedness kept them up, and so on.

Some druids suggested that there were certain flaws in this theory, but senior druids explained very pointedly that there was indeed room for informed argument, the cut and thrust of exciting scientific debate, and basically it lay on top of the next solstice bonfire.

"Ah, so you're an astronomer?" said Twoflower.

"Oh no," said Belafon, as the rock drifted gently

around the curve of a mountain, "I'm a computer hardware consultant."

"What's a computer hardware?"

"Well, this is," said the druid, tapping the rock with a sandalled foot. "Part of one, anyway. It's a replacement. I'm delivering it. They're having trouble with the big circles up on the Vortex Plains. So they say, anyway; I wished I had a bronze torc for every user who didn't read the manual." He shrugged.

"What use is it, then, exactly?" asked Rincewind. Anything to keep his mind off the drop below.

"You can use it to—to tell you what time of year it is," said Belafon.

"Ah. You mean if it's covered in snow then it must be winter?"

"Yes. I mean no. I mean, supposing you wanted to know when a particular star is going to rise—"

"Why?" said Twoflower, radiating polite interest.

"Well, maybe you want to know when to plant your crops," said Belafon, sweating a little, "or maybe—"

"I'll lend you my almanac, if you like," said Twoflower.

"Almanac?"

"It's a book that tells you what day it is," said Rincewind wearily. "It'd be right up your leyline."

Belafon stiffened. "Book?" he said. "Like, with paper?"

"Yes."

"That doesn't sound very reliable to me," said the druid nastily. "How can a book know what day it is? Paper can't count."

He stamped off to the front of the rock, causing it

to wallow alarmingly. Rincewind swallowed hard and beckoned Twoflower closer.

"Have you ever heard of culture shock?" he hissed.

"What's that?"

"It's what happens when people spend five hundred years trying to get a stone circle to work properly and then someone comes up with a little book with a page for every day and little chatty bits saying things like 'Now is a good time to plant broad beans' and 'Early to rise, early to bed, makes a man healthy, wealthy and dead,' and do you know what the most important thing to remember about culture shock," Rincewind paused for breath, and moved his lips silently trying to remember where the sentence had got to, "is?" he concluded.

"What?"

"Don't give it to a man flying a thousand ton rock."

"Has it gone?"

Trymon peered cautiously over the battlements of the Tower of Art, the great spire of crumbling masonry that loomed over Unseen University. The cluster of students and instructors of magic, far below, nodded.

"Are you sure?"

The bursar cupped his hands and shouted.

"It broke down the hubward door and escaped an hour ago, sir," he yelled.

"Wrong," said Trymon. "It left, we escaped. Well, I'll be getting down, then. Did it get anyone?"

The bursar swallowed. He was not a wizard, but a kind, good-natured man who should not have had to see the things he had witnessed in the past hour. Of course, it wasn't unknown for small demons, colored lights and various half-materialized imaginings to wander around the campus, but there had been something about the implacable onslaught of the Luggage that had unnerved him. Trying to stop it would have been like trying to wrestle a glacier.

"It—it swallowed the Dean of Liberal Studies, sir," he shouted.

Trymon brightened. "It's an ill wind," he murmured.

He started down the long spiral staircase. After a while he smiled, a thin, tight smile. The day was definitely improving.

There was a lot of organizing to do. And if there was something Trymon really liked, it was organizing.

The rock swooped across the high plains, whipping snow from the drifts a mere few feet below. Belafon scuttled about urgently, smearing a little mistletoe ointment here, chalking a rune there, while Rincewind cowered in terror and exhaustion and Twoflower worried about his Luggage.

"Up ahead!" screamed the druid above the noise of the slipstream. "Behold, the great computer of the skies!"

Rincewind peered between his fingers. On the distant skyline was an immense construction of gray and black slabs, arranged in concentric circles and mystic avenues, gaunt and forbidding against the snow. Surely men couldn't have moved those nascent mountains—surely a troop of giants had been turned to stone by some . . .

"It looks like a lot of rocks," said Twoflower.

Belafon hesitated in mid-gesture.

"What?" he said.

"It's very nice," added the tourist hurriedly. He sought for a word. "Ethnic," he decided.

The druid stiffened. "*Nice?*" he said. "A triumph of the silicon chunk, a miracle of modern masonic technology—*nice?*"

"Oh, yes," said Twoflower, to whom sarcasm was merely a seven-letter word beginning with S.

"What does ethnic mean?" said the druid.

"It means terribly impressive," said Rincewind hurriedly, "and we seem to be in danger of landing, if you don't mind—"

Belafon turned around, only slightly mollified. He raised his arms wide and shouted a series of untranslatable words, ending with "nice!" in a hurt whisper.

The rock slowed, drifted sideways in a billow of snow, and hovered over the circle. Down below a druid waved two bunches of mistletoe in complicated patterns, and Belafon skillfully brought the massive slab to rest across two giant uprights with the faintest of clicks.

Rincewind let his breath out in a long sigh. It hurried off to hide somewhere.

A ladder banged against the side of the slab and the head of an elderly druid appeared over the edge.

He gave the two passengers a puzzled glance, and then looked up at Belafon.

"About bloody time," he said. "Seven weeks to Hogswatchnight and it's gone down on us again."

"Hallo, Zakriah," said Belafon. "What happened this time?"

"It's all totally fouled up. Today it predicted sunrise three minutes early. Talk about a klutz, boy, this is it."

Belafon clambered onto the ladder and disappeared from view. The passengers looked at each other, and then stared down into the vast open space between the inner circle of stones.

"What shall we do now?" said Twoflower.

"We could go to sleep?" suggested Rincewind.

Twoflower ignored him, and climbed down the ladder.

Around the circle druids were tapping the megaliths with little hammers and listening intently. Several of the huge stones were lying on their sides, and each was surrounded by another crowd of druids who were examining it carefully and arguing amongst themselves. Arcane phrases floated up to where Rincewind sat:

"It can't be software incompatibility—the Chant of the Trodden Spiral was *designed* for concentric rings, idiot . . ."

"I say fire it up again and try a simple moon ceremony . . ."

". . . all right, all right, nothing's wrong with the stones, it's just that the universe has gone wrong, right? . . ."

Through the mists of his exhausted mind Rincewind remembered the horrible star they'd seen in the sky. Something *had* gone wrong with the universe last night.

How had he come to be back on the Disc?

He had a feeling that the answers were somewhere inside his head. And an even more unpleasant feeling began to dawn on him that something else was watching the scene below—watching it from behind his eyes.

The Spell had crept from its lair deep in the untrodden dirt roads of his mind, and was sitting bold as brass in his forebrain, watching the passing scene and doing the mental equivalent of eating popcorn.

He tried to push it back—and the world vanished . . .

He was in darkness; a warm, musty darkness, the darkness of the tomb, the velvet blackness of the mummy case.

There was a strong smell of old leather and the sourness of ancient paper. The paper rustled.

He felt that the darkness was full of unimaginable horrors—and the trouble with unimaginable horrors was that they were only too easy to imagine . . .

"Rincewind," said a voice. Rincewind had never heard a lizard speak, but if one did it would have a voice like that.

"Um," he said. "Yes?"

The voice chuckled—a strange sound, rather papery.

"You ought to say 'Where am I?'" it said.

"Would I like it if I knew?" said Rincewind. He

stared hard at the darkness. Now that he was accustomed to it, he could see something. Something vague, hardly bright enough to be anything at all, just the merest tracery in the air. Something strangely familiar.

"All right," he said. "Where am I?"

"You're dreaming."

"Can I wake up now, please?"

"No," said another voice, as old and dry as the first but still slightly different.

"We have something very important to tell you," said a third voice, if anything more corpse-dry than the others. Rincewind nodded stupidly. In the back of his mind the Spell lurked and peered cautiously over his mental shoulder.

"You've caused us a lot of trouble, young Rincewind," the voice went on. "All this dropping over the edge of the world with no thought for other people. We had to seriously distort reality, you know."

"Gosh."

"And now you have a very important task ahead of you."

"Oh. Good."

"Many years ago we arranged for one of our number to hide in your head, because we could foresee a time coming when you would need to play a very important role."

"Me? Why?"

"You run away a lot," said one of the voices. "That is good. You are a survivor."

"Survivor? I've nearly been killed dozens of times!"

"Exactly."

"Oh."

"But try not to fall off the Disc again. We really can't have that."

"Who are *we*, exactly?" said Rincewind.

There was a rustling in the darkness.

"In the beginning was the word," said a dry voice right behind him.

"It was the Egg," corrected another voice. "I distinctly remember. The Great Egg of the Universe. Slightly rubbery."

"You're both wrong, in fact. I'm sure it was the primordial slime."

A voice by Rincewind's knee said: "No, that came afterward. There was firmament first. Lots of firmament. Rather sticky, like candyfloss. Very syrupy, in fact—"

"*In case anyone's interested,*" said a crackly voice on Rincewind's left, "you're all wrong. In the beginning was the Clearing of the Throat—"

"—then the word—"

"Pardon me, the slime—"

"Distinctly rubbery, I thought—"

There was a pause. Then a voice said carefully, "Anyway, whatever it was, we remember it distinctly."

"Quite so."

"Exactly."

"And our task is to see that nothing dreadful happens to it, Rincewind."

Rincewind squinted into the blackness. "Would you kindly explain what you're talking about?"

There was a papery sigh. "So much for metaphor," said one of the voices. "Look, it is very important you safeguard the Spell in your head and bring it back to us at the right time, you understand, so that when the moment is precisely right we can be said. Do you understand?"

Rincewind thought: we can be *said?*

And it dawned on him what the tracery was, ahead of him. It was writing on a page, seen from underneath.

"I'm in the Octavo?" he said.

"In certain metaphysical respects," said one of the voices in offhand tones. It came closer. He could feel the dry rustling right in front of his nose . ...

He ran away.

The single red dot glowed in its patch of darkness. Trymon, still wearing the ceremonial robes from his inauguration as head of the Order, couldn't rid himself of the feeling that it had grown slightly while he watched. He turned away from the window with a shudder.

"Well?" he said.

"It's a star," said the Professor of Astrology, "I think."

"You think?"

The astrologer winced. They were standing in Unseen University's observatory, and the tiny ruby pinpoint on the horizon wasn't glaring at him any worse than his new master.

"Well, you see, the point is that we've always believed stars to be pretty much the same as our sun—"

"You mean balls of fire about a mile across?"

"Yes. But this new one is, well—big."

"Bigger than the sun?" said Trymon. He'd always considered a mile-wide ball of fire quite impressive, although he disapproved of stars on principle. They made the sky look untidy.

"A lot bigger," said the astrologer slowly.

"Bigger than Great A'Tuin's head, perhaps?"

The astrologer looked wretched.

"Bigger than Great A'Tuin and the Disc together," he said. "We've checked," he added hurriedly, "and we're quite sure."

"That is big," agreed Trymon. "The word 'huge' comes to mind."

"Massive," agreed the astrologer hurriedly.

"Hmm."

Trymon paced the broad mosaic floor of the observatory, which was inlaid with the signs of the Disc zodiac. There were sixty-four of them, from Wezen the Double-headed Kangaroo to Gahoolie, the Vase of Tulips (a constellation of great religious significance whose meaning, alas, was now lost).

He paused on the blue and gold tilework of Mubbo the Hyaena, and turned suddenly.

"We're going to hit it?" he asked.

"I am afraid so, sir," said the astrologer.

"Hmm." Trymon walked a few paces forward, stroking his beard thoughtfully. He paused on the cusp of Okjock the Salesman and The Celestial Parsnip.

"I'm not an expert in these matters," he said, "but I imagine this would not be a good thing?"

"No, sir."

"Very hot, stars?"

The astrologer swallowed. "Yes, sir."

"We'd be burned up?"

"Eventually. Of course, before that there would be discquakes, tidal waves, gravitational disruption and probably the atmosphere would be stripped away."

"Ah. In a word, lack of decent organization."

The astrologer hesitated, and gave in. "You could say so, sir."

"People would panic?"

"Fairly briefly, I'm afraid."

"Hmm," said Trymon, who was just passing over The Perhaps Gate and orbiting smoothly toward the Cow of Heaven. He squinted up again at the red gleam on the horizon. He appeared to reach a decision.

"We can't find Rincewind," he said, "and if we can't find Rincewind we can't find the eighth spell of the Octavo. But we believe that the Octavo must be read to avert catastrophe—otherwise why did the Creator leave it behind?"

"Perhaps He was just forgetful," suggested the astrologer.

Trymon glared at him.

"The other Orders are searching all the lands between here and the Hub," he continued, counting the points on his fingers, "because it seems unreasonable that a man can fly into a cloud and not come out . . ."

"Unless it was stuffed with rocks," said the astrologer, in a wretched and, as it turned out, entirely unsuccessful attempt to lighten the mood.

"But come down he must—somewhere. Where? we ask ourselves."

"Where?" said the astrologer loyally.

"And immediately a course of action suggests itself to us."

"Ah," said the astrologer, running in an attempt to keep up as the wizard stalked across The Two Fat Cousins.

"And that course is . . . ?"

The astrologer looked up into two eyes as gray and bland as steel.

"Um. We stop looking?" he ventured.

"Precisely! We use the gifts the Creator has given us, to whit, we look down and what is it we see?"

The astrologer groaned inwardly. He looked down.

"Tiles?" he hazarded.

"Tiles, yes, which together make up the . . . ?" Trymon looked expectant.

"Zodiac?" ventured the astrologer, a desperate man.

"Right! And therefore all we need do is cast Rincewind's precise horoscope and we will know exactly where he is!"

The astrologer grinned like a man who, having tap-danced on quicksand, feels the press of solid rock under his feet.

"I shall need to know his precise place and time of birth," he said.

"Easily done. I copied them out of the University files before I came up here."

The astrologer looked at the notes, and his forehead wrinkled. He crossed the room and pulled out a wide drawer full of charts. He read the notes again. He picked up a complicated pair of compasses and made some passes across the charts. He picked up a small brass astrolobe and cranked it carefully. He whistled between his teeth. He picked up a piece of chalk and scribbled some numbers on a blackboard.

Trymon, meanwhile, had been staring out at the new star. He thought: the legend in the Pyramid of Tsort says that whoever says the Eight Spells together when the Disc is in danger will obtain all that he truly desires. And it will be so soon!

And he thought: I remember Rincewind, wasn't he the scruffy boy who always came bottom of the class when we were training? Not a magical bone in his body. Let me get him in front of me, and we'll see if we can't get all eight—

The astrologer said "Gosh" under his breath. Trymon spun around.

"Well?"

"Fascinating chart," said the astrologer, breathlessly. His forehead wrinkled. "Bit strange, really," he said.

"How strange?"

"He was born under The Small Boring Group of Faint Stars which, as you know, lies between The Flying Moose and The Knotted String. It is said that even the ancients couldn't find anything interesting to say about the sign, which—"

"Yes, yes, get on with it," said Trymon irritably.

"It's the sign traditionally associated with chess board makers, sellers of onions, manufacturers of plaster images of small religious significance, and people allergic to pewter. Not a wizard's sign at all. And at the time of his birth the shadow of Cori Celesti—"

"I don't want to know all the mechanical details," growled Trymon. "Just give me his horoscope."

The astrologer, who had been rather enjoying himself, sighed and made a few additional calculations.

"Very well," he said. "It reads as follows: 'Today is a good time for making new friends. A good deed may have unforeseen consequences. Don't upset any druids. You will soon be going on a very strange journey. Your lucky food is small cucumbers. People pointing knives at you are probably up to no good. PS, we really mean it about druids.'"

"Druids?" said Trymon. "I wonder . . ."

"Are you all right?" said Twoflower.

Rincewind opened his eyes.

The wizard sat up hurriedly and grabbed Twoflower by the shirt.

"I want to leave here!" he said urgently. "Right now!"

"But there's going to be an ancient and traditional ceremony!"

"I don't care how ancient! I want the feel of honest cobbles under my feet, I want the old familiar smell of cesspits, I want to go where there's lots of people and fires and roofs and walls and friendly things like that! I want to go *home!*"

He found that he had this sudden desperate longing for the fuming, smoky streets of Ankh-Morpork, which was always at its best in the spring, when the gummy sheen on the turbid waters of the Ankh River had a special iridescence and the eaves were full of birdsong, or at least birds coughing rhythmically.

A tear sprang to his eye as he recalled the subtle play of light on the Temple of Small Gods, a noted local landmark, and a lump came to his throat when he remembered the fried fish stall on the junction of Midden Street and The Street of Cunning Artificers. He thought of the gherkins they sold there, great green things lurking at the bottom of their jar like drowned whales. They called to Rincewind across the miles, promising to introduce him to the pickled eggs in the next jar.

He thought of the cozy livery stable lofts and warm gratings where he spent his nights. Foolishly, he had sometimes jibed at this way of life. It seemed incredible now, but he had found it boring.

Now he'd had enough. He was going home. Pickled gherkins, I hear you calling . . .

He pushed Twoflower aside, gathered his tattered robe around him with great dignity, set his face toward that area of horizon he believed to contain the city of his birth, and with intense determination and considerable absentmindedness stepped right off the top of a thirty-foot trilithon.

Some ten minutes later, when a worried and rather contrite Twoflower dug him out of the large snowdrift at the base of the stones, his expression hadn't changed. Twoflower peered at him.

"Are you all right?" he said. "How many fingers am I holding up?"

"I want to go home!"

"Okay."

"No, don't try and talk me out of it, I've had enough, I'd like to say it's been great fun but I can't, and—what?"

"I said okay," said Twoflower. "I'd quite like to see Ankh-Morpork again. I expect they've rebuilt quite a lot of it by now."

It should be noted that the last time the two of them had seen the city it was burning quite fiercely, a fact which had a lot to do with Twoflower introducing the concept of fire insurance to a venial but ignorant populace. But devastating fires were a regular feature of Morporkian life and it had always been cheerfully and meticulously rebuilt, using the traditional local materials of tinder-dry wood and thatch waterproofed with tar.

"Oh," said Rincewind, deflating a bit. "Oh, right. Right then. Good. Perhaps we'd better be off, then."

He scrambled up and brushed the snow off himself.

"Only I think we should wait until morning," added Twoflower.

"Why?"

"Well, because it's freezing cold, we don't really know where we are, the Luggage has gone missing, it's getting dark—"

Rincewind paused. In the deep canyons of his mind he thought he heard the distant rustle of ancient paper. He had a horrible feeling that his dreams were going to be very repetitive from now on, and he had much better things to do than be lectured by a bunch of ancient spells who couldn't even agree on how the universe began—

A tiny dry voice at the back of his brain said: *What things?*

"Oh, shut up," he said.

"I only said it's freezing cold and—" Twoflower began.

"I didn't mean you, I meant me."

"What?"

"Oh, shut up," said Rincewind wearily. "I don't suppose there's anything to eat around here?"

The giant stones were black and menacing against the dying green light of sunset. The inner circle was full of druids, scurrying around by the light of several bonfires and tuning up all the necessary peripherals of a stone computer, like rams' skulls on poles topped with mistletoe, banners embroidered with twisted snakes and so on. Beyond the circles of firelight a large number of plains people had gathered; druidic festivals were always popular, especially when things went wrong.

Rincewind stared at them.

"What's going on?"

"Oh, well," said Twoflower enthusiastically, "apparently there's this ceremony dating back for thousands of years to celebrate the, um, rebirth of the moon, or possibly the sun. No, I'm pretty certain it's the moon. Apparently it's very solemn and beautiful and invested with a quiet dignity."

Rincewind shivered. He always began to worry

when Twoflower started to talk like that. At least he hadn't said "picturesque" or "quaint" yet; Rincewind had never found a satisfactory translation for those words, but the nearest he had been able to come was "trouble."

"I wish the Luggage was here," said the tourist regretfully. "I could use my picture box. It sounds very quaint and picturesque."

The crowd stirred expectantly. Apparently things were about to start.

"Look," said Rincewind urgently. "Druids are priests. You must remember that. Don't do anything to upset them."

"But—"

"Don't offer to buy the stones."

"But I—"

"Don't start talking about quaint native folkways."

"I thought—"

"*Really* don't try to sell them insurance, that always upsets them."

"But they're priests!" wailed Twoflower. Rincewind paused.

"Yes," he said. "That's the whole point, isn't it?"

At the far side of the outer circle some sort of procession was forming up.

"But priests are good kind men," said Twoflower. "At home they go around with begging bowls. It's their only possession," he added.

"Ah," said Rincewind, not certain he understood. "This would be for putting the blood in, right?"

"Blood?"

"Yes, from sacrifices." Rincewind thought about

the priests he had known at home. He was, of course, anxious not to make an enemy of any god and had attended any number of temple functions and, on the whole, he thought that the most accurate definition of any priest in the Circle Sea Regions was someone who spent quite a lot of time gory to the armpits.

Twoflower looked horrified.

"Oh no," he said. "Where I come from priests are holy men who have dedicated themselves to lives of poverty, good works and the study of the nature of God."

Rincewind considered this novel proposition.

"No sacrifices?" he said.

"Absolutely not."

Rincewind gave up. "Well," he said, "they don't sound very holy to *me*."

There was a loud blarting noise from a band of bronze trumpets. Rincewind looked around. A line of druids marched slowly past, their long sickles hung with sprays of mistletoe. Various junior druids and apprentices followed them, playing a variety of percussion instruments that were traditionally supposed to drive away evil spirits and quite probably succeeded.

Torchlight made excitingly dramatic patterns on the stones, which stood ominously against the green-lit sky. Hubward, the shimmering curtains of the aurora coriolis began to wink and glitter among the stars as a million ice crystals danced in the Disc's magical field.

"Belafon explained it all to me," whispered Two-flower. "We're going to see a time-honored ceremony that celebrates the Oneness of Man with the Universe, that was what he said."

Rincewind looked sourly at the procession. As the druids spread out around a great flat stone that dominated the center of the circle he couldn't help noticing the attractive if rather pale young lady in their midst. She wore a long white robe, a gold tore around her neck, and an expression of vague apprehension.

"Is she a druidess?" said Twoflower.

"I don't think so," said Rincewind slowly.

The druids began to chant. It was, Rincewind felt, a particularly nasty and rather dull chant which sounded very much as if it was going to build up to an abrupt crescendo. The sight of the young woman lying down on the big stone didn't do anything to derail his train of thought.

"I want to stay," said Twoflower. "I think ceremonies like this hark back to a primitive simplicity which—"

"Yes, yes," said Rincewind, "but they're going to sacrifice her, if you must know."

Twoflower looked at him in astonishment.

"What, kill her?"

"Yes."

"Why?"

"Don't ask me. To make the crops grow or the moon rise or something. Or maybe they're just keen on killing people. That's religion for you."

He became aware of a low humming sound, not so much heard as felt. It seemed to be coming from the stone next to them. Little points of light flickered under its surface, like mica specks.

Twoflower was opening and shutting his mouth.

"Can't they just use flowers and berries and things?" he said. "Sort of symbolic?"

"Nope."

"Has anyone ever tried?"

Rincewind sighed. "Look," he said. "No self-respecting High Priest is going to go through all the business with the trumpets and the processions and the banners and everything, and then shove his knife into a daffodil and a couple of plums. You've got to face it, all this stuff about golden boughs and the cycles of nature and stuff just boils down to sex and violence, usually at the same time."

To his amazement Twoflower's lip was trembling. Twoflower didn't just look at the world through rose-tinted spectacles, Rincewind knew—he looked at it through a rose-tinted brain, too, and heard it through rose-tinted ears.

The chant was rising inexorably to a crescendo. The head druid was testing the edge of his sickle and all eyes were turned to the finger of stone on the snowy hills beyond the circle where the moon was due to make a guest appearance.

"It's no use you—"

But Rincewind was talking to himself.

However, the chilly landscape outside the circle was not entirely devoid of life. For one thing a party of wizards was even now drawing near, alerted by Trymon.

But a small and solitary figure was also watching from the cover of a handy fallen stone. One of the

Disc's greatest legends watched the events in the stone circle with considerable interest.

He saw the druids circle and chant, saw the chief druid raise his sickle . . .

Heard the voice.

"I say! Excuse me! Can I have a word?"

Rincewind looked around desperately for a way of escape. There wasn't one. Twoflower was standing by the altar stone with one finger in the air and an attitude of polite determination.

Rincewind remembered one day when Twoflower had thought a passing drover was beating his cattle too hard, and the case he had made for decency toward animals had left Rincewind severely trampled and lightly gored.

The druids were looking at Twoflower with the kind of expression normally reserved for mad sheep or the sudden appearance of a rain of frogs. Rincewind couldn't quite hear what Twoflower was saying, but a few phrases like "ethnic folkways" and "nuts and flowers" floated across the hushed circle.

Then fingers like a bunch of cheese straws clamped over the wizard's mouth and an extremely sharp cutting edge pinked his Adam's apple and a damp voice right by his ear said, "Not a shound, or you ish a dead man."

Rincewind's eyes swiveled in their sockets as if trying to find a way out.

"If you don't want me to say anything, how will you know I understand what you just said?" he hissed.

"Shut up and tell me what the other idiot ish doing!"

"No, but look, if I've got to shut up, how can I—" The knife at his throat became a hot streak of pain and Rincewind decided to give logic a miss.

"His name's Twoflower. He isn't from these parts."

"Doeshn't look like it. Friend of yoursh?"

"We've got this sort of hate-hate relationship, yes."

Rincewind couldn't see his captor, but by the feel of it he had a body made of coat hangers. He also smelled strongly of peppermints.

"He hash got guts, I'll give him that. Do exshactly what I shay and it ish just poshible he won't end up with them wrapped around a shtone."

"Urrr."

"They're not very ecumenical around here, you shee."

It was at that moment that the moon, in due obedience to the laws of persuasion, rose, although in deference to the laws of computing it wasn't anywhere near where the stones said it should be.

But what was there, peeking through ragged clouds, was a glaring red star. It hung exactly over the circle's holiest stone, glittering away like the sparkle in the eye socket of Death. It was sullen and awful and, Rincewind couldn't help noticing, just a little bit bigger than it was last night.

A cry of horror went up from the assembled priests. The crowd on the surrounding banks pressed forward; this looked quite promising.

Rincewind felt a knife handle slip into his hand,

and the squelchy voice behind him said, "You ever done this short of thing before?"

"What sort of thing?"

"Rushed into a temple, killed the prieshts, shtolen the gold and reshcued the girl."

"No, not in so many words."

"You do it like thish."

Two inches from Rincewind's left ear a voice broke into a sound like a baboon with its foot trapped in an echo canyon, and a small but wiry shape rushed past him.

By the light of the torches he saw that it was a very old man, the skinny variety that generally gets called "spry," with a totally bald head, a beard almost down to his knees, and a pair of matchstick legs on which varicose veins had traced the street map of quite a large city. Despite the snow he wore nothing more than a studded leather holdall and a pair of boots that could have easily accommodated a second pair of feet.

The two druids closest to him exchanged glances and hefted their sickles. There was a brief blur and they collapsed into tight balls of agony, making rattling noises.

In the excitement that followed Rincewind sidled along toward the altar stone, holding his knife gingerly so as not to attract any unwelcome comment. In fact no one was paying a great deal of attention to him; the druids that hadn't fled the circle, generally the younger and more muscular ones, had congregated around the old man in order to discuss the whole subject of sacrilege as it pertained to stone circles, but judging by the cackling and sounds of gristle he was carrying the debate.

Twoflower was watching the fight with interest. Rincewind grabbed him by the shoulder.

"Let's go," he said.

"Shouldn't we help?"

"I'm sure we'd only get in the way," said Rincewind hurriedly. "You know what it's like to have people looking over your shoulder when you're busy."

"At least we must rescue the young lady," said Twoflower firmly.

"All right, but get a move on!"

Twoflower took the knife and hurried up to the altar stone. After several inept slashes he managed to cut the ropes that bound the girl, who sat up and burst into tears.

"It's all right—" he began.

"It bloody well isn't!" she snapped, glaring at him through two red-rimmed eyes. "Why do people always go and spoil things?" She blew her nose resentfully on the edge of her robe.

Twoflower looked up at Rincewind in embarrassment.

"Um, I don't think you quite understand," he said. "I mean, we just saved you from absolutely certain death."

"It's not easy around here," she said. "I mean, keeping yourself—" She blushed, and twisted the hem of her robe wretchedly. "I mean, staying . . . not letting yourself be . . . not losing your qualifications . . ."

"Qualifications?" said Twoflower, earning the Rincewind Cup for the slowest person on the uptake in the entire multiverse. The girl's eyes narrowed.

"I could have been up there with the Moon Goddess by now, drinking mead out of a silver bowl," she said petulantly. "Eight years of staying home on Saturday nights right down the drain!"

She looked up at Rincewind and scowled.

Then he sensed something. Perhaps it was a barely heard footstep behind him, perhaps it was movement reflected in her eyes—but he ducked.

Something whistled through the air where his neck had been and glanced off Twoflower's bald head. Rincewind spun around to see the archdruid readying his sickle for another swing and, in the absence of any hope of running away, lashed out desperately with a foot.

It caught the druid squarely on the kneecap. As the man screamed and dropped his weapon there was a nasty little fleshy sound and he fell forward. Behind him the little man with the long beard pulled his sword from the body, wiped it with a handful of snow, and said, "My lumbago is giving me gyp. You can carry the treashure."

"Treasure?" said Rincewind weakly.

"All the necklashes and shtuff. All the gold collarsh. They've got lotsh of them. Thatsh prieshts for you," said the old man wetly. "Nothing but torc, torc, torc. Who'she the girl?"

"She won't let us rescue her," said Rincewind. The

girl looked at the old man defiantly through her smudged eye shadow.

"Bugger that," he said, and with one movement picked her up, staggered a little, screamed at his arthritis and fell over.

After a moment he said, from his prone position, "Don't just shtand there, you daft bitcsh—help me up." Much to Rincewind's amazement, and almost certainly to hers as well, she did so.

Rincewind, meanwhile, was trying to rouse Two-flower. There was a graze across his temple which didn't look too deep, but the little man was unconscious with a faintly worried smile plastered across his face. His breathing was shallow and—strange.

And he felt light. Not simply underweight, but weightless. The wizard might as well have been holding a shadow.

Rincewind remembered that it was said that druids used strange and terrible poisons. Of course, it was often said, usually by the same people, that crooks always had close-set eyes, lightning never struck twice in the same place and if the gods had wanted men to fly they'd have given them an airline ticket. But something about Twoflower's lightness frightened Rincewind. Frightened him horribly.

He looked up at the girl. She had the old man slung over one shoulder, and gave Rincewind an apologetic half-smile. From somewhere around the small of her back a voice said, "Got everything? Letsh get out of here before they come back."

Rincewind tucked Twoflower under one arm and

jogged along after them. It seemed the only thing to do.

The old man had a large white horse tethered to a withered tree in a snow-filled gully some way from the circles. It was sleek, glossy and the general effect of a superb battle charger was only very slightly spoiled by the hemorrhoid ring tied to the saddle.

"Okay, put me down. There'sh a bottle of shome liniment shtuff in the shaddle bag, if you wouldn't mind . . ."

Rincewind propped Twoflower as nicely as possible against the tree, and by moonlight—and, he realized, by the faint red light of the menacing new star—took the first real look at his rescuer.

The man had only one eye; the other was covered by a black patch. His thin body was a network of scars and, currently, twanging white-hot with tendonitis. His teeth had obviously decided to quit long ago.

"Who are you?" he said.

"Bethan," said the girl, rubbing a handful of nasty-smelling green ointment into the old man's back. She wore the air of one who, if asked to consider what sort of events might occur after being rescued from virgin sacrifice by a hero with a white charger, would probably not have mentioned liniment, but who, now that liniment was apparently what did happen to you after all, was determined to be good at it.

"I meant him," said Rincewind.

One star-bright eye looked up at him.

"Cohen ish my name, boy." Bethan's hands stopped moving.

"Cohen?" she said. "Cohen the Barbarian?"

"The very shame."

"Hang on, hang on," said Rincewind. "Cohen's a great big chap, neck like a bull, got chest muscles like a sack of footballs. I mean, he's the Disc's greatest warrior, a legend in his own lifetime. I remember my granddad telling me he saw him . . . my granddad telling me he . . . my granddad . . ."

He faltered under the gimlet gaze.

"Oh," he said. "Oh. Of course. Sorry."

"Yesh," said Cohen, and sighed. "Thatsh right, boy. I'm a lifetime in my own legend."

"Gosh," said Rincewind. "How old are you, exactly?"

"Eighty-sheven."

"But you were the greatest!" said Bethan. "Bards still sing songs about you."

Cohen shrugged, and gave a little yelp of pain.

"I never get any royaltiesh," he said. He looked moodily at the snow. "That'sh the shaga of my life. Eighty yearsh in the bushiness and what have I got to show for it? Backache, pilesh, bad digeshtion and a hundred different recipesh for shoop. Shoop! I hate shoop!"

Bethan's forehead wrinkled. "Shoop?"

"Soup," explained Rincewind.

"Yeah, shoop," said Cohen, miserably. "It'sh my teeths, you shee. No one takes you sheriously when you've got no teeths, they shay 'Shit down by the fire, granddad, and have shome shoo—'" Cohen looked sharply at Rincewind. "That'sh a nashty cough you have there, boy."

Rincewind looked away, unable to look Bethan in the face. Then his heart sank. Twoflower was still leaning against the tree, peacefully unconscious, and looking as reproachful as was possible in the circumstances.

Cohen appeared to remember him, too. He got unsteadily to his feet and shuffled over to the tourist. He thumbed both eyes open, examined the graze, felt the pulse.

"He'sh gone," he said.

"Dead?" said Rincewind. In the debating chamber of his mind a dozen emotions got to their feet and started shouting. Relief was in full spate when Shock cut in on a point of order and then Bewilderment, Terror and Loss started a fight which was ended only when Shame slunk in from next door to see what all the row was about.

"No," said Cohen thoughtfully, "not exshactly. Just—gone."

"Gone where?"

"I don't know," said Cohen, "but I think I know shomeone who might have a map."

Far out on the snowfield half a dozen pinpoints of red light glowed in the shadows.

"He's not far away," said the leading wizard, peering into a small crystal sphere.

There was general mutter from the ranks behind him which roughly meant that however far away

Rincewind was he couldn't be further than a nice hot bath, a good meal and a warm bed.

Then the wizard who was tramping along in the rear stopped and said, "Listen!"

They listened. There were the subtle sounds of winter beginning to close its grip on the land, the creak of rocks, the muted scuffling of small creatures in their tunnels under the blanket of snow. In a distant forest a wolf howled, felt embarrassed when no one joined in, and stopped. There was the silver sleeting sound of moonlight. There was also the wheezing noise of half a dozen wizards trying to breathe quietly.

"I can't hear a thing—" one began.

"Ssshh!"

"All right, all right—"

Then they all heard it; a tiny distant crunching, like something moving very quickly over the snow crust.

"Wolves?" said a wizard. They all thought about hundreds of lean, hungry bodies leaping through the night.

"N-no," said the leader. "It's too regular. Perhaps it's a messenger?"

It was louder now, a crisp rhythm like someone eating celery very fast.

"I'll send up a flare," said the leader. He picked up a handful of snow, rolled it into a ball, threw it up into the air and ignited it with a stream of octarine fire from his fingertips. There was a brief, fierce blue glare.

There was silence. Then another wizard said, "You daft bugger, I can't see a thing now."

That was the last thing they heard before something fast, hard and noisy cannoned into them out of the darkness and vanished into the night.

When they dug one another out of the snow all they could find was a tight-pressed trail of little footprints. Hundreds of little footprints, all very close together and heading across the snow as straight as a searchlight.

"A necromancer!" said Rincewind.

The old woman across the fire shrugged and pulled a pack of greasy cards from some unseen pocket.

Despite the deep frost outside, the atmosphere inside the yurt was like a blacksmith's armpit and the wizard was already sweating heavily. Horse dung made a good fuel, but the Horse People had a lot to learn about air conditioning, starting with what it meant.

Bethan leaned sideways.

"What's neck romance?" she whispered.

"Necromancy. Talking to the dead," he explained.

"Oh," she said, vaguely disappointed.

They had dined on horse meat, horse cheese, horse black pudding, horse d'oeuvres and a thin beer that Rincewind didn't want to speculate about. Cohen (who'd had horse soup) explained that the Horse Tribes of the Hubland steppes were born in the saddle, which Rincewind considered was a gynecological impossibility, and they were particularly adept at natural magic, since life on the open steppe makes you realize how neatly the sky fits the land all around the edges and this naturally inspires the mind to deep thoughts like "Why?," "When?" and "Why don't we try beef for a change?"

The chieftain's grandmother nodded at Rincewind and spread the cards in front of her.

Rincewind, as it has already been noted, was the worst wizard on the Disc: no other spells would stay in his mind once the Spell had lodged in there, in much the same way that fish don't hang around in a pike pool. But he still had his pride, and wizards don't like to see women perform even simple magic. Unseen University had never admitted women, muttering something about problems with the plumbing, but the real reason was an unspoken dread that if women were allowed to mess around with magic they would probably be embarrassingly good at it . . .

"Anyway, I don't believe in Caroc cards," he muttered. "All that stuff about it being the distilled wisdom of the universe is a load of rubbish."

The first card, smoke-yellowed and age-crinkled, was . . .

It should have been The Star. But instead of the familiar round disc with crude little rays, it had become a tiny red dot. The old woman muttered and scratched at the card with a fingernail, then looked sharply at Rincewind.

"Nothing to do with me," he said.

She turned up the Importance of Washing the Hands, the Eight of Octograms, the Dome of the

Sky, the Pool of Night, the Four of Elephants, the Ace of Turtles, and—Rincewind had been expecting it—Death.

And something was wrong with Death, too. It should have been a fairly realistic drawing of Death on his white horse, and indeed He was still there. But the sky was red lit, and coming over a distant hill was a tiny figure, barely visible by the light of the horsefat lamps. Rincewind didn't have to identify it, because behind it was a box on hundreds of little legs.

The Luggage would follow its owner anywhere.

Rincewind looked across the tent to Twoflower, a pale shape on a pile of horsehides.

"He's really dead?" he said. Cohen translated for the old woman, who shook her head. She reached down to a small wooden chest beside her and rummaged around in a collection of bags and bottles until she found a tiny green bottle which she tipped into Rincewind's beer. He looked at it suspiciously.

"She shays it's sort of medicine," said Cohen. "I should drink it if I were you, theshe people get a bit upshet if you don't accshept hoshpitality."

"It's not going to blow my head off?" said Rincewind.

"She shays it's esshential you drink it."

"Well, if you're sure it's okay. It can't make the beer taste any worse."

He took a swig, aware of all eyes on him.

"Um," he said. "Actually, it's not at all ba—"

* * *

Something picked him up and threw him into the air. Except that in another sense he was still sitting by the fire—he could see himself there, a dwindling figure in the circle of firelight that was rapidly getting smaller. The toy figures around it were looking intently at his body. Except for the old woman. She was looking right up at *him*, and grinning.

The Circle Sea's senior wizards were not grinning at all. They were becoming aware that they were confronted with something entirely new and fearsome: a young man on the make.

Actually none of them were quite sure how old Trymon really was, but his sparse hair was still black and his skin had a waxy look to it that could be taken, in a poor light, to be the bloom of youth.

The six surviving heads of the Eight Orders sat at the long, shiny and new table in what had been Galder Weatherwax's study and each one wondered precisely what it was about Trymon that made them want to kick him.

It wasn't that he was ambitious and cruel. Cruel men were stupid; they all knew how to use cruel men, and they certainly knew how to bend other men's ambitions. You didn't stay an Eighth Level magus for long unless you were adept at a kind of mental judo.

It wasn't that he was bloodthirsty, power-hungry or especially wicked. These things were not necessarily drawbacks in a wizard. The wizards were, on the whole, no more wicked than, say, the committee of the average Rotary Club, and each had risen to preeminence in his chosen profession not so much by skill at magic but by never neglecting to capitalize on the weaknesses of opponents.

It wasn't that he was particularly wise. Every wizard considered himself a fairly hot property, wisewise; it went with the job.

It wasn't even that he had charisma. They all knew charisma when they encountered it, and Trymon had all the charisma of a duck egg.

That was it, in fact . . .

He wasn't good or evil or cruel or extreme in any way but one, which was that he had elevated grayness to the status of a fine art and cultivated a mind that was as bleak and pitiless and logical as the slopes of Hell.

And what was so strange was that each of the wizards, who had in the course of their work encountered many a fire-spitting, bat-winged, tiger-taloned entity in the privacy of a magical octogram, had never before had quite the same uncomfortable feeling as they had when, ten minutes late, Trymon strode into the room.

"Sorry I'm late, gentlemen," he lied, rubbing his hands briskly. "So many things to do, so much to organize, I'm sure you know how it is."

The wizards looked sidelong at one another as Trymon sat down at the head of the table and shuffled busily through some papers.

"What happened to old Galder's chair, the one with the lion arms and the chicken feet?" said Jiglad Wert. It had gone, along with most of the other familiar furniture, and in its place were a number of low leather chairs that appeared to be incredibly comfortable until you'd sat in them for five minutes.

"That? Oh, I had it burnt," said Trymon, not looking up.

"Burnt? But it was a priceless magical artifact, a genuine—"

"Just a piece of junk, I'm afraid," said Trymon, treating him to a fleeting smile. "I'm sure real wizards don't really need that sort of thing, now if I may draw your attention to the business of the day—"

"What's this paper?" said Jiglad Wert, of the Hoodwinkers, waving the document that had been left in front of him, and waving it all the more forcefully because his own chair, back in his cluttered and comfortable tower, was if anything more ornate than Galder's had been.

"It's an agenda, Jiglad," said Trymon, patiently.

"And what does a gender do?"

"It's just a list of the things we've got to discuss. It's very simple, I'm sorry if you feel that—"

"We've never needed one before!"

"I think perhaps you *have* needed one, you just haven't used one," said Trymon, his voice resonant with reasonableness.

Wert hesitated. "Well, all right," he said sullenly, looking around the table for support, "but what's this here where it says—" he peered closely at the writing— "'Successor to Greyhald Spold.' It's going to be old Rhunlet Vard, isn't it? He's been waiting for years."

"Yes, but is he sound?" said Trymon.

"What?"

"I'm sure we all realize the importance of proper leadership," said Trymon. "Now, Vard is—well, worthy, of course, in his way, but—"

"It's not our business," said one of the other wizards.

"No, but it could be," said Trymon.

There was silence.

"Interfere with the affairs of another Order?" said Wert.

"Of course not," said Trymon. "I merely suggest that we could offer . . . advice. But let us discuss this later . . ."

The wizards had never heard of the words "power base," otherwise Trymon would never have been able to get away with all this. But the plain fact was that helping others to achieve power, even to strengthen your own hand, was quite alien to them. As far as they were concerned, every wizard stood alone. Never mind about hostile paranormal entities, an ambitious wizard had quite enough to do fighting his enemies in his own Order.

"I think we should now consider the matter of Rincewind," said Trymon.

"And the star," said Wert. "People are noticing, you know."

"Yes, they say we should be doing something," said Lumuel Panter, of the Order of Midnight. "What, I should like to know?"

"Oh, that's easy," said Wert. "They say we should read the Octavo. That's what they always say. Crops bad? Read the Octavo. Cows ill? Read the Octavo. The Spells will make everything all right."

"There could be something in that," said Trymon. "My, er, late predecessor made quite a study of the Octavo."

"We all have," said Panter, sharply, "but what's the use? The Eight Spells have to work together. Oh, I agree, if all else fails maybe we should risk it, but the Eight have to be said together or not at all—and one of them is inside this Rincewind's head."

"And we cannot find him," said Trymon. "That is the case, isn't it? I'm sure we've all tried, privately."

The wizards looked at one another, embarrassed. Eventually Wert said, "Yes. All right. Cards on the table. I can't seem to locate him."

"I've tried scrying," said another. "Nothing."

"*I've* sent familiars," said a third. The others sat up. If confessing failure was the order of the day, then they were damn well going to make it clear that they had failed heroically.

"Is that all? *I've* sent demons."

"*I've* looked into the Mirror of Oversight."

"Last night I sought him out in the Runes of M'haw."

"I'd like to make it clear that I tried both the Runes and the Mirror *and* the entrails of a manic-reach."

"*I've* spoken to the beasts of the field and the birds of the Air."

"Any good?"

"Nah."

"Well, I've questioned the very bones of the country, yea, and the deep stones and the mountains thereof."

There was a sudden chilly silence. Everyone looked at the wizard who had spoken. It was Ganmack Treehallet, of the Venerable Seers, who shifted uneasily in his seat.

"Yes, with bells on, I expect," said someone.

"I never said they answered, did I?"

Trymon looked along the table.

"*I've* sent someone to find him," he said.

Wert snorted. "That didn't work out so well the last two times, did it?"

"That was because we relied on magic, but it is obvious that Rincewind is somehow hidden from magic. But he can't hide his footprints."

"You've set a tracker?"

"In a manner of speaking."

"A *hero?*" Wert managed to pack a lot of meaning into the one word. In such a tone of voice, in another universe, would a Southerner say "damnyankee."

The wizards looked at Trymon, open-mouthed.

"Yes," he said calmly.

"On whose authority?" demanded Wert. Trymon turned his gray eyes on him.

"Mine. I needed no other."

"It's—it's highly irregular! Since when have wizards needed to hire heroes to do their work for them?"

"Ever since wizards found their magic wouldn't work," said Trymon.

"A temporary setback, nothing more."

Trymon shrugged. "Maybe," he said, "but we haven't the time to find out. Prove me wrong. Find Rincewind by scrying or talking to birds. But as for me, I know I'm meant to be wise. And wise men do what the times demand."

It is a well-known fact that warriors and wizards do not get along, because one side considers the other side to be a collection of bloodthirsty idiots who can't walk and think at the same time, while the other side is naturally suspicious of a body of men who mumble a lot and wear long dresses. Oh, say the wizards, if we're going to be like that, then, what about all those studded collars and oiled muscles down at the Young Men's Pagan Association? To which the heroes reply, that's a pretty good allegation coming from a bunch of wimp-soes who won't go near a woman on account, can you believe it, of their mystical power being sort of drained out. Right, say the wizards, that just about does it, you and your leather posing pouches. Oh yeah, say the heroes, why don't you . . .

And so on. This sort of thing has been going on for centuries, and caused a number of major battles which have left large tracts of land uninhabitable because of magical harmonics.

In fact, the hero even at this moment galloping toward the Vortex Plains didn't get involved in this kind of argument, because they didn't take it seriously but mainly because this particular hero was a heroine. A redheaded one.

Now, there is a tendency at a point like this to

look over one's shoulder at the cover artist and start going on at length about leather, thighboots and naked blades.

Words like "full," "round" and even "pert" creep into the narrative, until the writer has to go and have a cold shower and a lie down.

Which is all rather silly, because any woman setting out to make a living by the sword isn't about to go around looking like something off the cover of the more advanced kind of lingerie catalogue for the specialized buyer.

Oh well, all right. The point that must be made is that although Herrena the Henna-Haired Harridan would look quite stunning after a good bath, a heavy-duty manicure, and the pick of the leather racks in Woo Hun Ling's Oriental Exotica and Martial Aids on Heroes Street, she was currently quite sensibly dressed in light chain mail, soft boots and a short sword.

All right, maybe the boots were leather. But not black.

Riding with her were a number of swarthy men that will certainly be killed before too long anyway, so a description is probably not essential. There was absolutely nothing pert about any of them.

Look, they can wear leather if you like.

Herrena wasn't too happy about them, but they were all that was available for hire in Morpork. Many of the citizens were moving out and heading for the hills, out of fear of the new star.

But Herrena was heading for the hills for a different reason. Just turnwise and rimward of the Plains were the bare Trollbone Mountains. Herrena, who had for many years availed herself of the uniquely equal opportunities available to any woman who could make a sword sing, was trusting to her instincts.

This Rincewind, as Trymon had described him, was a rat, and rats like cover. Anyway, the mountains were a long way from Trymon and, for all that he was currently her employer, Herrena was very happy about that. There was something about his manner that made her fists itch.

Rincewind knew he ought to be panicking, but that was difficult because, although he wasn't aware of it, emotions like panic and terror and anger are all to do with stuff sloshing around in glands and all Rincewind's glands were still in his body.

It was difficult to be certain where his real body was, but when he looked down he could see a fine blue line trailing from what for the sake of sanity he would still call his ankle into the blackness around him, and it seemed reasonable to assume that his body was on the other end.

It was not a particularly good body, he'd be the first to admit, but one or two bits of it had sentimental value and it dawned on him that if the little blue line snapped he'd have to spend the rest of his li—his existence hanging around Ouija boards pretending to be people's dead aunties and all the other things lost souls do to pass the time.

The sheer horror of this so appalled him he hardly felt his feet touch the ground. *Some* ground, anyway; he decided that it almost certainly wasn't *the* ground, which as far as he could remember wasn't black and didn't swirl in such a disconcerting way.

He took a look around.

Sheer sharp mountains speared up around him into a frosty sky hung with cruel stars, stars which appeared on no celestial chart in the multiverse, but right in there among them was a malevolent red disc. Rincewind shivered, and looked away. The land ahead of him sloped down sharply, and a dry wind whispered across the frost-cracked rocks.

It really did whisper. As gray eddies caught at his robe and tugged at his hair Rincewind thought he could hear voices, faint and far off, saying things like "Are you sure those were mushrooms in the stew? I feel a bit—" and "There's a lovely view if you lean over this—" and "Don't fuss, it's only a scratch—" and "Watch where you're pointing that bow, you nearly—" and so on.

He stumbled down the slope, with his fingers in his ears, until he saw a sight seen by very few living men.

The ground dipped sharply until it became a vast funnel, fully a mile across, into which the whispering wind of the souls of the dead blew with a vast, echoing susurration, as though the Disc itself was breathing. But a narrow spur of rock arched out and over the hole, ending in an outcrop perhaps a hundred feet across.

There was a garden up there, with orchards and flowerbeds, and a quite small black cottage.

A little path led up to it.

Rincewind looked behind him. The shiny blue line was still there.

So was the Luggage.

It squatted on the path, watching him.

Rincewind had never got on with the Luggage, it had always given him the impression that it thoroughly disapproved of him. But just for once it wasn't glaring at him. It had a rather pathetic look, like a dog that's just come home after a pleasant roll in the cowpats to find that the family has moved to the next continent.

"All right," said Rincewind. "Come on."

It extended its legs and followed him up the path.

Somehow Rincewind had expected the garden on the outcrop to be full of dead flowers, but it was in fact well kept and had obviously been planted by someone with an eye for color, always provided the color was deep purple, night black or shroud white. Huge lilies perfumed the air. There was a sundial without a gnomon in the middle of a freshly scythed lawn.

With the Luggage trailing behind him Rincewind crept along a path of marble chippings until he was at the rear of the cottage, and pushed open a door.

Four horses looked at him over the top of their nosebags. They were warm and alive, and some of the best-kept beasts Rincewind had ever seen. A big white one had a stall all to itself, and a silver and black harness hung over the door. The other three were tethered in front of a hay rack on the opposite wall, as if visitors had just dropped by. They regarded Rincewind with vague animal curiosity.

The Luggage bumped into his ankle. He spun around and hissed, "Push off, you!"

The Luggage backed away. It looked abashed.

Rincewind tiptoed to the far door and cautiously pushed it open. It gave onto a stone-flagged passageway, which in turn opened onto a wide entrance hall.

He crept forward with his back pressed tightly against a wall. Behind him the Luggage rose up on tiptoes and skittered along nervously.

The hall itself . . .

Well, it wasn't the fact that it was considerably bigger than the whole cottage had appeared from the outside that worried Rincewind; the way things were these days, he'd have laughed sarcastically if anyone had said you couldn't get a quart into a pint pot. And it wasn't the decor, which was Early Crypt and ran heavily to black drapes.

It was the clock. It was very big, and occupied a space between two curving wooden staircases covered with carvings of things that normal men only see after a heavy session on something illegal.

It had a very long pendulum, and the pendulum swung with a slow tick-tock that set his teeth on edge, because it was the kind of deliberate, annoying ticking that wanted to make it abundantly clear that every tick and every tock was stripping another second off your life. It was the kind of sound that suggested very pointedly that in some hypothetical hourglass, somewhere, another few grains of sand had dropped out from under you.

Needless to say, the weight on the pendulum was knife-edged and razor sharp.

Something tapped him in the small of the back. He turned angrily.

"Look, you son of a suitcase, I told you—"

It wasn't the Luggage. It was a young woman— silver haired, silver eyed, rather taken aback.

"Oh," said Rincewind. "Um. Hallo?"

"Are you alive?" she said. It was the kind of voice associated with beach umbrellas, suntan oil and long cool drinks.

"Well, I hope so," said Rincewind, wondering if his glands were having a good time wherever they were. "Sometimes I'm not so sure. What is this place?"

"This is the house of Death," she said.

"Ah," said Rincewind. He ran a tongue over his dry lips. "Well, nice to meet you, I think I ought to be getting along—"

She clapped her hands. "Oh, you mustn't go!" she said. "We don't often have living people here. Dead people are so boring, don't you think?"

"Uh, yes," Rincewind agreed fervently, eyeing the doorway. "Not much conversation, I imagine."

"It's always 'When I was alive—' and 'We really knew how to breathe in my day—'" she said, laying a small white hand on his arm and smiling at him. "They're always so set in their ways, too. No fun at all. So formal."

"Stiff?" suggested Rincewind. She was propelling him toward an archway.

"Absolutely. What's your name? My name is Ysa-bell."

"Um, Rincewind. Excuse me, but if this is the house of Death, what are you doing here? You don't look dead to me."

"Oh, I live here." She looked intently at him. "I say, you haven't come to rescue your lost love, have you? That always annoys daddy, he says it's a good job he never sleeps because if he did he'd be kept awake by the tramp, tramp, tramp of young heroes coming down here to carry back a lot of silly girls, he says."

"Goes on a lot, does it?" said Rincewind weakly, as they walked along a black-hung corridor.

"All the time. I think it's very romantic. Only when you leave, it's very important not to look back."

"Why not?"

She shrugged. "I don't know. Perhaps the view isn't very good. Are you a hero, actually?"

"Um, no. Not as such. Not at all, really. Even less than that, in fact. I just came to look for a friend of mine," he said wretchedly. "I suppose you haven't seen him? Little fat man, talks a lot, wears eye-glasses, funny sort of clothes?"

As he spoke he was aware that he may have missed something vital. He shut his eyes and tried to recall the last few minutes of conversation. Then it hit him like a sandbag.

"Daddy?"

She looked down demurely. "Adopted, actually,"

she said. "He found me when I was a little girl, he says. It was all rather sad." She brightened. "But come and meet him—he's got his friends in tonight, I'm sure he'll be interested to see you. He doesn't meet many people socially. Nor do I, actually," she added.

"Sorry," said Rincewind. "Have I got it right? We're talking about Death, yes? Tall, thin, empty eye sockets, handy in the scythe department?"

She sighed. "Yes. His looks are against him, I'm afraid."

While it was true that, as has already been indicated, Rincewind was to magic what a bicycle is to a bumblebee, he nevertheless retained one privilege available to practitioners of the art, which was that at the point of death it would be Death himself who turned up to claim him (instead of delegating the job to a lesser mythological anthropomorphic personification, as is usually the case). Owing largely to inefficiency Rincewind had consistently failed to die at the right time, and if there is one thing that Death does not like it is unpunctuality.

"Look, I expect my friend has just wandered off somewhere," he said. "He's always doing that, story of his life, nice to have met you, must be going—"

But she had already stopped in front of a tall door padded with purple velvet. There were voices on the other side—eldritch voices, the sort of voices that mere typography will remain totally unable to convey until someone can make a linotype machine with echo-reverb and, possibly, a typeface that looks like something said by a slug.

This is what the voices were saying:

WOULD YOU MIND EXPLAINING THAT AGAIN?

"Well, if you return anything *except* a trump, South will be able to get in his two ruffs, losing only one Turtle, one Elephant and one Major Arcana, then—"

"That's Twoflower!" hissed Rincewind. "I'd know that voice anywhere!"

JUST A MINUTE—PESTILENCE IS SOUTH?

"*Oh, come on, Mort. He explained that. What if Famine had played a—what was it—a trump return?*" It was a breathy, wet voice, practically contagious all by itself.

"Ah, then you'd only be able to ruff one Turtle instead of two," said Twoflower enthusiastically.

"But if War had chosen a trump lead originally, then the contract would have gone two down?"

"Exactly!"

I DIDN'T QUITE FOLLOW THAT. TELL ME ABOUT PSYCHIC BIDS AGAIN, I THOUGHT I WAS GETTING THE HANG OF THAT. It was a heavy, hollow voice, like two large lumps of lead smashing together.

"That's when you make a bid primarily to deceive your opponents, but of course it might cause problems for your partner—"

Twoflower's voice rambled on in its enthusiastic way. Rincewind looked blankly at Ysabell as words like "rebiddable suit," "double finesse" and "grand slam" floated through the velvet.

"Do you understand any of that?" she asked.

"Not a word," he said.

"It sounds awfully complicated."

On the other side of the door the heavy voice said: DID YOU SAY HUMANS PLAY THIS FOR FUN?

Some of them get to be very good at it, yes. I'm only an amateur, I'm afraid.

BUT THEY ONLY LIVE EIGHTY OR NINETY YEARS!

"You should know, Mort," said a voice that Rincewind hadn't heard before and certainly never wanted to hear again, especially after dark.

It's certainly very—intriguing.

DEAL AGAIN AND LET'S SEE IF I'VE GOT THE HANG OF IT.

"Do you think perhaps we should go in?" said Ysabell. A voice behind the door said, I BID . . . . THE KNAVE OF TERRAPINS.

"No, sorry, I'm sure you're wrong, let's have a look at your—"

Ysabell pushed the door open.

It was, in fact, a rather pleasant study, perhaps a little on the somber side, possibly created on a bad day by an interior designer who had a headache and a craving for putting large hourglasses on every flat surface and also a lot of large, fat, yellow and extremely runny candles he wanted to get rid of.

The Death of the Disc was a traditionalist who prided himself on his personal service and spent most of the time being depressed because this was not appreciated. He would point out that no one feared death itself, just pain and separation and oblivion, and that it was quite unreasonable to take against someone just because he had empty eye sockets and a quiet pride in his work. He still used a scythe, he'd point out, while the Deaths of other worlds had long ago invested in combine harvesters.

Death sat at one side of a black baize table in the center of the room, arguing with Famine, War and Pestilence. Twoflower was the only one to look up and notice Rincewind.

"Hey, how did you get here?" he said.

"Well, some say the Creator took a handful—oh, I see, well, it's hard to explain but I—"

"Have you got the Luggage?"

The wooden box pushed past Rincewind and settled down in front of its owner, who opened its lid and rummaged around inside until he came up with a small, leatherbound book which he handed to War, who was hammering the table with a mailed fist.

"It's 'Nosehinger on the Laws of Contract,'" he said. "It's quite good, there's a lot in it about double finessing and how to—"

Death snatched the book with a bony hand and flipped through the pages, quite oblivious to the presence of the two men.

RIGHT, he said, PESTILENCE, OPEN ANOTHER PACK OF CARDS. I'M GOING TO GET TO THE BOTTOM OF THIS IF IT KILLS ME, FIGURATIVELY SPEAKING OF COURSE.

Rincewind grabbed Twoflower and pulled him out of the room. As they jogged down the corridor with the Luggage galloping behind them he said:

"What was all that about?"

"Well, they've got lots of time and I thought they might enjoy it," panted Twoflower.

"What, playing with cards?"

"It's a special kind of playing," said Twoflower. "It's called—" he hesitated. Language wasn't his strong point. "In your language it's called a thing you put across a river, for example," he concluded, "I think."

"Aqueduct?" hazarded Rincewind. "Fishing line? Weir? Dam?"

"Yes, possibly."

They reached the hallway, where the big clock still shaved the seconds off the lives of the world.

"And how long do you think that'll keep them occupied?"

Twoflower paused. "I'm not sure," he said thoughtfully. "Probably until the last trump—what an amazing clock . . ."

"Don't try to buy it," Rincewind advised. "I don't think they'd appreciate it around here."

"Where is here, exactly?" said Twoflower, beckoning the Luggage and opening its lid.

Rincewind looked around. The hall was dark and deserted, its tall narrow windows whorled with ice. He looked down. There was the faint blue line stretching away from his ankle. Now he could see that Twoflower had one too.

"We're sort of informally dead," he said. It was the best he could manage.

"Oh." Twoflower continued to rummage.

"Doesn't that worry you?"

"Well, things tend to work out in the end, don't you think? Anyway, I'm a firm believer in reincarnation. What would you like to come back as?"

"I don't want to go," said Rincewind firmly. "Come on, let's get out of—oh, no. Not that."

Twoflower had produced a box from the depths of the Luggage. It was large and black and had a handle on one side and a little round window in front and a strap so that Twoflower could put it around his neck, which he did.

There was a time when Rincewind had quite liked the iconoscope. He believed, against all experience, that the world was fundamentally understandable, and that if he could only equip himself with the right mental toolbox he could take the back off and see how it worked. He was, of course, dead wrong. The iconoscope didn't take pictures by letting light fall onto specially treated paper, as he had surmised, but by the far simpler method of imprisoning a small demon with a good eye for color and a speedy hand with a paintbrush. He had been very upset to find that out.

"You haven't got time to take pictures!" he hissed.

"It won't take long," said Twoflower firmly, and rapped on the side of the box. A tiny door flew open and the imp poked his head out.

"Bloody hell," it said. "Where are we?"

"It doesn't matter," said Twoflower. "The clock first, I think."

The demon squinted.

"Poor light," he said. "Three bloody years at f8, if you ask me." He slammed the door shut. A second later there was the tiny scraping noise of his stool being dragged up to his easel.

Rincewind gritted his teeth.

"You don't need to take pictures, you can just remember it!" he shouted.

"It's not the same," said Twoflower calmly.

"It's better! It's more real!"

"It isn't really. In years to come, when I'm sitting by the fire—"

"You'll be sitting by the fire forever if we don't get out of here!"

"Oh, I do hope you're not going."

They both turned. Ysabell was standing in the archway, smiling faintly. She held a scythe in one hand, a scythe with a blade of proverbial sharpness. Rincewind tried not to look down at his blue lifeline; a girl holding a scythe shouldn't smile in that unpleasant, knowing and slightly deranged way.

"Daddy seems a little preoccupied at the moment but I'm sure he wouldn't dream of letting you go off just like that," she added. "Besides, I'd have no one to talk to."

"Who's this?" said Twoflower.

"She sort of lives here," mumbled Rincewind. "She's a sort of girl," he added.

He grabbed Twoflower's shoulder and tried to shuffle imperceptibly toward the door into the dark, cold garden. It didn't work; largely because Twoflower wasn't the sort of person who went in for nuances of expression and somehow never assumed that anything bad might apply to him.

"Charmed, I'm sure," he said. "Very nice place, you have here. Interesting baroque effect with the bones and skulls."

Ysabell smiled. Rincewind thought: if Death ever

does hand over the family business, she'll be better at it than he is—she's bonkers.

"Yes, but we must be going," he said.

"I really won't hear of it," she said. "You must stay and tell me all about yourselves. There's plenty of time and it's so boring here."

She darted sideways and swung the scythe at the shining threads. It screamed through the air like a neutered tomcat—and stopped sharply.

There was the creak of wood. The Luggage had snapped its lid shut on the blade.

Twoflower looked up at Rincewind in astonishment. And the wizard, with great deliberation and a certain amount of satisfaction, hit him smartly on the chin. As the little man fell backward Rincewind caught him, threw him over a shoulder and ran.

Branches whipped at him in the starlit garden, and small, furry and probably horrible things scampered away as he pounded desperately along the faint lifeline that shone eerily on the freezing grass.

From the building behind him came a shrill scream of disappointment and rage. He cannoned off a tree and sped on.

Somewhere there was a path, he remembered. But in this maze of silver light and shadows, tinted now with red as the terrible new star made its presence felt even in the netherworld, nothing looked right. Anyway, the lifeline appeared to be going in quite the wrong direction.

There was the sound of feet behind him. Rincewind wheezed with effort; it sounded like the Luggage, and at the moment he didn't want to meet the

Luggage, because it might have got the wrong idea about him hitting its master, and generally the Luggage bit people it didn't like. Rincewind had never had the nerve to ask where it was they actually went when the heavy lid slammed shut on them, but they certainly weren't there when it opened again.

In fact he needn't have worried. The Luggage overtook him easily, its little legs a blur of movement. It seemed to Rincewind to be concentrating very heavily on running, as if it had some inkling of what was coming up behind it and didn't like the idea at all.

Don't look back, he remembered. The view probably isn't very nice.

The Luggage crashed through a bush and vanished.

A moment later Rincewind saw why. It had careened over the edge of the outcrop and was dropping toward the great hole underneath, which he could now see was faintly red lit at the bottom. Stretching from Rincewind, out over the edge of the rocks and down into the hole, were two shimmering blue lines.

He paused uncertainly, although that isn't precisely true because he was totally certain of several things, for example that he didn't want to jump, and that he certainly didn't want to face whatever it was coming up behind him, and that in the spirit world Twoflower was quite heavy, and that there were worse things than being dead.

"Name two," he muttered, and jumped.

A few seconds later the horsemen arrived and

didn't stop when they reached the edge of the rock but simply rode into the air and reined their horses over nothingness.

Death looked down.

THAT ALWAYS ANNOYS ME, he said. I MIGHT AS WELL INSTALL A REVOLVING DOOR.

"*I wonder what they wanted?*" said Pestilence.

"Search me," said War. "Nice game, though."

"Right," agreed Famine. "Compelling, I thought."

WE'VE GOT TIME FOR ANOTHER FONDLE, said Death.

"Rubber," corrected War.

RUBBER WHAT?

"You call them rubbers," said War.

RIGHT, RUBBERS, said Death. He looked up at the new star, puzzled as to what it might mean.

I THINK WE'VE GOT TIME, he repeated, a trifle uncertainly.

Mention has already been made of an attempt to inject a little honesty into reporting on the Disc, and how poets and bards were banned on pain of—well, pain—from going on about babbling brooks and rosy-fingered dawn and could only say, for example, that a face had launched a thousand ships if they were able to produce certified dockyard accounts.

And therefore, out of a passing respect for this tradition, it will not be said of Rincewind and Twoflower that they became an ice-blue sinewave arcing through the dark dimensions, or that there was a sound like the twanging of a monstrous tusk, or that their lives passed in front of their eyes (Rincewind had in any case seen his past life flash in front of his eyes so many times that he could sleep through the boring bits) or that the universe dropped on them like a large jelly.

It will be said, because experiment has proven it to be true, that there was a noise like a wooden ruler being struck heavily with a C-sharp tuning fork, possibly B-flat, and a sudden sensation of absolute stillness.

This was because they were absolutely still, and it was absolutely dark.

It occurred to Rincewind that something had gone wrong.

Then he saw the faint blue tracery in front of him.

He was inside the Octavo again. He wondered what would happen if anyone opened the book; would he and Twoflower appear like a color plate?

Probably not, he decided. The Octavo they were in was something a bit different from the mere book chained to its lectern deep in Unseen University, which was merely a three-dimensional representation of a multidimensional reality, and—

Hold on, he thought. I don't think like this. Who's thinking for me?

"Rincewind," said a voice like the rustle of old pages.

"Who? Me?"

"Of course you, you daft sod."

A flicker of defiance flared very briefly in Rincewind's battered heart.

"Have you managed to recall how the universe started yet?" he said nastily. "The Clearing of the Throat, wasn't it, or the Drawing of the Breath, or the Scratching of the Head and Trying to Remember It, It was On the Tip of the Tongue?"

Another voice, dry as tinder, hissed, "You would do well to remember where you are." It should be impossible to hiss a sentence with no sibilants in it, but the voice made a very good attempt.

"Remember where I am? Remember where I am?" shouted Rincewind. "Of course I remember where I am, I'm inside a bloody book talking to a load of voices I can't see, why do you think I'm screaming?"

"I expect you're wondering why we brought you here again," said a voice by his ear.

"No."

"No?"

"What did he say?" said another disembodied voice.

"He said no."

"He really said no?"

"Yes."

"Oh."

"Why?"

"This sort of thing happens to me all the time," said Rincewind. "One minute I'm falling off the world, then I'm inside a book, then I'm on a flying rock, then I'm watching Death learn how to play Weir or Dam or whatever it was, why should I wonder about anything?"

"Well, we imagine you will be wondering why we

don't want anyone to say us," said the first voice, aware that it was losing the initiative.

Rincewind hesitated. The thought had crossed his mind, only very fast and looking nervously from side to side in case it got knocked over.

"Why should anyone want to say you?"

"It's the star," said the spell. "The red star. Wizards are already looking for you; when they find you they want to say all eight Spells together to change the future. They think the Disc is going to collide with the star."

Rincewind thought about this. "Is it?"

"Not exactly, but in a—*What's that?*"

Rincewind looked down. The Luggage padded out of the darkness. There was a long sliver of scytheblade in its lid.

"It's just the Luggage," he said.

"But we didn't summon it here!"

"No one summons it anywhere," said Rincewind. "It just turns up. Don't worry about it."

"Oh. What were we talking about?"

"This red star thing."

"Right. It's very important that you—"

"Hallo? Hallo? Anyone out there?"

It was a small and squeaky voice and came from the picture box still slung around Twoflower's inert neck.

The picture imp opened his hatch and squinted up at Rincewind.

"Where's this, squire?" it said.

"I'm not sure."

"We still dead?"

"Maybe."

"Well, let's hope we go somewhere where we don't need too much black, because I've run out." The hatch slammed shut.

Rincewind had a fleeting vision of Twoflower handing around his pictures and saying things like "This is me being tormented by a million demons" and "This is me with that funny couple we met on the freezing slopes of the Underworld." Rincewind wasn't certain about what happened to you after you really died, the authorities were a little unclear on the subject; a swarthy sailor from the rimward lands had said that he was confident of going to a paradise where there was sherbet and houris. Rincewind wasn't certain what a houri was, but after some thought he came to the conclusion that it was a little licorice tube for sucking up the sherbet. Anyway, sherbet made him sneeze.

"Now that interruption is over," said a dry voice firmly, "perhaps we can get on. It is most important that you don't let the wizards take the spell from you. Terrible things will happen if all eight spells are said too soon."

"I just want to be left in peace," said Rincewind.

"Good, good. We knew we could trust you from the day you first opened the Octavo."

Rincewind hesitated. "Hang on a minute," he said. "You want me to run around keeping the wizards from getting all the spells together?"

"Exactly."

"That's why one of you got into my head?"

"Precisely."

"You totally ruined my life, you know that?" said Rincewind hotly. "I could have really made it as a wizard if you hadn't decided to use me as a sort of portable spellbook. I can't remember any other spells, they're too frightened to stay in the same head as you!"

"We're sorry."

"I just want to go home! I want to go back to where—" a trace of moisture appeared in Rincewind's eye— "to where there's cobbles under your feet and some of the beer isn't too bad and you can get quite a good piece of fried fish of an evening, with maybe a couple of big green gherkins, and even an eel pie and a dish of whelks, and there's always a warm stable somewhere to sleep in and in the morning you are always in the same place as you were the night before and there wasn't all this weather all over the place. I mean, I don't mind about the magic, I'm probably not, you know, the right sort of material for a wizard, I just want to go home!—"

"But you must—" one of the spells began.

It was too late. Homesickness, the little elastic band in the subconscious that can wind up a salmon and propel it three thousand miles through strange seas, or send a million lemmings running joyfully back to an ancestral homeland which, owing to a slight kink in the continental drift, isn't there anymore—homesickness rose up inside Rincewind like a late-night prawn biriani, flowed along the tenuous thread linking his tortured soul to his body, dug its heels in and tugged . . .

The spells were alone inside their Octavo.

Alone, at any rate, apart from the Luggage.

They looked at it, not with eyes, but with consciousness as old as the Discworld itself.

"And you can bugger off too," they said.

"—bad."

Rincewind knew it was himself speaking, he recognized the voice. For a moment he was looking out through his eyes not in any normal way, but as a spy might peer through the cut-out eyes of a picture. Then he was back.

"You okay, Rinshwind?" said Cohen. "You looked a bit gone there."

"You did look a bit white," agreed Bethan. "Like someone had walked over your grave."

"Uh, yes, it was probably me," he said. He held up his fingers and counted them. There appeared to be the normal amount.

"Um, have I moved at all?" he said.

"You just looked at the fire as if you had seen a ghost," said Bethan.

There was a groan behind them. Twoflower was sitting up, holding his head in his hands.

His eyes focused on them. His lips moved soundlessly.

"That was a really strange . . . dream," he said. "What's this place? Why am I here?"

"Well," said Cohen, "shome shay the Creator of the Univershe took a handful of clay and—"

"No, I mean here," said Twoflower. "Is that you, Rincewind?"

"Yes," said Rincewind, giving it the benefit of the doubt.

"There was this . . . a clock that . . . and these people who . . ." said Twoflower. He shook his head. "Why does everything smell of horses?"

"You've been ill," said Rincewind. "Hallucinating."

"Yes . . . I suppose I was." Twoflower looked down at his chest. "But in that case, why have I—"

Rincewind jumped to his feet.

"Sorry, very close in here, got to have a breath of fresh air," he said. He removed the picture box's strap from Twoflower's neck, and dashed for the tent flap.

"I didn't notice that when he came in," said Bethan. Cohen shrugged.

Rincewind managed to get a few yards from the yurt before the ratchet of the picture box began to click. Very slowly, the box extruded the last picture that the imp had taken.

Rincewind snatched at it.

What it showed would have been quite horrible even in broad daylight. By freezing starlight, tinted red with the fires of the evil new star, it was a lot worse.

"No," said Rincewind softly. "No, it wasn't like that, there was a house, and this girl, and . . ."

"You see what you see and I paint what I see," said the imp from its hatch. "What I see is real. I was bred for it. I only see what's really there."

A dark shape crunched over the snowcrust toward Rincewind. It was the Luggage. Rincewind, who normally hated and distrusted it, suddenly felt it was the most refreshingly normal thing he had ever seen.

"I see you made it, then," said Rincewind. The Luggage rattled its lid.

"Okay, but what did *you* see?" said Rincewind. "Did you look behind?"

The Luggage said nothing. For a moment they were silent, like two warriors who have fled the field of carnage and have paused for a return of breath and sanity.

Then Rincewind said, "Come on, there's a fire inside." He reached out to pat the Luggage's lid. It snapped irritably at him, nearly catching his fingers. Life was back to normal again.

The next day dawned bright and clear and cold. The sky became a blue dome stuck on the white sheet of the world, and the whole effect would have been as fresh and clean as a toothpaste advert if it wasn't for the pink dot on the horizon.

"You can shee it in daylight now," said Cohen. "What is it?"

He looked hard at Rincewind, who reddened.

"Why does everyone look at me?" he said. "I don't know what it is, maybe it's a comet or something."

"Will we all be burned up?" said Bethan.

"How should I know? I've never been hit by a comet before."

They were riding in single file across the brilliant snowfield. The Horse people, who seemed to hold Cohen in high regard, had given them their mounts and directions to the River Smarl, a hundred miles rimward, where Cohen reckoned Rincewind and Twoflower could find a boat to take them to the Circle Sea. He had announced that he was coming with them, on account of his chilblains.

Bethan had promptly announced that she was going to come too, in case Cohen wanted anything rubbed.

Rincewind was vaguely aware of some sort of chemistry bubbling away. For one thing, Cohen had made an effort to comb his beard.

"I think she's rather taken with you," he said. Cohen sighed.

"If I wash twenty yearsh younger," he said wistfully.

"Yes?"

"I'd be shixty-sheven."

"What's that got to do with it?"

"Well—how can I put it? When I wash a young man, carving my name in the world, well, then I liked my women red-haired and fiery."

"Ah."

"And then I grew a little older and for preference I looked for a woman with blonde hair and the glint of the world in her eye."

"Oh? Yes?"

"But then I grew a little older again and I came to see the point of dark women of a sultry nature."

He paused. Rincewind waited.

"And?" he said. "Then what? What is it that you look for in a woman now?"

Cohen turned one rheumy blue eye on him.

"Patience," he said.

"I can't believe it!" said a voice behind them. "Me riding with Cohen the Barbarian!"

It was Twoflower. Since early morning he had been like a monkey with the key to the banana plantation after discovering he was breathing the same air as the greatest hero of all time.

"Is he perhapsh being sharcashtic?" said Cohen to Rincewind.

"No. He's always like that."

Cohen turned in his saddle. Twoflower beamed at him, and waved proudly. Cohen turned back, and grunted.

"He's got eyesh, hashn't he?"

"Yes, but they don't work like other people's. Take it from me. I mean—well, you know the Horse people's yurt, where we were last night?"

"Yesh."

"Would you say it was a bit dark and greasy and smelled like a very ill horse?"

"Very accurate deshcription, I'd shay."

"He wouldn't agree. He'd say it was a magnificent barbarian tent, hung with the pelts of the great beasts hunted by the lean-eyed warriors from the edge of civilization, and smelled of the rare and curious resins plundered from the caravans as they crossed the trackless—well, and so on. I mean it," he added.

"He'sh mad?"

"Sort of mad. But mad with lots of money."

"Ah, then he can't be mad. I've been around; if a man hash lotsh of money he'sh just ecshentric."

Cohen turned in his saddle again. Twoflower was

telling Bethan how Cohen had single-handed defeated the snake warriors of the witch lord of S'belinde and stolen the sacred diamond from the giant statue of Offler the Crocodile God.

A weird smile formed among the wrinkles of Cohen's face.

"I could tell him to shut up, if you like," said Rincewind.

"Would he?"

"No, not really."

"Let him babble," said Cohen. His hand fell to the handle of his sword, polished smooth by the grip of decades.

"Anyway, I *like* his eyes," he said. "They can see for fifty years."

A hundred yards behind them, hopping rather awkwardly through the soft snow, came the Luggage. No one ever asked its opinion about anything.

By evening they had come to the edge of the high plains, and rode down through gloomy pine forests that had only been lightly dusted by the snowstorm. It was a landscape of huge cracked rocks, and valleys so narrow and deep that the days only lasted about twenty minutes. A wild, windy country, the sort where you might expect to find—

"Trollsh," said Cohen, sniffing the air.

Rincewind stared around him in the red evening light. Suddenly rocks that had seemed perfectly normal looked suspiciously alive. Shadows that he wouldn't have looked at twice now began to look horribly occupied.

"I like trolls," said Twoflower.

"No you don't," said Rincewind firmly. "You can't. They're big and knobbly and they eat people."

"No they don't," said Cohen, sliding awkwardly off his horse and massaging his knees. "Well-known mishapprehenshion, that ish. Trollsh never ate anybody."

"No?"

"No, they alwaysh spit the bitsh out. Can't digesht people, see? Your average troll don't want any more out of life than a nice lump of granite, maybe, with perhapsh a nice slab of limeshtone for aftersh. I heard someone shay it's becosh they're a shilicashe—a shillycaysheou—" Cohen paused, and wiped his beard, "made out of rocks."

Rincewind nodded. Trolls were not unknown in Ankh-Morpork, of course, where they often got employment as bodyguards. They tended to be a bit expensive to keep until they learned about doors and didn't simply leave the house by walking aimlessly through the nearest wall.

As they gathered firewood Cohen went on, "Trollsh teeth, that'sh the thingsh."

"Why?" said Bethan.

"Diamonds. Got to be, you shee. Only thing that can shtand the rocksh, and they shtill have to grow a new shet every year."

"Talking of teeth—" said Twoflower.

"Yesh?"

"I can't help noticing—"

"Yesh?"

"Oh, nothing," said Twoflower.

"Yesh? Oh. Let'sh get thish fire going before we loshe the light. And then," Cohen's face fell, "I supposhe we'd better make some shoop."

"Rincewind's good at that," said Twoflower enthusiastically. "He knows all about herbs and roots and things."

Cohen gave Rincewind a look which suggested that he, Cohen, didn't believe that.

"Well, the Horshe people gave us shome horse jerky," he said. "If you can find shome wild onionsh and stuff, it might make it tashte better."

"But I—" Rincewind began, and gave up. Anyway, he reasoned, I know what an onion looks like, it's a sort of saggy white thing with a green bit sticking out of the top, should be fairly conspicuous.

"I'll just go and have a look, shall I?" he said.

"Yesh."

"Over there in all that thick, shadowy undergrowth?"

"Very good playshe, yesh."

"Where all the deep gullies and things are, you mean?"

"Ideal shpot, I'd shay."

"Yes, I thought so," said Rincewind bitterly. He set off, wondering how you attracted onions. After all, he thought, although you see them hanging in ropes on market stalls they probably don't grow like that, perhaps peasants or whatever use onion hounds or something, or sing songs to attract onions.

There were a few early stars out as he started to poke aimlessly among the leaves and grass. Luminous fungi, unpleasantly organic and looking like marital aids for gnomes, squished under his feet. Small flying things bit him. Other things, fortunately invisible, hopped or slithered away under the bushes and croaked reproachfully at him.

"Onions?" whispered Rincewind. "Any onions here?"

"There's a patch of them by that old yew tree," said a voice beside him.

"Ah," said Rincewind. "Good."

There was a long silence, except for the buzzing of the mosquitoes around Rincewind's ears.

He was standing perfectly still. He hadn't even moved his eyes.

Eventually he said, "Excuse me."

"Yes?"

"Which one's the yew?"

"Small gnarly one with the little dark green needles."

"Oh, yes. I see it. Thanks again."

He didn't move. Eventually the voice said conversationally, "Anything more I can do for you?"

"You're not a tree, are you?" said Rincewind, still staring straight ahead.

"Don't be silly. Trees can't talk."

"Sorry. It's just that I've been having a bit of difficulty with trees lately, you know how it is."

"Not really. I'm a rock."

Rincewind's voice hardly changed.

"Fine, fine," he said slowly. "Well, I'll just be getting those onions, then."

"Enjoy them."

He walked forward in a careful and dignified

fashion, spotted a clump of stringy white things huddling in the undergrowth, uprooted them carefully, and turned around.

There was a rock a little way away. But there were rocks everywhere, the very bones of the Disc were near the surface here.

He looked hard at the yew tree, just in case it had been speaking. But the yew, being a fairly solitary tree, hadn't heard about Rincewind the arborial savior, and in any case was asleep.

"If that was you, Twoflower, I knew it was you all along," said Rincewind. His voice sounded suddenly clear and very alone in the gathering dusk.

Rincewind remembered the only fact he knew for sure about trolls, which was that they turned to stone when exposed to sunlight, so that anyone who employed trolls to work during daylight had to spend a fortune in barrier cream.

But now that he came to think about it, it didn't say *anywhere* what happened to them after the sun had gone down again . . .

The last of the daylight trickled out of the landscape. And there suddenly seemed to be a great many rocks about.

"He's an awful long time with those onions," said Twoflower. "Do you think we'd better go and look for him?"

"Wishards know how to look after themshelves," said Cohen. "Don't worry." He winced. Bethan was cutting his toenails.

"He's not a terribly good wizard, actually," said

Twoflower, drawing nearer the fire. "I wouldn't say this to his face, but—" he leaned toward Cohen— "I've never actually seen him do any magic."

"Right, let's have the other one," said Bethan.

"Thish is very kind of you."

"You'd have quite nice feet if only you'd look after them."

"Can't sheem to bend down like I used to," said Cohen, sheepishly. "Of courshe, you don't get to meet many chiropodishts in my line of work. Funny, really. I've met any amount of snake prieshts, mad godsh, warlordsh, never any chiropodishts. I shupposhe it wouldn't look right, really—Cohen Against The Chiropodishts . . ."

"Or Cohen And The Chiropractors Of Doom," suggested Bethan. Cohen cackled.

"Or Cohen And The Mad Dentists!" laughed Twoflower.

Cohen's mouth snapped shut.

"What'sh sho funny about that?" he asked, and his voice had knuckles in it.

"Oh, er, well," said Twoflower. "Your teeth, you see . . ."

"What about them?" snapped Cohen.

Twoflower swallowed. "I can't help noticing that they're, um, not in the same geographical location as your mouth."

Cohen glared at him. Then he sagged, and looked very small and old.

"True, of corsh," he muttered. "I don't blame you. It'sh hard to be a hero with no teethsh. It don't matter what elsh you loosh, you can get by with one eye even, but you show 'em a mouth full of gumsh and no one hash any reshpect."

"I do," said Bethan loyally.

"Why don't you get some more?" said Twoflower brightly.

"Yesh, well, if I wash a shark or something, yesh, I'd grow shome," said Cohen sarcastically.

"Oh, no, you buy them," said Twoflower. "Look, I'll show you—er, Bethan, do you mind looking the other way?" He waited until she had turned around and then put his hand to his mouth.

"You shee?" he said.

Bethan heard Cohen gasp.

"You can take yoursh out?"

"Oh yesh. I've got sheveral shets. Excushe me—" there was a swallowing noise, and then in a more normal voice Twoflower said, "It's very convenient, of course."

Cohen's very voice radiated awe, or as much awe as is possible without teeth, which is about the same amount as with teeth but sounds a great deal less impressive.

"I should think show," he said. "When they ache, you jusht take them out and let them get on with it, yesh? Teach the little buggersh a lesshon, shee how they like being left to ache all by themshelvesh!"

"That's not quite right," said Twoflower carefully. "They're not mine, they just belong to me."

"You put shomeone elshe's teethsh in your mouth?"

"No, someone made them, lots of people wear them where I come from, it's a—"

But Twoflower's lecture on dental appliances
went ungiven, because somebody hit him.

The Disc's little moon toiled across the sky. It
shone by its own light, owing to the cramped and
rather inefficient astronomical arrangements made
by the Creator, and was quite crowded with assorted
lunar goddesses who were not, at this particular
time, paying much attention to what went on in the
Disc but were getting up a petition about the Ice
Giants.

Had they looked down, they would have seen
Rincewind talking urgently to a bunch of rocks.

Trolls are one of the oldest life-forms in the multiverse, dating from an early attempt to get the
whole life thing on the road without all that squashy
protoplasm. Individual trolls live for a long time,
hibernating during the summertime and sleeping
during the day, since heat affects them and makes
them slow. They have a fascinating geology. One
could talk about tribology, one could mention the
semiconductor effects of impure silicon, one could
talk about the giant trolls of prehistory who make
up most of the Disc's major mountain ranges and
will cause some real problems if they ever awake,
but the plain fact is that without the Disc's powerful and pervasive magical field trolls would have
died out a long time ago.

Psychiatry hadn't been invented on the Disc. No
one had ever shoved an inkblot under Rincewind's
nose to see if he had any loose toys in the attic. So
the only way he'd have been able to describe the

rocks turning back into trolls was by gabbling vaguely about how pictures suddenly form when you look at the fire, or clouds.

One minute there'd be a perfectly ordinary rock, and suddenly a few cracks that had been there all along took on the definite appearance of a mouth or a pointed ear. A moment later, and without anything actually changing at all, a troll would be sitting there, grinning at him with a mouth full of diamonds.

They wouldn't be able to digest me, he told himself. I'd make them awfully ill.

It wasn't much of a comfort.

"So you're Rincewind the wizard," said the nearest one. It sounded like someone running over gravel. "I dunno. I thought you'd be taller."

"Perhaps he's eroded a bit," said another one. "The legend is awfully old."

Rincewind shifted awkwardly. He was pretty certain the rock he was sitting on was changing shape, and a tiny troll—hardly any more than a pebble—was sitting companionably on his foot and watching him with extreme interest.

"Legend?" he said. "What legend?"

"It's been handed down from mountain to gravel since the sunset* of time," said the first troll. "'When the red star lights the sky Rincewind the wizard will come looking for onions. Do not bite him. It is very important that you help him stay alive.'"

---

* An interesting metaphor. To nocturnal trolls, of course, the dawn of time lies in the future.

There was a pause.

"That's it?" said Rincewind.

"Yes," said the troll. "We've always been puzzled about it. Most of our legends are much more exciting. It was more interesting being a rock in the old days."

"It was?" said Rincewind weakly.

"Oh yes. No end of fun. Volcanoes all over the place. It really meant something, being a rock then. There was none of this sedimentary nonsense, you were igneous or nothing. Of course, that's all gone now. People call themselves trolls today, well, sometimes they're hardly more than slate. Chalk even. I wouldn't give myself airs if you could use me to draw with, would you?"

"No," said Rincewind quickly. "Absolutely not, no. This, er, this legend thing. It said you shouldn't bite me?"

"That's right!" said the little troll on his foot, "and it was me who told you where the onions were!"

"We're rather glad you came along," said the first troll, which Rincewind couldn't help noticing was the biggest one there. "We're a bit worried about this new star. What does it mean?"

"I don't know," said Rincewind. "Everyone seems to think I know about it, but I don't—"

"It's not that we would mind being melted down," said the big troll. "That's how we all started, anyway. But we thought, maybe, it might mean the end of everything and that doesn't seem a very good thing."

"It's getting bigger," said another troll. "Look at it now. Bigger than last night."

Rincewind looked. It was *definitely* bigger than last night.

"So we thought you might have some suggestions?" said the head troll, as meekly as it is possible to sound with a voice like a granite gargle.

"You could jump over the Edge," said Rincewind. "There must be lots of places in the universe that could do with some extra rocks."

"We've heard about that," said the troll. "We've met rocks that tried it. They say you float about for millions of years and then you get very hot and burn away and end up at the bottom of a big hole in the scenery. That doesn't sound very bright."

It stood up with a noise like coal rattling down a chute, and stretched its thick, knobbly arms.

"Well, we're supposed to help you," it said. "Anything you want doing?"

"I was supposed to be making some soup," said Rincewind. He waved the onions vaguely. It was probably not the most heroic or purposeful gesture ever made.

"Soup?" said the troll. "Is that all?"

"Well, maybe some biscuits too."

The trolls looked at one another, exposing enough mouth jewelry to buy a medium-sized city.

Eventually the biggest troll said, "Soup it is, then." It shrugged grittily. "It's just that we imagined that the legend would, well, be a little more— I don't know, somehow I thought—still, I expect it doesn't matter."

It extended a hand like a bunch of fossil bananas.

"I'm Kwartz," it said. "That's Krysoprase over there, and Breccia, and Jasper, and my wife Beryl—she's a bit metamorphic, but who isn't these days? Jasper, get off his foot."

Rincewind took the hand gingerly, bracing himself for the crunch of crushed bone. It didn't come. The troll's hand was rough and a bit lichenous around the fingernails.

"I'm sorry," said Rincewind. "I never really met trolls before."

"We're a dying race," said Kwartz sadly, as the party set off under the stars. "Young Jasper's the only pebble in our tribe. We suffer from philosophy, you know."

"Yes?" said Rincewind, trying to keep up. The troll band moved very quickly, but also very quietly, big round shapes moving like wraiths through the night. Only the occasional flat squeak of a night creature who hadn't heard them approaching marked their passage.

"Oh, yes. Martyrs to it. It comes to all of us in the end. One evening, they say, you start to wake up and then you think 'Why bother?' and you just don't. See those boulders over there?"

Rincewind saw some huge shapes lying in the grass.

"The one on the end's my aunt. I don't know what she's thinking about, but she hasn't moved for two hundred years."

"Gosh, I'm sorry."

"Oh, it's no problem with us around to look after

them," said Kwartz. "Not many humans around here, you see. I know it's not your fault, but you don't seem to be able to spot the difference between a thinking troll and an ordinary rock. My great-uncle was actually quarried, you know."

"That's terrible!"

"Yes, one minute he was a troll, the next he was an ornamental fireplace."

They paused in front of a familiar-looking cliff. The scuffed remains of a fire smoldered in the darkness.

"It looks like there's been a fight," said Beryl.

"They're all gone!" said Rincewind. He ran to the end of the clearing. "The horses, too! Even the Luggage!"

"One of them's leaked," said Kwartz, kneeling down. "That red watery stuff you have in your insides. Look."

"Blood!"

"Is that what it's called? I've never really seen the point of it."

Rincewind scuttled about in the manner of one totally at his wits' end, peering behind bushes in case anyone was hiding there. That was why he tripped over a small green bottle.

"Cohen's liniment!" he moaned. "He never goes anywhere without it!"

"Well," said Kwartz, "you humans have something you can do, I mean like when we slow right down and catch philosophy, only you just fall to bits—"

"Dying, it's called!" screamed Rincewind.

"That's it. They haven't done that, because they're not here."

"Unless they were eaten!" suggested Jasper excitedly.

"Hmm," said Kwartz, and, "Wolves?" said Rincewind.

"We flattened all the wolves around here years ago," said the troll. "Old Grandad did, anyway."

"He didn't like them?"

"No, he just didn't used to look where he was going. Hmm." The trolls looked at the ground again.

"There's a trail," he said. "Quite a lot of horses." He looked up at the nearby hills, where sheer cliffs and dangerous crags loomed over the moonlit forests.

"Old Grandad lives up there," he said quietly.

There was something about the way he said it that made Rincewind decide that he didn't ever want to meet Old Grandad.

"Dangerous, is he?" he ventured.

"He's very old and big and mean. We haven't seen him about for years," said Kwartz.

"Centuries," corrected Beryl.

"He'll squash them all flat!" added Jasper, jumping up and down on Rincewind's toes.

"It just happens sometimes that a really old and big troll will go off by himself into the hills, and—um— the rock takes over, if you follow me."

"No?"

Kwartz sighed. "People sometimes act like animals, don't they? And sometimes a troll will start thinking like a rock, and rocks don't like people much."

Breccia, a skinny troll with a sandstone finish, rapped on Kwartz's shoulder.

"Are we going to follow them, then?" he said. "The legend says we should help this Rincewind squashy."

Kwartz stood up, thought for a moment, then picked Rincewind up by the scruff of his neck and with a big gritty movement placed him on his shoulders.

"We go," he said firmly. "If we meet Old Grandad I'll try to explain . . ."

Two miles away a string of horses trotted through the night. Three of them carried captives, expertly gagged and bound. A fourth pulled a rough travois on which the Luggage lay trussed and netted and silent.

Herrena softly called the column to a halt and beckoned one of her men to her.

"Are you quite sure?" she said. "I can't hear anything."

"I saw troll shapes," he said flatly.

She looked around. The trees had thinned out here, there was a lot of scree, and ahead of them the track led toward a bald, rocky hill that looked especially unpleasant by red starlight.

She was worried about that track. It was extremely old, but something had made it, and trolls took a lot of killing.

She sighed. Suddenly it looked as though that secretarial career was not such a bad option, at that.

Not for the first time she reflected that there were

many drawbacks to being a swordswoman, not least of which was that men didn't take you seriously until you'd actually killed them, by which time it didn't really matter anyway. Then there was all the leather, which brought her out in a rash but seemed to be unbreakably traditional. And then there was the ale. It was all right for the likes of Hrun the Barbarian or Cimbar the Assassin to carouse all night in low bars, but Herrena drew the line at it unless they sold proper drinks in small glasses, preferably with a cherry in. As for the toilet facilities . . .

But she was too big to be a thief, too honest to be an assassin, too intelligent to be a wife, and too proud to enter the only other female profession generally available.

So she'd become a swordswoman and had been a good one, amassing a modest fortune that she was carefully husbanding for a future that she hadn't quite worked out yet but which would certainly include a bidet if she had anything to say about it.

There was a distant sound of splintering timber. Trolls had never seen the point of walking around trees.

She looked up at the hill again. Two arms of high ground swept away to right and left, and up ahead was a large outcrop with—she squinted—some caves in it?

Troll caves. But maybe a better option than blundering around at night. And come sunup, there'd be no problem.

She leaned across to Gancia, leader of the gang of Morpork mercenaries. She wasn't very happy about him. It was true that he had the muscles of an ox and the stamina of an ox, the trouble was that he seemed to have the brains of an ox. And the viciousness of a ferret. Like most of the lads in downtown Morpork he'd have cheerfully sold his granny for glue, and probably had.

"We'll head for the caves and light a big fire in the entrance," she said. "Trolls don't like fire."

He gave her a look which suggested he had his own ideas about who should be giving the orders, but his lips said, "You're the boss."

"Right."

Herrena looked back at the three captives. That was the box all right—Trymon's description had been absolutely accurate. But neither of the men looked like a wizard. Not even a failed wizard.

"Oh, dear," said Kwartz.

The trolls halted. The night closed in like velvet. An owl hooted eerily—at least Rincewind assumed it was an owl, he was a little hazy on ornithology. Perhaps a nightingale hooted, unless it was a thrush. A bat flittered overhead. He was quite confident about that.

He was also very tired and quite bruised.

"Why oh dear?" he said.

He peered into the gloom. There was a distant speck in the hills that might have been a fire.

"Oh," he said. "You don't like fires, do you?"

Kwartz nodded. "It destroys the superconductivity of our brains," he said, "but a fire that small wouldn't have much effect on Old Grandad."

Rincewind looked around cautiously, listening for the sound of a rogue troll. He'd seen what normal trolls could do to a forest. They weren't naturally destructive, they just treated organic matter as a sort of inconvenient fog.

"Let's hope he doesn't find it, then," he said fervently.

Kwartz sighed. "Not much chance of that," he said. "They've lit it in his mouth."

"It'sh a judgeshment on me!" moaned Cohen. He tugged ineffectually at his bonds.

Twoflower peered at him muzzily. Gancia's slingshot had raised quite a lump on the back of his head and he was a little uncertain about things, starting with his name and working upward.

"I should have been lisshening out," said Cohen. "I should have been paying attenshion and not being shwayed by all this talk about your wosshnames, your din-chewers. I musht be getting shoft."

He levered himself up by his elbows. Herrena and the rest of the gang were standing around the fire in the cave mouth. The Luggage was still and silent under its net in a corner.

"There's something funny about this cave," said Bethan.

"What?" said Cohen.

"Well, look at it. Have you ever seen rocks like those before?"

Cohen had to agree that the semicircle of stones around the cave entrance were unusual; each one

was higher than a man, and heavily worn, and surprisingly shiny. There was a matching semicircle
on the ceiling. The whole effect was that of a stone
computer built by a druid with a vague idea of
geometry and no sense of gravity.

"Look at the walls, too."

Cohen squinted at the wall next to him. There
were veins of red crystal in it. He couldn't be quite
certain, but it was almost as if little points of light
kept flashing on and off deep within the rock itself.

It was also extremely drafty. A steady breeze blew
out of the black depths of the cave.

"I'm sure it was blowing the other way when we
came in," whispered Bethan. "What do you think,
Twoflower?"

"Well, I'm not a cave expert," he said, "but I was
just thinking, that's a very interesting stalag-thingy
hanging from the ceiling up there. Sort of bulbous,
isn't it?"

They looked at it.

"I can't quite put my finger on why," said Twoflower, "but I think it might be a rather good idea to
get out of here."

"Oh yesh," said Cohen sarcastically, "I shupposhe
we'd jusht better ashk theesh people to untie ush
and let us go, eh?"

Cohen hadn't spent much time in Twoflower's
company, otherwise he would not have been surprised when the little man nodded brightly and said,
in the loud, slow and careful voice he employed as
an alternative to actually speaking other people's

languages: "Excuse me? Could you please untie us and let us go? It's rather damp and drafty here. Sorry."

Bethan looked sidelong at Cohen.

"Was he supposed to say that?"

"It'sh novel, I'll grant you."

And, indeed, three people detached themselves from the group around the fire and came toward them. They did not look as if they intended to untie anyone. The two men, in fact, looked the sort of people who, when they see other people tied up, start playing around with knives and making greasy suggestions and leering a lot.

Herrena introduced herself by drawing her sword and pointing it at Twoflower's heart.

"Which one of you is Rincewind the wizard?" she said. "There were four horses. Is he here?"

"Um, I don't know where he is," said Twoflower. "He was looking for some onions."

"Then you are his friends and he will come looking for you," said Herrena. She glanced at Cohen and Bethan, then looked closely at the Luggage.

Trymon had been emphatic that they shouldn't touch the Luggage. Curiosity may have killed the cat, but Herrena's curiosity could have massacred a pride of lions.

She slit the netting and grasped the lid of the box. Twoflower winced.

"Locked," she said eventually. "Where is the key, fat one?"

"It—it hasn't got a key," said Twoflower.

"There is a keyhole," she pointed out.

"Well, yes, but if it wants to stay locked, it stays locked," said Twoflower uncomfortably.

Herrena was aware of Gancia's grin. She snarled.

"I want it open," she said. "Gancia, see to it." She strode back to the fire.

Gancia drew a long thin knife and leaned down close to Twoflower's face.

"She wants it open," he said. He looked up at the other man and grinned.

"She wants it open, Weems."

"Yah."

Gancia waved the knife slowly in front of Twoflower's face.

"Look," said Twoflower patiently, "I don't think you understand. No one can open the Luggage if it's feeling in a locked mood."

"Oh yes, I forgot," said Gancia thoughtfully. "Of course, it's a magic box, isn't that right? With little legs, they say. I say, Weems, any legs your side? No?"

He held his knife to Twoflower's throat.

"I'm really upset about that," he said. "So's Weems. He doesn't say much but what he does is, he tears bits off people. So open—the—box!"

He turned and planted a kick on the side of the box, leaving a nasty gash in the wood.

There was a tiny little click.

Gancia grinned. The lid swung up slowly, ponderously. The distant firelight gleamed off gold—lots of gold, in plate, chain, and coin, heavy and glistening in the flickering shadows.

"All right," said Gancia softly.

He looked back at the unheeding men around the

fire, who seemed to be shouting at someone outside the cave. Then he looked speculatively at Weems. His lips moved soundlessly with the unaccustomed effort of mental arithmetic.

He looked down at his knife.

Then the floor moved.

"I heard someone," said one of the men. "Down there. Among the—uh—rocks."

Rincewind's voice floated up out of the darkness.

"I say," he said.

"Well?" said Herrena.

"You're in great danger!" shouted Rincewind. "You must put the fire out!"

"No, no," said Herrena. "You've got it wrong, you're in great danger. And the fire stays."

"There's this big old troll—"

"Everyone knows trolls keep away from fire," said Herrena. She nodded. A couple of men drew their swords and slipped out into the darkness.

"Absolutely true!" shouted Rincewind desperately. "Only this specific troll can't, you see."

"Can't?" Herrena hesitated. Something of the terror in Rincewind's voice hit her.

"Yes, because, you see, you've lit it on his tongue."

Then the floor moved.

Old Grandad awoke very slowly from his centuries-old slumber. He nearly didn't awake at all, in fact a few decades later none of this could have happened. When a troll gets old and starts to think seriously about the universe it normally finds a quiet spot and gets down to some hard philosophizing, and after a while starts to forget about its extremities. It begins to crystallize around the edges until nothing remains except a tiny flicker of life inside quite a large hill with some unusual rock strata.

Old Grandad hadn't quite got that far. He awoke from considering quite a promising line of inquiry about the meaning of truth and found a hot ashy taste in what, after a certain amount of thought, he remembered as being his mouth.

He began to get angry. Commands skittered along neural pathways of impure silicon. Deep within his silicaceous body stone slipped smoothly along special fracture lines. Trees toppled, turf split, as fingers the size of ships unfolded and gripped the ground. Two enormous rockslides high on his cliff face marked the opening of eyes like great crusted opals.

Rincewind couldn't see all this, of course, since his own eyes were daylight issue only, but he did see the whole dark landscape shake itself slowly and then begin to rise impossibly against the stars.

The sun rose.

However, the sunlight didn't. What did happen was that the famous Discworld sunlight, which as has already been indicated travels very slowly through the Disc's powerful magical field, sloshed gently over the lands around the Rim and began its soft, silent battle against the retreating armies of the night. It poured like molten gold* across the sleeping landscape—bright, clean and, above all, slow.

Herrena didn't hesitate. With great presence of mind she ran to the edge of Old Grandad's bottom lip and jumped, rolling as she hit the earth. The men followed her, cursing as they landed among the debris.

Like a fat man trying to do push-ups the old troll pushed himself upward.

This wasn't apparent from where the prisoners were lying. All they knew was that the floor kept rolling under them and that there was a lot of noise going on, most of it unpleasant.

Weems grabbed Gancia's arm.

"It's a herthquake," he said. "Let's get out of here!"

"Not without that gold," said Gancia.

"What?"

"The gold, the gold. Man, we could be as rich as Creosote!"

Weems might have had a room-temperature IQ, but he knew idiocy when he saw it. Gancia's eyes gleamed more than gold, and he appeared to be staring at Weems's left ear.

Weems looked desperately at the Luggage. It was still open invitingly, which was odd—you'd have

---

* Not precisely, of course. Trees didn't burst into flame, people didn't suddenly become very rich and extremely dead, and the seas didn't flash into steam. A better simile, in fact, would be "not like molten gold."

thought all this shaking would have slammed the lid shut.

"We'd never carry it," he suggested. "It's too heavy," he added.

"We'll damn well carry some of it!" shouted Gancia, and leapt toward the chest as the floor shook again.

The lid snapped shut. Gancia vanished.

And just in case Weems thought it was accidental the Luggage's lid snapped open again, just for a second, and a large tongue as red as mahogany licked across broad teeth as white as sycamore. Then it slammed shut again.

To Weems's further horror hundreds of little legs extruded from the underside of the box. It rose very deliberately and, carefully arranging its feet, shuffled around to face him. There was a particularly malevolent look about its keyhole, the sort of look that says "Go on—make my day . . ."

He backed away and looked imploringly at Twoflower.

"I think it might be a good idea if you untied us," suggested Twoflower. "It's really quite friendly once it gets to know you."

Licking his lips nervously, Weems drew his knife. The Luggage gave a warning creak.

He slashed through their bonds and stood back quickly.

"Thank you," said Twoflower.

"I think my back'sh gone again," complained Cohen, as Bethan helped him to his feet.

"What do we do with this man?" said Bethan.

"We take hish knife and tell him to bugger off," said Cohen. "Right?"

"Yes, sir! Thank you, sir!" said Weems, and bolted toward the cavemouth. For a moment he was outlined against the gray predawn sky, and then he vanished. There was a distant cry of "aaargh."

The sunlight roared silently across the land like surf. Here and there, where the magic field was slightly weaker, tongues of morning raced ahead of the day, leaving isolated islands of night that contracted and vanished as the bright ocean flowed onward.

The uplands around the Vortex Plains stood out ahead of the advancing tide like a great gray ship.

It is possible to stab a troll, but the technique takes practice and no one ever gets a chance to practice more than once. Herrena's men saw the trolls loom out of the darkness like very solid ghosts. Blades shattered as they hit silica skins, there were one or two brief, flat screams, and then nothing more but shouts far away in the forest as they put as much distance as they could between themselves and the avenging earth.

Rincewind crept out from behind a tree and looked around. He was alone, but the bushes behind him rustled as the trolls lumbered after the gang.

He looked up.

High above him two great crystalline eyes focused in hatred of everything soft and squelchy and, above all, warm. Rincewind cowered in horror as a hand the size of a house rose, curled into a fist, and dropped toward him.

Day came with a silent explosion of light. For a moment the huge terrifying bulk of Old Grandad was a breakwater of shadow as the daylight streamed past. There was a brief grinding noise.

There was silence.

Several minutes passed. Nothing happened.

A few birds started singing. A bumblebee buzzed over the boulder that was Old Grandad's fist and alighted on a patch of thyme that had grown under a stone fingernail.

There was a scuffling down below. Rincewind slid awkwardly out of the narrow gap between the fist and the ground like a snake leaving a burrow.

He lay on his back, staring up at the sky past the frozen shape of the troll. It hadn't changed in any way, apart from the stillness, but already the eye started to play tricks. Last night Rincewind had looked at cracks in stone and seen them become mouths and eyes; now he looked at the great cliff face and saw the features become, like magic, mere blemishes in the rock.

"Wow!" he said.

That didn't seem to help. He stood up, dusted himself off, and looked around. Apart from the bumblebee, he was completely alone.

After poking around for a bit he found a rock that, from certain angles, looked like Beryl.

He was lost and lonely and a long way from home. He—

There was a crunch high above him, and shards of rock spattered into the earth. High up on the face of Old Grandad a hole appeared; there was a brief sight of the Luggage's backside as it struggled to regain its footing, and then Twoflower's head poked out of the mouth cave.

"Anyone down there? I say?"

"Hey!" shouted the wizard. "Am I glad to see you!"

"I don't know. Are you?" said Twoflower.

"Am I what?"

"Gosh, there's a wonderful view from up here!"

It took them half an hour to get down. Fortunately Old Grandad had been quite craggy with plenty of handholds, but his nose would have presented a tricky obstacle if it hadn't been for the luxuriant oak tree that flourished in one nostril.

The Luggage didn't bother to climb. It just jumped, and bounced its way down with no apparent harm.

Cohen sat in the shade, trying to catch his breath and waiting for his sanity to catch up with him. He eyed the Luggage thoughtfully.

"The horses have all gone," said Twoflower.

"We'll find 'em," said Cohen. His eyes bored into the Luggage, which began to look embarrassed.

"They were carrying all our food," said Rince-wind.

"Plenty of food in the foreshts."

"I have some nourishing biscuits in the Luggage," said Twoflower. "Traveler's Digestives. Always a comfort in a tight spot."

"I've tried them," said Rincewind. "They've got a mean edge on them, and—"

Cohen stood up, wincing.

"Excushe me," he said flatly. "There'sh shomething I've got to know."

He walked over to the Luggage and gripped its lid. The box backed away hurriedly, but Cohen stuck out a skinny foot and tripped up half its legs. As it twisted to snap at him he gritted his teeth and heaved, jerking the Luggage onto its curved lid where it rocked angrily like a maddened tortoise.

"Hey, that's my Luggage!" said Twoflower. "Why's he attacking my Luggage?"

"I think I know," said Bethan quietly. "I think it's because he's scared of it."

Twoflower turned to Rincewind, openmouthed. Rincewind shrugged.

"Search me," he said. "I run away from things I'm scared of, myself."

With a snap of its lid the Luggage jerked into the air and came down running, catching Cohen a crack on the shins with one of its brass corners. As it wheeled around he got a grip on it just long enough to send it galloping full tilt into a rock.

"Not bad," said Rincewind, admiringly.

The Luggage staggered back, paused for a moment, then came at Cohen waving its lid menacingly. He jumped and landed on it, with both his hands and feet caught in the gap between the box and the lid.

This severely puzzled the Luggage. It was even more astonished when Cohen took a deep breath and heaved, muscles standing out on his skinny arms like a sock full of coconuts.

They stood locked there for some time, tendon versus hinge. Occasionally one or other would creak.

Bethan elbowed Twoflower in the ribs.

"Do something," she said.

"Um," said Twoflower. "Yes. That's about enough, I think. Put him down, please."

The Luggage gave a creak of betrayal at the sound of its master's voice. Its lid flew up with such force that Cohen tumbled backward, but he scrambled to his feet and flung himself toward the box.

Its contents lay open to the skies.

Cohen reached inside.

The Luggage creaked a bit, but had obviously weighed up the chances of being sent to the top of that Great Wardrobe in the Sky. When Rincewind dared to peek through his fingers Cohen was peering into the Luggage and cursing under his breath.

"Laundry?" he shouted. "Is that it? Just laundry?" He was shaking with rage.

"I think there's some biscuits too," said Twoflower in a small voice.

"But there wash gold! And I shaw it eat shomebody!" Cohen looked imploringly at Rincewind.

The wizard sighed. "Don't ask me," he said. "I don't own the bloody thing."

"I bought it in a shop," said Twoflower defensively. "I said I wanted a traveling trunk."

"That's what you got, all right," said Rincewind.

"It's very loyal," said Twoflower.

"Oh yes," agreed Rincewind. "If loyalty is what you look for in a suitcase."

"Hold on," said Cohen, who had sagged onto a rock. "Wash it one of thoshe shopsh—I mean, I bet you hadn't noticed it before and when you went back again it washn't there?"

Twoflower brightened. "That's right!"

"Shopkeeper a little wizened old guy? Shop full of strange shtuff?"

"Exactly! Never could find it again, I thought I must have got the wrong street, nothing but a brick wall where I thought it was, I remember thinking at the time it was rather—"

Cohen shrugged. "One of *those* shops,"* he said. "That explainsh it, then." He felt his back, and grimaced. "Bloody horshe ran off with my liniment!"

Rincewind remembered something, and fumbled in the depths of his torn and now very grubby robe. He held up a green bottle.

"That'sh the shtuff!" said Cohen. "You're a marvel." He looked sideways at Twoflower.

"I would have beaten it," he said quietly, "even if

---

* No one knows why, but all the most truly mysterious and magical items are bought from shops that appear and, after a trading life even briefer than a double-glazing company, vanish like smoke. There had been various attempts to explain this, all of which don't fully account for the observed facts. These shops turn up anywhere in the universe, and their immediate nonexistence in any particular city can normally be deduced from crowds of people wandering the streets clutching defunct magical items, ornate guarantee cards, and looking very suspiciously at brick walls.

you hadn't called it off, I would have beaten it in the end."

"That's right," said Bethan.

"You two can make yourshelf usheful," he added. "That Luggage broke through a troll tooth to get ush out. That wash diamond. Shee if you can find the bitsh. I've had an idea about them."

As Bethan rolled up her sleeves and uncorked the bottle Rincewind took Twoflower to one side. When they were safely hidden behind a shrub he said, "He's gone barmy."

"That's Cohen the Barbarian you're talking about!" said Twoflower, genuinely shocked. "He is the greatest warrior that—"

"Was," said Rincewind urgently. "All that stuff with the warrior priests and man-eating zombies was years ago. All he's got now is memories and so many scars you could play noughts-and-crosses on him."

"He is rather more elderly than I imagined, yes," said Twoflower. He picked up a fragment of diamond.

"So we ought to leave them and find our horses and move on," said Rincewind.

"That's a bit of a mean trick, isn't it?"

"They'll be all right," said Rincewind heartily. "The point is, would you feel happy in the company of someone who would attack the Luggage with his bare hands?"

"That is a point," said Twoflower.

"They'll probably be better off without us anyway."

"Are you sure?"

"Positive," said Rincewind.

They found the horses wandering aimlessly in the scrub, breakfasted on badly dried horse jerky, and set off in what Rincewind believed was the right direction. A few minutes later the Luggage emerged from the bushes and followed them.

The sun rose higher in the sky, but still failed to blot out the light of the star.

"It's got bigger overnight," said Twoflower. "Why isn't anybody doing something?"

"Such as what?"

Twoflower thought. "Couldn't somebody tell Great A'Tuin to avoid it?" he said. "Sort of go around it?"

"That sort of thing has been tried before," said Rincewind. "Wizards tried to tune in to Great A'Tuin's mind."

"It didn't work?"

"Oh, it worked all right," said Rincewind. "Only . . ."

Only there had been certain unforeseen risks in reading a mind as great as the World Turtle's, he explained. The wizards had trained up on tortoises and giant sea turtles first, to get the hang of the chelonian frame of mind, but although they knew that Great A'Tuin's mind would be big they hadn't realized that it would be *slow*.

"There's a bunch of wizards that have been reading it in shifts for thirty years," said Rincewind.

"All they've found out is that Great A'Tuin is looking forward to something."

"What?"

"Who knows?"

They rode in silence for a while through a rough country where huge limestone blocks lined the track. Eventually Twoflower said, "We ought to go back, you know."

"Look, we'll reach the Smarl tomorrow," said Rincewind. "Nothing will happen to them out here, I don't see why—"

He was talking to himself. Twoflower had wheeled his horse and was trotting back, demonstrating all the horsemanship of a sack of potatoes.

Rincewind looked down. The Luggage regarded him owlishly.

"What are you looking at?" said the wizard. "He can go back if he wants, why should I bother?"

The Luggage said nothing.

"Look, he's not my responsibility," said Rincewind. "Let's be absolutely clear about that."

The Luggage said nothing, but louder this time.

"Go on—follow him. You're nothing to do with me."

The Luggage retracted its little legs and settled down on the track.

"Well, I'm going," said Rincewind. "I mean it," he added.

He turned the horse's head back toward the new horizon, and glanced down. The Luggage sat there.

"It's no good trying to appeal to my better nature.

You can stay there all day for all I care. I'm just going to ride off, okay?"

He glared at the Luggage. The Luggage looked back.

"I thought you'd come back," said Twoflower.

"I don't want to talk about it," said Rincewind.

"Shall we talk about something else?"

"Yeah, well, discussing how to get these ropes off would be favorite," said Rincewind. He wrenched at the bonds around his wrists.

"I can't imagine why you're so important," said Herrena. She sat on a rock opposite them, sword across her knees. Most of the gang laying among the rocks high above, watching the road. Rincewind and Twoflower had been a pathetically easy ambush.

"Weems told me what your box did to Gancia," she added. "I can't say that's a great loss, but I hope it understands that if it comes within a mile of us I will personally cut both your throats, yes?"

Rincewind nodded violently.

"Good," said Herrena. "You're wanted dead or alive, I'm not really bothered which, but some of the lads might want to have a little discussion with you about those trolls. If the sun hadn't come up when it did—"

She left the words hanging, and walked away.

"Well, here's another fine mess," said Rincewind. He had another pull at the ropes that bound him. There was a rock behind him, and if he could bring his wrists up—yes, as he thought, it lacerated him while at the same time being too blunt to have any effect on the rope.

"But why us?" said Twoflower. "It's to do with that star, isn't it?"

"I don't know anything about the star," said Rincewind. "I never even attended astrology lessons at the University!"

"I expect everything will turn out all right in the end," said Twoflower.

Rincewind looked at him. Remarks like that always threw him.

"Do you really believe that?" he said. "I mean, really?"

"Well, things generally do work out satisfactorily, when you come to think about it."

"If you think the total disruption of my life for the last year is satisfactory then you might be right. I've lost count of the times I've nearly been killed—"

"Twenty-seven," said Twoflower.

"What?"

"Twenty-seven times," said Twoflower helpfully. "I worked it out. But you never actually have."

"What? Worked it out?" said Rincewind, who was beginning to have the familiar feeling that the conversation had been mugged.

"No. Been killed. Doesn't that seem a bit suspicious?"

"I've never objected to it, if that's what you mean," said Rincewind. He glared at his feet. Twoflower was right, of course. The Spell was keeping him alive, it was obvious. No doubt if he jumped over a cliff a passing cloud would cushion his fall.

The trouble with that theory, he decided, was that it only worked if he didn't believe it was true. The moment he thought he was invulnerable he'd be dead.

So, on the whole it was wisest not to think about it at all.

Anyway, he might be wrong.

The only thing he could be certain of was that he was getting a headache. He hoped that the Spell was somewhere in the area of the headache and really suffering.

When they rode out of the hollow both Rincewind and Twoflower were sharing a horse with one of their captors. Rincewind perched uncomfortably in front of Weems, who had sprained an ankle and was not in a good mood. Twoflower sat in front of Herrena which, since he was fairly short, meant that at least he kept his ears warm. She rode with a drawn knife and a sharp eye out for any walking boxes; Herrena hadn't quite worked out what the Luggage was, but she was bright enough to know that it wouldn't let Twoflower be killed.

After about ten minutes they saw it in the middle of the road. Its lid lay open invitingly. It was full of gold.

"Go around it," said Herrena.

"But—"

"It's a trap."

"That's right," said Weems, white-faced. "You take it from me."

Reluctantly they reined their horses around the glittering temptation and trotted on along the track. Weems glanced back fearfully, dreading to see the chest coming after him.

What he saw was almost worse. It had gone.

Far off to one side of the path the long grass moved mysteriously and was still.

Rincewind wasn't much of a wizard and even less of a fighter, but he was an expert at cowardice and he knew fear when he smelled it. He said, quietly, "It'll follow you, you know."

"What?" said Weems, distractedly. He was still peering at the grass.

"It's very patient and it never gives up. That's sapient pearwood you're dealing with. It'll let you think it's forgotten you, then one day you'll be walking along a dark street and you'll hear these little footsteps behind you—shlup, shlup, they'll go, then you'll start running and they'll speed up, shlup-shlupSHLUP—"

"Shut up!" shouted Weems.

"It's probably already recognized you, so—"

"I said shut up!"

Herrena turned around in her saddle and glared at them. Weems scowled and pulled Rincewind's ear until it was right in front of his mouth, and said hoarsely, "I'm afraid of nothing, understand? This wizard stuff, I spit on it."

"They all say that until they hear the footsteps,"

said Rincewind. He stopped. A knifepoint was pricking his ribs.

Nothing happened for the rest of the day but, to Rincewind's satisfaction and Weems's mounting paranoia, the Luggage showed itself several times. Here it would be perched incongruously on a crag, there it would be half-hidden in a ditch with moss growing over it.

By late afternoon they came to the crest of a hill and looked down on the broad valley of the upper Smarl, the longest river on the Disc. It was already half a mile across, and heavy with the silt that made the lower valley the most fertile area on the continent. A few wisps of early mist wreathed its banks.

"Shlup," said Rincewind. He felt Weems jerk upright in the saddle.

"Eh?"

"Just clearing my throat," said Rincewind, and grinned. He had put a lot of thought into that grin. It was the sort of grin people use when they stare at your left ear and tell you in an urgent tone of voice that they are being spied on by secret agents from the next galaxy. It was not a grin to inspire confidence. More horrible grins had probably been seen, but only on the sort of grinner that is orange with black stripes, has a long tail and hangs around in jungles looking for victims to grin at.

"Wipe that off," said Herrena, trotting up.

Where the track led down to the river bank there was a crude jetty and a big bronze gong.

"It'll summon the ferryman," said Herrena. "If we cross here we can cut off a big bend in the river. Might even make it to a town tonight."

Weems looked doubtful. The sun was getting fat and red, and the mists were beginning to thicken.

"Or maybe you want to spend the night this side of the water?"

Weems picked up the hammer and hit the gong so hard that it spun right around on its hanger and fell off.

They waited in silence. Then with a wet clinking sound a chain sprang out of the water and pulled taut against an iron peg set into the bank. Eventually the slow flat shape of the ferry emerged from the mist, its hooded ferryman heaving on a big wheel set in its center as he winched his way toward the shore.

The ferry's flat bottom grated on the gravel, and the hooded figure leaned against the wheel panting.

"Two at a time," it muttered. "That'sh all. Jusht two, with horshesh."

Rincewind swallowed, and tried not to look at Twoflower. The man would probably be grinning and mugging like an idiot. He risked a sideways glance.

Twoflower was sitting with his mouth open.

"You're not the usual ferryman," said Herrena. "I've been here before, the usual man is a big fellow, sort of—"

"It'sh hish day off."

"Well, okay," she said doubtfully. "In that case— *What's he laughing at?*"

Twoflower's shoulders were shaking, his face had

gone red, and he was emitting muffled snorts. Herrena glared at him, then looked hard at the ferryman.

"Two of you—grab him!"

There was a pause. Then one of the men said, "What, the ferryman?"

"Yes!"

"Why?"

Herrena looked blank. This sort of thing wasn't supposed to happen. It was accepted that when someone yelled something like "Get him!" or "Guards!" people jumped to it, they weren't supposed to sit around discussing things.

"Because I said so!" was the best she could manage. The two men nearest to the bowed figure looked at each other, shrugged, dismounted, and each took a shoulder. The ferryman was about half their size.

"Like this?" said one of them. Twoflower was choking for breath.

"Now I want to see what he's got under that robe."

The two men exchanged glances.

"I'm not sure that—" said one.

He got no further because a knobbly elbow jerked into his stomach like a piston. His companion looked down incredulously and got the other elbow in the kidneys.

Cohen cursed as he struggled to untangle his sword from his robe while hopping crabwise toward Herrena. Rincewind groaned, gritted his teeth, and jerked his head backward hard. There was a scream from Weems and Rincewind rolled sideways, landed heavily in the mud, scrambled up madly and looked around for somewhere to hide.

With a cry of triumph Cohen managed to free his sword and waved it triumphantly, severely wounding a man who had been creeping up behind him.

Herrena pushed Twoflower off her horse and fumbled for her own blade. Twoflower tried to stand up and caused the horse of another man to rear, throwing him off and bringing his head down to the right level for Rincewind to kick it as hard as possible. Rincewind would be the first to call himself a rat, but even rats fight in a corner.

Weems's hands dropped onto his shoulder and a fist like a medium-sized rock slammed into his head.

As he went down he heard Herrena say, quite quietly, "Kill them both. I'll deal with this old fool."

"Right!" said Weems, and turned toward Twoflower with his sword drawn.

Rincewind saw him hesitate. There was a moment of silence, and then even Herrena could hear the splashing as the Luggage surged ashore, water pouring from it.

Weems stared at it in horror. His sword fell from his hand. He turned and ran into the mists. A moment later the Luggage bounded over Rincewind and followed him.

Herrena lunged at Cohen, who parried the thrust and grunted as his arm twinged. The blades clanged wetly, and then Herrena was forced to back away as

a cunning upward sweep from Cohen nearly dis-
armed her.

Rincewind staggered toward Twoflower and
tugged at him ineffectually.

"Time to be going," he muttered.

"This is great!" said Twoflower. "Did you see the
way he—"

"Yes, yes, come on."

"But I want— I say, well done!"

Herrena's sword spun out of her hand and stood
quivering in the dirt. With a snort of satisfaction
Cohen brought his own sword back, went momentarily crosseyed, gave a little yelp of pain, and stood
absolutely motionless.

Herrena looked at him, puzzled. She made an experimental move in the direction of her own sword
and when nothing happened she grasped it, tested
its balance, and stared at Cohen. Only his agonized
eyes moved to follow her as she circled him cautiously.

"His back's gone again!" whispered Twoflower.
"What can we do?"

"We can see if we can catch the horses?"

"Well," said Herrena, "I don't know who you are
or why you're here, and there's nothing personal
about this, you understand."

She raised her sword in both hands.

There was a sudden movement in the mists and
the dull thud of a heavy piece of wood hitting a
head. Herrena looked bewildered for a moment, and
then fell forward.

Bethan dropped the branch she had been holding

and looked at Cohen. Then she grabbed him by the shoulders, stuck her knee in the small of his back, gave a businesslike twist and let him go.

An expression of bliss passed across his face. He gave an experimental bend.

"It's gone!" he said. "The back! Gone!"

Twoflower turned to Rincewind.

"My father used to recommend hanging from the top of a door," he said conversationally.

Weems crept very cautiously through the scrubby, mist-laden trees. The pale damp air muffled all sounds, but he was certain that there had been nothing to hear for the past ten minutes. He turned around very slowly, and then allowed himself the luxury of a long, heartfelt sigh. He stepped back into the cover of the bushes.

Something nudged the back of his knees, very gently. Something angular.

He looked down. There seemed to be more feet down there than there ought to be.

There was a short, sharp snap.

The fire was a tiny dot of light in a dark landscape. The moon wasn't up yet, but the star was a lurking glow on the horizon.

"It's circular now," said Bethan. "It looks like a tiny sun. I'm sure it's getting hotter, too."

"Don't," said Rincewind. "As if I hadn't got enough to worry about."

"What I don't undershtand," said Cohen, who was having his back massaged, "ish how they captured you without ush hearing it. We wouldn't have known at all if your Luggage hadn't kept jumping up and down."

"And whining," said Bethan. They all looked at her.

"Well, it *looked* as if it was whining," she said. "I think it's rather sweet, really."

Four pairs of eyes turned toward the Luggage, which was squatting on the other side of the fire. It got up, and very pointedly moved back into the shadows.

"Eashy to feed," said Cohen.

"Hard to lose," agreed Rincewind.

"Loyal," suggested Twoflower.

"Roomy," said Cohen.

"But I wouldn't say sweet," said Rincewind.

"I shuppose you wouldn't want to shell it?" said Cohen.

Twoflower shook his head. "I don't think it would understand," he said.

"No, I shupposhe not," said Cohen. He sat up, and bit his lip. "I wash looking for a preshent for Bethan, you shee. We're getting married."

"We thought you ought to be the first to know," said Bethan, and blushed.

Rincewind didn't catch Twoflower's eye.

"Well, that's very, er—"

"Just as soon as we find a town where there's a priest," said Bethan. "I want it done properly."

"That's very important," said Twoflower seriously. "If there were more morals about we wouldn't be crashing into stars."

They considered this for a moment. Then Two-flower said brightly, "This calls for a celebration. I've got some biscuits and water, if you've still got some of that jerky."

"Oh, good," said Rincewind weakly. He beckoned Cohen to one side. With his beard trimmed the old man could easily have passed for seventy on a dark night.

"This is, uh, serious?" he said. "You're really going to marry her?"

"Shure thing. Any objections?"

"Well, no, of course not, but—I mean, she's seventeen and you're, you're, how can I put it, you're of the elderly persuasion."

"Time I shettled down, you mean?"

Rincewind groped for words. "You're seventy years older than her, Cohen. Are you sure that—"

"I have been married before, you know. I've got quite a good memory," said Cohen reproachfully.

"No, what I mean is, well, I mean physically, the point is, what about, you know, the age difference and everything, it's a matter of health, isn't it, and—"

"Ah," said Cohen slowly, "I shee what you mean. The strain. I hadn't looked at it like that."

"No," said Rincewind, straightening up. "No, well, that's only to be expected."

"You've given me something to think about and no mishtake," said Cohen.

"I hope I haven't upset anything."

"No, no," said Cohen vaguely. "Don't apologishe. You were right to point it out."

He turned and looked at Bethan, who waved at him, and then he looked up at the star that glared through the mists.

Eventually he said, "Dangerous times, these."

"That's a fact."

"Who knows what tomorrow may bring?"

"Not me."

Cohen clapped Rincewind on the shoulder. "Shometimesh we jusht have to take rishks," he said. "Don't be offended, but I think we'll go ahead with the wedding anyway and, well," he looked at Bethan and sighed, "we'll just have to hope she's shtrong enough."

Around noon the following day they rode into a small, mud-walled city surrounded by fields still lush and green. There seemed to be a lot of traffic going the other way, though. Huge carts rumbled past them. Herds of livestock ambled along the crown of the road. Old ladies stomped past carrying entire households and haystacks on their backs.

"Plague?" said Rincewind, stopping a man pushing a handcart full of children.

He shook his head. "It's the star, friend," he said. "Haven't you seen it in the sky?"

"We couldn't help noticing it, yes."

"They say that it'll hit us on Hogswatchnight and the seas will boil and the countries of the Disc will be broken and kings will be brought down and the cities will be as lakes of glass," said the man. "I'm off to the mountains."

"That'll help, will it?" said Rincewind doubtfully.

"No, but the view will be better."

Rincewind rode back to the others.

"Everyone's worried about the star," he said. "Apparently there's hardly anyone left in the cities, they're all frightened of it."

"I don't want to worry anyone," said Bethan, "but hasn't it struck you as unseasonably hot?"

"That's what I said last night," said Twoflower. "Very warm, I thought."

"I shuspect it'll get a lot hotter," said Cohen. "Let'sh get on into the city."

They rode through echoing streets that were practically deserted. Cohen kept peering at merchants' signs until he reined his horse and said, "Thish ish what I've been looking for. You find a temple and a priesht, I'll join you shortly."

"A jeweler?" said Rincewind.

"It's a shuprishe."

"I could do with a new dress, too," said Bethan.

"I'll shteal you one."

There was something very oppressive about the city, Rincewind decided. There was also something very odd.

Almost every door was painted with a large red star.

"It's creepy," said Bethan. "As if people wanted to bring the star here."

"Or keep it away," said Twoflower.

"That won't work. It's too big," said Rincewind. He saw their faces turned toward him.

"Well, it stands to reason, doesn't it?" he said lamely.

"No," said Bethan.

"Stars are small lights in the sky," said Twoflower. "One fell down near my home once—big white thing, size of a house, glowed for weeks before it went out."

"This star is different," said a voice. "Great A'Tuin has climbed the beach of the universe. This is the great ocean of space."

"How do you know?" said Twoflower.

"Know what?" said Rincewind.

"What you just said. About beaches and oceans."

"I didn't say anything!"

"Yes you did, you silly man!" yelled Bethan. "We saw your lips going up and down and everything!"

Rincewind shut his eyes. Inside his mind he could feel the Spell scuttling off to hide behind his conscience, and muttering to itself.

"All right, all right," he said. "No need to shout. I—I don't know how I know, I just know—"

"Well, I wish you'd tell us."

They turned the corner.

All the cities around the Circle Sea had a special area set aside for the gods, of which the Disc had an elegant sufficiency. Usually they were crowded and not very attractive from an architectural point of view. The most senior gods, of course, had large and splendid temples, but the trouble was that later gods demanded equality and soon the holy areas were sprawling with lean-tos, annexes, loft conversions, subbasements, bijou flatlets, ecclesiastical infilling and trans-temporal timesharing, since no god would dream of living outside the holy quarter or, as it had become, three-eighths. There were usually three hundred different types of incense being burned and the noise was normally at pain threshold because of all the priests vying with each other to call their share of the faithful to prayer.

But this street was deathly quiet, that particularly unpleasant quiet that comes when hundreds of frightened and angry people are standing very still.

A man at the edge of the crowd turned around and scowled at the newcomers. He had a red star painted on his forehead.

"What's—" Rincewind began, and stopped as his voice seemed far too loud, "what's this?"

"You're strangers?" said the man.

"Actually we know one another quite—" Twoflower began, and fell silent. Bethan pointed up the street.

Every temple had a star painted on it. There was a particularly big one daubed across the stone eye outside the temple of Blind Io, leader of the gods.

"Urgh," said Rincewind. "Io is going to be really pissed when he sees that. I don't think we ought to hang around here, friends."

The crowd was facing a crude platform that had been built in the center of the wide street. A big banner had been draped across the front of it.

"I always heard that Blind Io can see everything that happens everywhere," said Bethan quietly. "Why hasn't—"

"Quiet!" said the man beside them. "Dahoney speaks!"

A figure had stepped up on the platform, a tall thin man with hair like a dandelion. There was no cheer from the crowd, just a collective sigh. He began to speak.

Rincewind listened in mounting horror. Where were the gods? said the man. They had gone. Perhaps they had never been. Who, actually, could remember seeing them? And now the star had been sent—

It went on and on, a quiet, clear voice that used words like "cleanse" and "scouring" and "purify" and drilled into the brain like a hot sword. Where were the wizards? Where was magic? Had it ever really worked, or had it all been a dream?

Rincewind began to be really afraid that the gods might get to hear about this and be so angry that they'd take it out on anyone who happened to have been around at the time.

But somehow even the wrath of the gods would have been better than the sound of that voice. The star was coming, it seemed to say, and its fearful fire could only be averted by—by—Rincewind couldn't be certain, but he had visions of swords and banners and blank-eyed warriors. The voice didn't believe in gods, which in Rincewind's book was fair enough, but it didn't believe in people either.

A tall, hooded stranger on Rincewind's left jostled him. He turned—and looked up into a grinning skull under a black hood.

Wizards, like cats, can see Death.

Compared to the sound of that voice, Death

seemed almost pleasant. He leaned against a wall, his scythe propped up beside him. He nodded at Rincewind.

"Come to gloat?" whispered Rincewind. Death shrugged.

I HAVE COME TO SEE THE FUTURE, he said.

"This is the future?"

A FUTURE, said Death.

"It's horrible," said Rincewind.

I'M INCLINED TO AGREE, said Death.

"I would have thought you'd be all for it!"

NOT LIKE THIS. THE DEATH OF THE WARRIOR OR THE OLD MAN OR THE LITTLE CHILD, THIS I UNDERSTAND, AND I TAKE AWAY THE PAIN AND END THE SUFFERING. I DO NOT UNDERSTAND THIS DEATH-OF-THE-MIND.

"Who are you talking to?" said Twoflower. Several members of the congregation had turned around and were looking suspiciously at Rincewind.

"Nobody," said Rincewind. "Can we go away? I've got a headache."

Now a group of people at the edge of the crowd were muttering and pointing to them. Rincewind grabbed the other two and hurried them around the corner.

"Mount up and let's go," he said. "I've got a bad feeling that—"

A hand landed on his shoulder. He turned around. A pair of cloudy gray eyes set in a round bald head on top of a large muscular body were staring hard at his left ear. The man had a star painted on his forehead.

"You look like a wizard," he said, in a tone of voice that suggested this was very unwise and quite possibly fatal.

"Who, me? No, I'm—a clerk. Yes. A clerk. That's right," said Rincewind.

He gave a little laugh.

The man paused, his lips moving soundlessly, as though he was listening to a voice in his head. Several other star people had joined him. Rincewind's left ear began to be widely regarded.

"I think you're a wizard," said the man.

"Look," said Rincewind, "if I was a wizard I'd be able to do magic, right? I'd just turn you into something, and I haven't, so I'm not."

"We killed all our wizards," said one of the men. "Some ran away, but we killed quite a lot. They waved their hands and nothing came out."

Rincewind stared at him.

"And we think you're a wizard too," said the man holding Rincewind in an ever-tightening grip. "You've got the box on legs and you look like a wizard."

Rincewind became aware that the three of them and the Luggage had somehow become separated from their horses, and that they were now in a contracting circle of gray-faced, solemn people.

Bethan had gone pale. Even Twoflower, whose ability to recognize danger was as good as Rincewind's ability to fly, was looking worried.

Rincewind took a deep breath.

He raised his hands in the classic pose he'd learned years before, and rasped, "Stand back! Or I'll fill you full of magic!"

"The magic has faded," said the man. "The star has taken it away. All the false wizards said their funny words and then nothing happened and they looked at their hands in horror and very few of them, in fact, had the sense to run away."

"I mean it!" said Rincewind.

He's going to kill me, he thought. That's it. I can't even bluff any more. No good at magic, no good at bluffing, I'm just a—

The Spell stirred in his mind. He felt it trickle into his brain like iced water and brace itself. A cold tingle coursed down his arm.

His arm raised of its own volition, and he felt his own mouth opening and shutting and his own tongue moving as a voice that wasn't his, a voice that sounded old and dry, said syllables that puffed into the air like steam clouds.

Octarine fire flashed from under his fingernails. It wrapped itself around the horrified man until he was lost in a cold, spitting cloud that rose above the street, hung there for a long moment, and then exploded into nothingness.

There wasn't even a wisp of greasy smoke.

Rincewind stared at his hand in horror.

Twoflower and Bethan each grabbed him by an arm and hustled him through the shocked crowd until they reached the open street. There was a painful moment as they each chose to run down a

different alley, but they hurried on with Rincewind's feet barely touching the cobbles.

"Magic," he mumbled excitedly, drunk with power.
"I did magic . . ."

"That's right," said Twoflower soothingly.

"Would you like me to do a spell?" said Rincewind. He pointed a finger at a passing dog and said
"Wheeee!" It gave him a hurt look.

"Making your feet run a lot faster'd be favorite,"
said Bethan grimly.

"Sure!" slurred Rincewind. "Feet! Run faster!
Hey, look, they're doing it!"

"They've got more sense than you," said Bethan.
"Which way now?"

Twoflower peered at the maze of alleyways around
them. There was a lot of shouting going on, some
way off.

Rincewind lurched out of their grasp, and tottered uncertainly down the nearest alley.

"I can do it!" he shouted wildly. "Just you all
watch out—"

"He's in shock," said Twoflower.

"Why?"

"He's never done a spell before."

"But he's a wizard!"

"It's all a bit complicated," said Twoflower, running after Rincewind. "Anyway, I'm not sure that
was actually him. It certainly didn't sound like him.
Come along, old fellow."

Rincewind looked at him with wild, unseeing
eyes.

"I'll turn you into a rosebush," he said.

"Yes, yes, jolly good. Just come along," said Twoflower soothingly, pulling gently at his arm.

There was a pattering of feet from several alleyways and suddenly a dozen star people were advancing on them.

Bethan grabbed Rincewind's limp hand and held it up threateningly.

"That's far enough!" she screamed.

"Right!" shouted Twoflower. "We've got a wizard and we're not afraid to use him!"

"I mean it!" screamed Bethan, spinning Rincewind around by his arm, like a capstan.

"Right! We're heavily armed! What?" said Twoflower.

"I said, where's the Luggage?" hissed Bethan behind Rincewind's back.

Twoflower looked around. The Luggage was missing.

Rincewind was having the desired effect on the star people, though. As his hand waved vaguely around they treated it like a rotary scythe and tried to hide behind one another.

"Well, where's it gone?"

"How should I know?" said Twoflower.

"It's *your* Luggage!"

"I often don't know where my Luggage is, that's what being a tourist is all about," said Twoflower. "Anyway, it often wanders off by itself. It's probably best not to ask why."

It began to dawn on the mob that nothing was actually happening, and that Rincewind was in no condition to hurl insults, let alone magical fire. They advanced, watching his hands cautiously.

Twoflower and Bethan backed away. Twoflower looked around.

"Bethan?"

"What?" said Bethan, not taking her eyes off the advancing figures.

"This is a dead end."

"Are you sure?"

"I think I know a brick wall when I see one," said Twoflower reproachfully.

"That's about it, then," said Bethan.

"Do you think perhaps if I explain—?"

"No."

"Oh."

"I don't think these are the sort of people who listen to explanations," Bethan added.

Twoflower stared at them. He was, as has been mentioned, usually oblivious to personal danger. Against the whole of human experience Twoflower believed that if only people would talk to each other, have a few drinks, exchange pictures of their grandchildren, maybe take in a show or something, then everything could be sorted out. He also believed that people were basically good but sometimes had their bad days. What was coming down the street was having about the same effect on him as a gorilla in a glass factory.

There was the faintest of sounds behind him, not so much a sound in fact as a change in the texture of the air.

The faces in front of him gaped open, turned, and disappeared rapidly down the alley.

"Eh?" said Bethan, still propping up the now-unconscious Rincewind.

Twoflower was looking the other way, at a big glass window full of strange wares, and a beaded doorway, and a large sign above it all which now said, after its characters had finished writhing into position:

SKILLET, WANG, YRXLE!YT, BUNGLESTIFF, CWM-
LAD AND PATEL

ESTBLSHD: VARIOUS
PURVEYORS

The jeweler turned the gold slowly over the tiny anvil, tapping the last strangely-cut diamond into place.

"From a troll's tooth, you say?" he muttered, squinting closely at his work.

"Yesh," said Cohen, "and as I shay, you can have all the resht." He was fingering a tray of gold rings.

"Very generous," murmured the jeweler, who was dwarvish and knew a good deal when he saw one. He sighed.

"Not much work lately?" said Cohen. He looked out through the tiny window and watched a group of empty-eyed people gathered on the other side of the narrow street.

"Times are hard, yes."

"Who are all theshe guysh with the starsh painted on?" said Cohen.

The dwarf jeweler didn't look up.

"Madmen," he said. "They say I should do no work because the star comes. I tell them stars have never hurt me, I wish I could say the same about people."

Cohen nodded thoughtfully as six men detached themselves from the group and came toward the shop. They were carrying an assortment of weapons, and had a driven, determined look about them.

"Strange," said Cohen.

"I am, as you can see, of the dwarvish persuasion," said the jeweler. "One of the magical races, it is said. The star people believe that the star will not destroy the Disc if we turn aside from magic. They're probably going to beat me up a bit. So it goes."

He held up his latest work in a pair of tweezers.

"The strangest thing I have ever made," he said, "but practical, I can see that. What did you say they were called again?"

"Din-chewersh," said Cohen. He looked at the horseshoe shapes nestling in the wrinkled palm of his hand, then opened his mouth and made a series of painful grunting noises.

The door burst open. The men strode in and took up positions around the walls. They were sweating and uncertain, but their leader pushed Cohen aside disdainfully and picked up the dwarf by his shirt.

"We tole you yesterday, small stuff," he said. "You go out feet down or feet up, we don't mind. So now we gonna get really—"

Cohen tapped him on the shoulder. The man looked around irritably.

"What do you want, grandad?" he snarled.

Cohen paused until he had the man's full attention, and then he smiled. It was a slow, lazy smile, unveiling about three hundred carats of mouth jewelry that seemed to light up the room.

"I will count to three," he said, in a friendly tone of voice. "One. Two." His bony knee came up and buried itself in the man's groin with a satisfyingly meaty noise, and he half turned to bring the full force of an elbow into the kidneys as the leader collapsed around his private universe of pain.

"Three," he told the ball of agony on the floor. Cohen had heard of fighting fair, and had long ago decided he wanted no part of it.

He looked up at the other men, and flashed his incredible smile.

They ought to have rushed him. Instead one of them, secure in the knowledge that he had a broadsword and Cohen didn't, sidled crabwise toward him.

"Oh, no," said Cohen, waving his hands. "Oh, come on, lad, not like that."

The man looked sideways at him.

"Not like what?" he asked suspiciously.

"You never held a sword before?"

The man half turned to his colleagues for reassurance.

"Not a lot, no," he said. "Not often." He waved his sword menacingly.

Cohen shrugged. "I may be going to die, but I should hope I could be killed by a man who could hold his sword like a warrior," he said.

The man looked at his hands. "Looks all right," he said, doubtfully.

"Look, lad, I know a little about these things. I mean, come here a minute and—do you mind?—right, your left hand goes *here*, around the pommel, and your right hand goes—that's right, just *here*—and the blade goes right into your leg."

As the man screamed and clutched at his foot Cohen kicked his remaining leg away and turned to the room at large.

"This is getting fiddly," he said. "Why don't you rush me?"

"That's right," said a voice by his waist. The jeweler had produced a very large and dirty ax, guaranteed to add tetanus to all the other terrors of warfare.

The four men gave these odds some consideration, and backed toward the door.

"And wipe those silly stars off," said Cohen. "You can tell everyone that Cohen the Barbarian will be very angry if he sees stars like that again, right?"

The door slammed shut. A moment later the ax thumped into it, bounced off, and took a sliver of leather off the toe of Cohen's sandal.

"Sorry," said the dwarf. "It belonged to my grandad. I only use it for splitting firewood."

Cohen felt his jaw experimentally. The dine chewers seemed to be settling in quite well.

"If I was you, I'd be getting out of here anyway," he said. But the dwarf was already scuttling around the room, tipping trays of precious metal and gems into a leather sack. A roll of tools went into one pocket, a packet of finished jewelry went into another, and with a grunt the dwarf stuck his arms through handles on either side of his little forge and heaved it bodily onto his back.

"Right," he said. "I'm ready."

"You're coming with me?"

"As far as the city gates, if you don't mind," he said. "You can't blame me, can you?"

"No. But leave the ax behind."

They stepped out into the afternoon sun and a deserted street. When Cohen opened his mouth little pinpoints of bright light illuminated all the shadows.

"I've got some friends around here to pick up," he said, and added, "I hope they're all right. What's your name?"

"Lackjaw."

"Is there anywhere around here where I can—" Cohen paused lovingly, savoring the words— "where I can get a steak?"

"The star people have closed all the inns. They said it's wrong to be eating and drinking when—"

"I know, I know," said Cohen. "I think I'm beginning to get the hang of it. Don't they approve of anything?"

Lackjaw was lost in thought for a moment. "Setting fire to things," he said at last. "They're quite good at that. Books and stuff. They have these great big bonfires."

Cohen was shocked.

"Bonfires of books?"

"Yes. Horrible, isn't it?"

"Right," said Cohen. He thought it was appalling. Someone who spent his life living rough under the sky knew the value of a good thick book, which ought to outlast at least a season of cooking fires if you were careful how you tore the pages out. Many a life had been saved on a snowy night by a handful of sodden kindling and a really dry book. If you felt like a smoke and couldn't find a pipe, a book was your man every time.

Cohen realized people wrote things in books. It had always seemed to him to be a frivolous waste of paper.

"I'm afraid if your friends met them they might be in trouble," said Lackjaw sadly as they walked up the street.

They turned the corner and saw the bonfire. It was in the middle of the street. A couple of star people were feeding it with books from a nearby house, which had its door smashed in and had been daubed with stars.

News of Cohen hadn't spread too far yet. The book burners took no notice as he wandered up and leaned against the wall. Curly flakes of burnt paper bounced in the hot air and floated away over the rooftops.

"What are you doing?" he said.

One of the star people, a woman, pushed her hair out of her eyes with a soot-blackened hand, gazed intently at Cohen's left ear, and said, "Ridding the Disc of wickedness."

Two men came out of the building and glared at Cohen, or at least at his ear.

Cohen reached out and took the heavy book the woman was carrying. Its cover was crusted with strange red and black stones that spelled out what Cohen was sure was a word. He showed it to Lackjaw.

"The Necrotelecomnicon," said the dwarf. "Wizards use it. It's how to contact the dead, I think."

"That's wizards for you," said Cohen. He felt a page between finger and thumb; it was thin, and quite soft. The rather unpleasant organic-looking writing didn't worry him at all. Yes, a book like this could be a real friend to a man—

"Yes? You want something?" he said to one of the star men, who had gripped his arm.

"All books of magic must be burned," said the man, but a little uncertainly, because something about Cohen's teeth was giving him a nasty feeling of sanity.

"Why?" said Cohen.

"It has been revealed to us." Now Cohen's smile was as wide as all outdoors, and rather more dangerous.

"I think we ought to be getting along," said Lackjaw nervously. A party of star people had turned into the street behind them.

"*I* think I would like to kill someone," said Cohen, still smiling.

"The star directs that the Disc must be cleansed," said the man, backing away.

"Stars can't talk," said Cohen, drawing his sword.

"If you kill me a thousand will take my place,"

said the man, who was now backed against the wall.

"Yes," said Cohen, in a reasonable tone of voice, "but that isn't the point, is it? The point is, *you'll* be dead."

The man's Adam's apple began to bob like a yo-yo. He squinted down at Cohen's sword.

"There is that, yes," he conceded. "Tell you what—how about if we put the fire out?"

"Good idea," said Cohen.

Lackjaw tugged at his belt. The other star people were running toward them. There were a lot of them, many of them were armed, and it began to look as though things would become a little more serious.

Cohen waved his sword at them defiantly, and turned and ran. Even Lackjaw had difficulty in keeping up.

"Funny," he gasped, as they plunged down another alley, "I thought—for a minute—you'd want to stand—and fight them."

"Blow that—for a—lark."

As they came out into the light at the other end of the alley Cohen flung himself against the wall, drew his sword, stood with his head on one side as he judged the approaching footsteps, and then brought the blade around in a dead flat sweep at stomach height. There was an unpleasant noise and several screams, but by then Cohen was well away up the street, moving in the unusual shambling run that spared his bunions.

With Lackjaw pounding along grimly beside him

he turned off into an inn painted with red stars, jumped onto a table with only a faint whimper of pain, ran along it—while, with almost perfect choreography, Lackjaw ran straight underneath without ducking—jumped down at the other end, kicked his way through the kitchens, and came out into another alley.

They scurried around a few more turnings and piled into a doorway. Cohen clung to the wall and wheezed until the little blue and purple lights went away.

"Well," he panted, "what did you get?"

"Um, the cruet," said Lackjaw.

"Just that?"

"Well, I had to go *under* the table, didn't I? You didn't do so well yourself."

Cohen looked disdainfully at the small melon he had managed to skewer in his flight.

"This must be pretty tough here," he said, biting through the rind.

"Want some salt on it?" said the dwarf.

Cohen said nothing. He just stood holding the melon, with his mouth open.

Lackjaw looked around. The cul-de-sac they were in was empty, except for an old box someone had left against a wall.

Cohen was staring at it. He handed the melon to the dwarf without looking at him and walked out into the sunlight. Lackjaw watched him creep stealthily around the box, or as stealthily as is possible with joints that creaked like a ship under full sail, and prod it once or twice with his sword, but very gingerly, as if he half expected it to explode.

"It's just a box," the dwarf called out. "What's so special about a box?"

Cohen said nothing. He squatted down painfully and peered closely at the lock on the lid.

"What's in it?" said Lackjaw.

"You wouldn't want to know," said Cohen. "Help me up, will you?"

"Yes, but this box—"

"This box," said Cohen, "this box is—" he waved his arms vaguely.

"Oblong?"

"*Eldritch*," said Cohen mysteriously.

"Eldritch?"

"Yup."

"Oh," said the dwarf. They stood looking at the box for a moment.

"Cohen?"

"Yes?"

"What does eldritch mean?"

"Well, eldritch is—" Cohen paused and looked down irritably. "Give it a kick and you'll see."

Lockjaw's steel-capped dwarfboot whammed into the side of the box. Cohen flinched. Nothing else happened.

"I see," said the dwarf. "Eldritch means wooden?"

"No," said Cohen. "It—it oughtn't to have done that."

"I see," said Lackjaw, who didn't, and was beginning to wish Cohen hadn't gone out into all this hot sunlight. "It ought to have run away, you think?"

"Yes. Or bitten your leg off."

"Ah," said the dwarf. He took Cohen gently by the arm. "It's nice and shady over here," he said. "Why don't you just have a little—"

Cohen shook him off.

"It's watching that wall," he said. "Look, that's why it's not taking any notice of us. It's staring at the wall."

"Yes, that's right," said Lackjaw soothingly. "Of course it's watching that wall with its little eyes—"

"Don't be an idiot, it hasn't got any eyes," snapped Cohen.

"Sorry, sorry," said Lackjaw hurriedly. "It's watching the wall without eyes, sorry."

"I think it's worried about something," said Cohen.

"Well, it would be, wouldn't it," said Lackjaw. "I expect it just wants us to go off somewhere and leave it alone."

"I think it's very puzzled," Cohen added.

"Yes, it certainly looks puzzled," said the dwarf. Cohen glared at him.

"How can *you* tell?" he snapped.

It struck Lackjaw that the roles were unfairly reversing. He looked from Cohen to the box, his mouth opening and shutting.

"How can *you* tell?" he said. But Cohen wasn't listening anyway. He sat down in front of the box, assuming that the bit with the keyhole was the front, and watched it intently. Lackjaw backed away.

Funny, said his mind, but the damn thing *is* looking at me.

"All right," said Cohen, "I know you and me don't see eye to eye, but we're all trying to find someone we care for, okay?"

"I'm—" said Lackjaw, and realized that Cohen was talking to the box.

"So tell me where they've gone."

As Lackjaw looked on in horror the Luggage extended its little legs, braced itself, and ran full tilt at the nearest wall. Clay bricks and dusty mortar exploded around it.

Cohen peered through the hole. There was a small grubby storeroom on the other side. The Luggage stood in the middle of the floor, radiating extreme bafflement.

"Shop!" said Twoflower.

"Anyone here?" said Bethan.

"Urrgh," said Rincewind.

"I think we ought to sit him down somewhere and get him a glass of water," said Twoflower. "If there's one here."

"There's everything else," said Bethan.

The room was full of shelves, and the shelves were full of everything. Things that couldn't be accommodated on them hung in bunches from the dark and shadowy ceiling; boxes and sacks of everything spilled onto the floor.

There was no sound from outside. Bethan looked around and found out why.

"I've never seen so much stuff," said Twoflower.

"There's one thing it's out of stock of," said Bethan, firmly.

"How can you tell?"

"You just have to look. It's fresh out of exits."

Twoflower turned around. Where the door and window had been there were shelves stacked with boxes; they looked as though they had been there for a long time.

Twoflower sat Rincewind down on a rickety chair by the counter and poked doubtfully at the shelves. There were boxes of nails, and hairbrushes. There were bars of soap, faded with age. There was a stack of jars containing deliquescent bath salts, to which someone had fixed a rather sad and jaunty little notice announcing, in the face of all the evidence, that one would make an Ideal Gift. There was also quite a lot of dust.

Bethan peered at the shelves on the other wall, and laughed.

"Would you look at this!" she said.

Twoflower looked. She was holding a—well, it was a little mountain chalet, but with seashells stuck all over it, and then the perpetrator had written "A Special Souvenir" in pokerwork on the roof (which, of course, opened so that cigarettes could be kept in it, and played a tinny little tune).

"Have you ever seen anything like it?" she said.

Twoflower shook his head. His mouth dropped open.

"Are you all right?" said Bethan.

"I think it's the most beautiful thing I've ever seen," he said.

There was a whirring noise overhead. They looked up.

A big black globe had lowered itself from the darkness of the ceiling. Little red lights flashed on and off on it, and as they stared it spun around and looked at them with a big glass eye. It was menacing, that eye. It seemed to suggest very emphatically that it was watching something distasteful.

"Hallo?" said Twoflower.

A head appeared over the edge of the counter. It looked angry.

"I hope you were intending to pay for that," it said nastily. Its expression suggested that it expected Rincewind to say yes, and that it wouldn't believe him.

"This?" said Bethan. "I wouldn't buy this if you threw in a hatful of rubies and—"

"I'll buy it. How much?" said Twoflower urgently, reaching into his pockets. His face fell.

"Actually, I haven't got any money," he said. "It's in my Luggage, but I—"

There was a snort. The head disappeared from behind the counter, and reappeared from behind a display of toothbrushes.

It belonged to a very small man almost hidden behind a green apron. He seemed very upset.

"No money?" he said. "You come into my shop—"

"We didn't mean to," said Twoflower quickly. "We didn't notice it was there."

"It wasn't," said Bethan firmly. "It's magical, isn't it?"

The small shopkeeper hesitated.

"Yes," he reluctantly agreed. "A bit."

"A bit?" said Bethan. "A *bit* magical?"

"Quite a bit, then," he conceded, backing away, and, "All right," he agreed, as Bethan continued to glare at him. "It's magical. I can't help it. The bloody door hasn't been and gone again, has it?"

"Yes, and we're not happy about that thing in the ceiling."

He looked up, and frowned. Then he disappeared through a little beaded doorway half-hidden among the merchandise. There was a lot of clanking and whirring, and the black globe disappeared into the shadows. It was replaced by, in succession, a bunch of herbs, a mobile advertising something Two-flower had never heard of but which was apparently a bedtime drink, a suit of armor and a stuffed croc-odile with a lifelike expression of extreme pain and surprise.

The shopkeeper reappeared.

"Better?" he demanded.

"It's an improvement," said Twoflower, doubt-fully. "I liked the herbs best."

At this point Rincewind groaned. He was about to wake up.

There have been three general theories put forward to explain the phenomenon of the wandering shops or, as they are generically known, *tabernae vagantes*.

The first postulates that many thousands of years ago there evolved somewhere in the multiverse a race whose single talent was to buy cheap and sell dear. Soon they controlled a vast galactic empire or, as they put it, Emporium, and the more advanced members of the species found a way to equip their very shops with unique propulsion units that could break the dark walls of space itself and open up vast new markets. And long after the worlds of the Emporium perished in the heat death of their particular universe, after one last defiant fire sale, the wandering starshops still ply their trade, eating their way through the pages of spacetime like a worm through a three-volume novel.

The second is that they are the creation of a sympathetic Fate, charged with the role of supplying exactly the right thing at the right time.

The third is that they are simply a very clever way of getting around the various Sunday Closing acts.

All these theories, diverse as they are, have two things in common. They explain the observed facts, and they are completely and utterly wrong.

Rincewind opened his eyes and lay for a moment looking up at the stuffed reptile. It was not the best thing to see when awakening from troubled dreams . . .

Magic! So that's what it felt like! No wonder wizards didn't have much truck with sex!

Rincewind knew what orgasms were, of course, he'd had a few in his time, sometimes even in company, but nothing in his experience even approximated to that tight, hot moment when every nerve in his body streamed with blue-white fire and raw magic had blazed forth from his fingers. It filled you and lifted you and you surfed down the rising, curling wave of elemental force. No wonder wizards fought for power . . .

And so on. The Spell in his head had been doing it, though, not Rincewind. He was really beginning to hate that Spell. He was sure that if it hadn't frightened away all the other spells he'd tried to learn he could have been a decent wizard in his own right.

Somewhere in Rincewind's battered soul the worm of rebellion flashed a fang.

Right, he thought. You're going back into the Octavo, first chance I get.

He sat up.

"Where the hell is this?" he said, grabbing his head to stop it exploding.

"A shop," said Twoflower mournfully.

"I hope it sells knives because I think I'd like to cut my head off," said Rincewind. Something about the expression of the two opposite him sobered him up.

"That was a joke," he said. "Mainly a joke, anyway. Why are we in this shop?"

"We can't get out," said Bethan.

"The door's disappeared," added Twoflower helpfully.

Rincewind stood up, a little shakily.

"Oh," he said. "One of those shops?"

"All right," said the shopkeeper testily. "It's magical, yes, it moves around, yes, no, I'm not telling you why—"

"Can I have a drink of water, please?" said Rincewind.

The shopkeeper looked affronted.

"First no money, then they want a glass of water," he snapped. "That's just about—"

Bethan snorted and strode across to the little man, who tried to back away. He was too late.

She picked him up by his apron straps and glared at him eye to eye. Torn though her dress was, disarrayed though her hair was, she became for a moment the symbol of every woman who has caught a man with his thumb on the scales of life.

"Time is money," she hissed. "I'll give you thirty seconds to get him a glass of water. I think that's a bargain, don't you?"

"I say," Twoflower whispered. "She's a real terror when she's roused, isn't she?"

"Yes," said Rincewind, without enthusiasm.

"All right, all right," said the shopkeeper, visibly cowed.

"And then you can let us out," Bethan added.

"That's fine by me, I wasn't open for business anyway, I just stopped for a few seconds to get my bearings and you barged in!"

He grumbled off through the bead curtains and returned with a cup of water.

"I washed it out special," he said, avoiding Bethan's gaze.

Rincewind looked at the liquid in the cup. It had probably been clean before it was poured in, now drinking it would be genocide for thousands of innocent germs.

He put it down carefully.

"Now I'm going to have a good wash!" stated Bethan, and stalked off through the curtain.

The shopkeeper waved a hand vaguely and looked appealingly at Rincewind and Twoflower.

"She's not bad," said Twoflower. "She's going to marry a friend of ours."

"Does he know?"

"Things not so good in the starshop business?" said Rincewind, as sympathetically as he could manage.

The little man shuddered. "You wouldn't believe it," he said. "I mean, you learn not to expect much, you make a sale here and there, it's a living, you know what I mean? But these people you've got these days, the ones with these star things painted on their faces, well, I hardly have time to open the store and they're threatening to burn it down. Too magical, they say. So I say, of course magical, what else?"

"Are there a lot of them about, then?" said Rincewind.

"All over the Disc, friend. Don't ask me why."

"They believe a star is going to crash into the Disc," said Rincewind.

"Is it?"

"Lots of people think so."

"That's a shame. I've done good business here. Too magical, they say! What's wrong with magic, that's what I'd like to know?"

"What will you do?" said Twoflower.

"Oh, go to some other universe, there's plenty around," said the shopkeeper airily. "Thanks for telling me about the star, though. Can I drop you off somewhere?"

The Spell gave Rincewind's mind a kick.

"Er, no," he said, "I think perhaps we'd better stay. To see it through, you know."

"You're not worried about this star thing, then?"

"The star is life, not death," said Rincewind.

"How's that?"

"How's what?"

"You did it again!" said Twoflower, pointing an accusing finger. "You say things and then don't know you've said them!"

"I just said we'd better stay," said Rincewind.

"You said the star was life, not death," said Twoflower. "Your voice went all crackly and far away. Didn't it?" He turned to the shopkeeper for confirmation.

"That's true," said the little man. "I thought his eyes crossed a bit, too."

"It's the Spell, then," said Rincewind. "It's trying to take me over. It knows what's going to happen, and I think it wants to go to Ankh-Morpork. I want to go too," he added defiantly. "Can you get us there?"

"Is that the big city on the Ankh? Sprawling place, smells of cesspits?"

"It has an ancient and honorable history," said Rincewind, his voice stiff with injured civic pride.

"That's not how you described it to *me*," said Twoflower. "You told me it was the only city that actually started out decadent."

Rincewind looked embarrassed. "Yes, but, well, it's my home, don't you see?"

"No," said the shopkeeper, "not really. I always say home is where you hang your hat."

"Um, no," said Twoflower, always anxious to

enlighten. "Where you hang your hat is a hatstand. A home is—"

"I'll just go and see about setting you on your way," said the shopkeeper hurriedly, as Bethan came in. He scooted past her.

Twoflower followed him.

On the other side of the curtain was a room with a small bed, a rather grubby stove, and a three-legged table. Then the shopkeeper did something to the table, there was a noise like a cork coming reluctantly out of a bottle, and the room contained a wall-to-wall universe.

"Don't be frightened," said the shopkeeper, as stars streamed past.

"I'm not frightened," said Twoflower, his eyes sparkling.

"Oh," said the shopkeeper, slightly annoyed. "Anyway, it's just imagery generated by the shop, it's not real."

"And you can go anywhere?"

"Oh no," said the shopkeeper, deeply shocked. "There's all kinds of fail-safes built in, after all, there'd be no point in going somewhere with insufficient per capita disposable income. And there's got to be a suitable wall, of course. Ah, here we are, this is your universe. Very bijou, I always think. A sort of universette . . ."

Here is the blackness of space, the myriad stars gleaming like diamond dust or, as some people would say, like great balls of exploding hydrogen a very long way off. But then, some people would say anything.

A shadow starts to blot out the distant glitter, and it is blacker than space itself.

From here it also looks a great deal bigger, because space is not really big, it is simply somewhere to be big *in*. Planets are big, but planets are meant to be big and there is nothing clever about being the right size.

But this shape blotting out the sky like the footfall of God isn't a planet.

It is a turtle, ten thousand miles long from its crater-pocked head to its armored tail.

And Great A'Tuin is *huge*.

Great flippers rise and fall ponderously, warping space into strange shapes. The Discworld slides across the sky like a royal barge. But even Great A'Tuin is struggling now as it leaves the free depths of space and must fight the tormenting pressures of the solar shallows. Magic is weaker here, on the littoral of light. Many more days of this and the Discworld will be stripped away by the pressures of reality.

Great A'Tuin knows this, but Great A'Tuin can recall doing all this before, many thousands of years ago.

The astrochelonian's eyes, glowing red in the light of the dwarf star, are not focused on it but at a little patch of space nearby . . .

"Yes, but where are we?" said Twoflower. The shopkeeper, hunched over his table, just shrugged.

"I don't think we're *anywhere*," he said. "We're in a cotangent incongruity, I believe. I could be wrong. The shop generally knows what it's doing."

"You mean you don't?"

"I pick a bit up, here and there." The shopkeeper blew his nose. "Sometimes I land on a world where they understand these things." He turned a pair of small, sad eyes on Twoflower. "You've got a kind face, sir. I don't mind telling you."

"Telling me what?"

"It's no life, you know, minding the Shop. Never settling down, always on the move, never closing."

"Why don't you stop, then?"

"Ah, that's it, you see, sir—I can't. I'm under a curse, I am. A terrible thing." He blew his nose again.

"Cursed to run a shop?"

"Forever, sir, forever. And never closing! For hundreds of years! There was this sorcerer, you see. I did a terrible thing."

"In a shop?" said Twoflower.

"Oh, yes. I can't remember what it was he wanted, but when he asked for it I—I gave one of those sucking-in noises, you know, like whistling only backward?" He demonstrated.

Twoflower looked somber, but he was at heart a kind man and always ready to forgive.

"I see," he said slowly. "Even so—"

"That's not all!"

"Oh."

"I told him there was no demand for it!"

"After making the sucking noise?"

"Yes. I probably grinned, too."

"Oh, dear. You didn't call him squire, did you?"

"I—I may have done."

"Um."

"There's more."

"Surely not?"

"Yes, I said I could order it and he could come back next day."

"That doesn't sound too bad," said Twoflower, who alone of all the people in the multiverse allowed shops to order things for him and didn't object at all to paying quite large sums of money to reimburse the shopkeeper for the inconvenience of having a bit of stock in his store often for several hours.

"It was early closing day," said the shopkeeper.

"Oh."

"Yes, and I heard him rattling the doorhandle, I had this sign on the door, you know, it said something like 'Closed even for the sale of Necromancer cigarettes,' anyway, I heard him banging and I laughed."

"You laughed?"

"Yes. Like this. Hnufhnufhnufblort."

"Probably not a wise thing to do," said Twoflower, shaking his head.

"I know, I know. My father always said, he said, Do not peddle in the affairs of wizards . . . Anyway, I heard him shouting something about never closing again, and a lot of words I couldn't understand, and then the shop—the shop—the shop came *alive*."

"And you've wandered like this ever since?"

"Yes. I suppose one day I might find the sorcerer and perhaps the thing he wanted will be in stock. Until then I must go from place to place—"

"That was a terrible thing to do," said Twoflower.

The shopkeeper wiped his nose on his apron. "Thank you," he said.

"Even so, he shouldn't have cursed you quite so badly," Twoflower added.

"Oh. Yes, well." The shopkeeper straightened his apron and made a brave little attempt to pull himself together. "Anyway, this isn't getting you to Ankh-Morpork, is it?"

"Funny thing is," said Twoflower, "that I bought my Luggage in a shop like this, once. Another shop, I mean."

"Oh yes, there's several of us," said the shopkeeper, turning back to the table, "that sorcerer was a very impatient man, I understand."

"Endlessly roaming through the universe," mused Twoflower.

"That's right. Mind you, there is a saving on the rates."

"Rates?"

"Yes, they're—" the shopkeeper paused, and wrinkled his forehead. "I can't quite remember, it was such a long time ago. Rates, rates—"

"Very large mice?"

"That's probably it."

"Hold on—it's thinking about something," said Cohen.

Lackjaw looked up wearily. It had been quite nice,

sitting here in the shade. He had just worked out that in trying to escape from a city of crazed madmen he had appeared to have allowed one mad man to give him his full attention. He wondered whether he would live to regret this.

He earnestly hoped so.

"Oh yes, it's definitely thinking," he said bitterly. "Anyone can see that."

"I think it's found them."

"Oh, good."

"Hold onto it."

"Are you mad?" said Lackjaw.

"I know this thing, trust me. Anyway, would you rather be left with all these star people? They might be interested in having a talk with you."

Cohen sidled over to the Luggage, and then flung himself astride it. It took no notice.

"Hurry up," he said. "I think it's going to go."

Lackjaw shrugged, and climbed on gingerly behind Cohen.

"Oh?" he said, "and how does it g—"

Ankh-Morpork!

Pearl of cities!

This is not a completely accurate description, of course—it was not round and shiny—but even its worst enemies would agree that if you had to liken Ankh-Morpork to anything, then it might as well be a piece of rubbish covered with the diseased secretions of a dying mollusc.

There have been bigger cities. There have been richer cities. There have certainly been prettier cities. But no city in the multiverse could rival Ankh-Morpork for its smell.

The Ancient Ones, who know everything about all the universes and have smelled the smells of Calcutta and !Xrc—! and dauntocum Marsport, have agreed that even these fine examples of nasal poetry are mere limericks when set against the glory of the Ankh-Morpork smell.

You can talk about ramps. You can talk about garlic. You can talk about France. Go on. But if you haven't smelled Ankh-Morpork on a hot day you haven't smelled anything.

The citizens are proud of it. They carry chairs outside to enjoy it on a really good day. They puff out their cheeks and slap their chests and comment cheerfully on its little distinctive nuances. They have even put up a statue to it, to commemorate the time when the troops of a rival state tried to invade by stealth one dark night and managed to get to the top of the walls before, to their horror, their nose plugs gave out. Rich merchants who have spent many years abroad sent back home for specially stoppered and sealed bottles of the stuff, which brings tears to their eyes.

It has that kind of effect.

There is only really one way to describe the effect the smell of Ankh-Morpork has on the visiting nose, and that is by analogy.

Take a tartan. Sprinkle it with confetti. Light it with strobe lights.

Now take a chameleon.

Put the chameleon on the tartan.

Watch it closely.

See?

Which explains why, when the shop finally materialized in Ankh-Morpork, Rincewind sat bolt upright and said "We're here," Bethan went pale and Twoflower, who had no sense of smell, said, "Really? How can you tell?"

It had been a long afternoon. They had broken into realspace in a number of walls in a variety of cities because, according to the shopkeeper, the Disc's magical field was playing up and upsetting everything.

All the cities were empty of most of their citizens and belonged to roaming gangs of crazed left-ear people.

"Where do they all come from?" said Twoflower, as they fled yet another mob.

"Inside every sane person there's a madman struggling to get out," said the shopkeeper. "That's what I've always thought. No one goes mad quicker than a totally sane person."

"That doesn't make sense," said Bethan, "or if it makes sense, I don't like it."

The star was bigger than the sun. There would be no night tonight. On the opposite horizon the Disc's own sunlet was doing its best to set normally, but the general effect of all that red light was to make the city, never particularly beautiful, look like something painted by a fanatical artist after a bad time on the shoe polish.

But it was *home*. Rincewind peered up and down the empty street and felt almost happy.

At the back of his mind the Spell was kicking up a ruckus, but he ignored it. Maybe it was true that magic was getting weaker as the star got nearer, or perhaps he'd had the Spell in his head for so long he had built up some kind of psychic immunity, but he found he *could* resist it.

"We're in the docks," he declared. "Just smell that sea air!"

"Oh," said Bethan, leaning against the wall, "yes."

"That's ozone, that is," said Rincewind. "That's air with character, is that." He breathed deeply.

Twoflower turned to the shopkeeper.

"Well, I hope you find your sorcerer," he said. "Sorry we didn't buy anything, but all my money's in my Luggage, you see."

The shopkeeper pushed something into his hand.

"A little gift," he said. "You'll need it."

He darted back into his shop, the bell jangled, the sign saying Call Again Tomorrow For Spoonfetcher's Leeches, the Little Suckers banged forlornly against the door, and the shop faded into the brickwork as though it had never been. Twoflower reached out gingerly and touched the wall, not quite believing it.

"What's in the bag?" said Rincewind.

It was a thick brown paper bag, with string handles.

"If it sprouts legs I don't want to know about it," said Bethan.

Twoflower peered inside, and pulled out the contents.

"Is that all?" said Rincewind. "A little house with shells on?"

"It's very useful," said Twoflower defensively. "You can keep cigarettes in it."

"And they're what you really need, are they?" said Rincewind.

"I'd plump for a bottle of really strong suntan oil," said Bethan.

"Come on," said Rincewind, and set off down the street. The others followed.

It occurred to Twoflower that some words of comfort were called for, a little tactful small talk to take Bethan out of herself, as he would put it, and generally cheer her up.

"Don't worry," he said. "There's just a chance that Cohen might still be alive."

"Oh, I expect he's alive all right," she said, stamping along the cobbles as if she nursed a personal grievance against each one of them. "You don't live to be eighty-seven in his job if you go around dying all the time. But he's not here."

"Nor is my Luggage," said Twoflower. "Of course, that's not the same thing."

"Do you think the star is going to hit the Disc?"

"No," said Twoflower confidently.

"Why not?"

"Because Rincewind doesn't think so."

She looked at him in amazement.

"You see," the tourist went on, "you know that thing you do with seaweed?"

Bethan, brought up on the Vortex Plains, had

only heard of the sea in stories, and had decided she
didn't like it. She looked blank.

"Eat it?"

"No, what you do is, you hang it up outside your
door, and it tells you if it's going to rain."

Another thing Bethan had learned was that there
was no real point in trying to understand anything
Twoflower said, and that all anyone could do was
run alongside the conversation and hope to jump
on as it turned a corner.

"I see," she said.

"Rincewind is like that, you see."

"Like seaweed."

"Yes. If there was anything at all to be frightened
about, he'd be frightened. But he's not. The star is
just about the only thing I've ever seen him not
frightened of. If he's not worried, then take it from
me, there's nothing to worry about."

"It's not going to rain?" said Bethan.

"Well, no. Metaphorically speaking."

"Oh." Bethan decided not to ask what "metaphorically" meant, in case it was something to do with
seaweed.

Rincewind turned around.

"Come on," he said. "Not far now."

"Where to?" said Twoflower.

"Unseen University, of course."

"Is that wise?"

"Probably not, but I'm still going—" Rincewind
paused, his face a mask of pain. He put his hand to
his ears and groaned.

"Spell giving you trouble?"

"Yargh."

"Try humming."

Rincewind grimaced. "I'm going to get rid of this thing," he said thickly. "It's going back into the book where it belongs. I want my head back!"

"But then—" Twoflower began, and stopped. They could all hear it—a distant chanting and the stamping of many feet.

"Do you think it's star people?" said Bethan.

It was. The lead marchers came around a corner a hundred yards away, behind a ragged white banner with an eight-pointed star on it.

"Not just star people," said Twoflower. "All kinds of people!"

The crowd swept them up in its passage. One moment they were standing in the deserted street, the next they were perforce moving with a tide of humanity that bore them onward through the city.

Torchlight flickered easily on the damp tunnels far under the University as the heads of the eight Orders of wizardry filed onward.

"At least it's cool down here," said one.

"We shouldn't *be* down here."

Trymon, who was leading the party, said nothing. But he was thinking very hard. He was thinking about the bottle of oil in his belt, and the eight keys the wizards carried—eight keys that would fit the eight locks that chained the Octavo to its lectern. He was thinking that old wizards who sense that magic is draining away are preoccupied with their own problems and are perhaps less alert than they should be. He was thinking that within a few minutes the Octavo, the greatest concentration of magic on the Disc, would be under his hands.

Despite the coolness of the tunnel he began to sweat.

They came to a lead-lined door set in the sheer stone. Trymon took a heavy key—a good, honest iron key, not like the twisted and disconcerting keys that would unlock the Octavo—gave the lock a squirt of oil, inserted the key, turned it. The lock squeaked open protestingly.

"Are we of one resolve?" said Trymon. There was a series of vaguely affirmative grunts.

He pushed at the door.

A warm gale of thick and somehow oily air rolled over them. The air was filled with a high-pitched and unpleasant chittering. Tiny sparks of octarine fire flared off every nose, fingernail and beard.

The wizards, their heads bowed against the storm of randomized magic that blew out of the room, pushed forward. Half-formed shapes giggled and fluttered around them as the nightmare inhabitants of the Dungeon Dimensions constantly probed (with things that passed for fingers only because they were at the ends of their arms) for an unguarded entry into the circle of firelight that passed for the universe of reason and order.

Even at this bad time for all things magical, even in a room designed to damp down all magical vibrations, the Octavo was still crackling with power.

There was no real need for the torches. The Octavo filled the room with a dull, sullen light, which wasn't strictly light at all but the opposite of light; darkness isn't the opposite of light, it is simply its absence, and what was radiating from the book was the light that lies on the far side of darkness, the light fantastic.

It was a rather disappointing purple color.

As has been noted before, the Octavo was chained to a lectern carved into the shape of something that looked vaguely avian, slightly reptilian and horribly alive. Two glittering eyes regarded the wizards with hooded hatred.

"I saw it move," said one of them.

"We're safe so long as we don't touch the book," said Trymon. He pulled a scroll out of his belt and unrolled it.

"Bring that torch here," he said, *"and put that cigarette out!"*

He waited for the explosion of infuriated pride. But none came. Instead, the offending mage removed the dogend from his lips with trembling fingers and ground it into the floor.

Trymon exulted. So, he thought, they do what I say. Just for now, maybe—but just for now is enough.

He peered at the crabby writing of a wizard long dead.

"Right," he said, "let's see: 'To Appease Yt, The Thynge That Ys The Guardian . . .'"

The crowd surged over one of the bridges that linked Morpork with Ankh. Below it the river, turgid at the best of times, was a mere trickle which steamed.

The bridge shook under their feet rather more than it should. Strange ripples ran across the muddy remains of the river. A few tiles slid off the roof of a nearby house.

"What was that?" said Twoflower.

Bethan looked behind them, and screamed.

The star was rising. As the Disc's own sun scurried for safety below the horizon the great bloated ball of the star climbed slowly into the sky until the whole of it was several degrees above the edge of the world.

They pulled Rincewind into the safety of a doorway. The crowd hardly noticed them, but ran on, terrified as lemmings.

"The star's got spots on," said Twoflower.

"No," said Rincewind. "They're . . . things. Things going around the star. Like the sun goes around the Disc. But they're close in, because, because . . ." he paused. "I nearly know!"

"Know what?"

"I've got to get rid of this Spell!"

"Which way is the University?" said Bethan.

"This way!" said Rincewind, pointing along the street.

"It must be very popular. That's where everyone's going."

"I wonder why?" said Twoflower.

"Somehow," said Rincewind, "I don't think it's to enroll for evening classes."

In fact Unseen University was under siege, or at least those parts of it that extruded into the usual, everyday dimensions were under siege. The crowds outside its gates were, generally, making one of two demands. They were demanding that either a) the wizards should stop messing about and get rid of the star or, and this was the demand favored by the star people, that b) they should cease all magic and commit suicide in good order, thus ridding the Disc of the curse of magic and warding off the terrible threat in the sky.

The wizards on the other side of the walls had no idea how to do a) and no intention of doing b) and many had in fact plumped for c), which largely consisted of nipping out of hidden side doors and having it away on their toes as far as possible, if not faster.

What reliable magic still remained in the University was being channeled into keeping the great gates secure. The wizards were learning that while it was all very fine and impressive to have a set of gates that were locked by magic, it ought to have occurred to the builders to include some sort of emergency backup device such as, for example, a pair of ordinary, unimpressive stout iron bolts.

In the square outside the gates several large bonfires had been lit, for effect as much as anything else, because the heat from the star was scorching.

"But you can still see the stars," said Twoflower, "the other stars, I mean. The little ones. In a black sky."

Rincewind ignored him. He was looking at the gates. A group of star people and citizens were trying to batter them down.

"It's hopeless," said Bethan. "We'll never get in. Where are you going?"

"For a walk," said Rincewind. He was setting off determinedly down a side street.

There were one or two freelance rioters here, mostly engaged in wrecking shops. Rincewind took no notice, but followed the wall until it ran parallel to a dark alley that had the usual unfortunate smell of all alleys, everywhere.

Then he started looking very closely at the stonework. The wall here was twenty feet high, and topped with cruel metal spikes.

"I need a knife," he said.

"You're going to cut your way through?" said Bethan.

"Just find me a knife," said Rincewind. He started to tap stones.

Twoflower and Bethan looked at each other, and shrugged. A few minutes later they returned with a selection of knives, and Twoflower had even managed to find a sword.

"We just helped ourselves," said Bethan.

"But we left some money," said Twoflower. "I mean, we would have left some money, if we'd had any—"

"So he insisted on writing a note," said Bethan wearily.

Twoflower drew himself up to his full height, which was hardly worth it.

"I see no reason—" he began, stiffly.

"Yes, yes," said Bethan, sitting down glumly. "I know you don't. Rincewind, all the shops have been smashed open, there was a whole bunch of people across the street helping themselves to musical instruments, can you believe that?"

"Yeah," said Rincewind, picking up a knife and testing its blade thoughtfully. "Luters, I expect."

He thrust the blade into the wall, twisted it, and stepped back as a heavy stone fell out. He looked up, counting under his breath, and levered another stone from its socket.

"How did you do that?" said Twoflower.

"Just give me a leg up, will you?" said Rincewind. A moment later, his feet wedged into the holes he had created, he was making further steps halfway up the wall.

"It's been like this for centuries," his voice floated down. "Some of the stones haven't got any mortar. Secret entrance, see? Watch out below."

Another stone cracked into the cobbles.

"Students made it long ago," said Rincewind. "Handy way in and out after lights out."

"Ah," said Twoflower, "I *understand*. Over the wall and out to brightly lit tavernas to drink and sing and recite poetry, yes?"

"Nearly right except for the singing and the poetry, yes," said Rincewind. "A couple of these spikes should be loose—" There was a clang.

"There's not much of a drop this side," came his voice after a few seconds. "Come on, then. If you're coming."

And so it was that Rincewind, Twoflower and Bethan entered Unseen University.

Elsewhere on the campus—

The eight wizards inserted their keys and, with many a worried glance at one another, turned them. There was a faint little snicking sound as the lock slid open.

The Octavo was unchained. A faint octarine light played across its bindings.

Trymon reached out and picked it up, and none of the others objected. His arm tingled.

He turned toward the door.

"Now to the Great Hall, brothers," he said, "if I may lead the way—"

And there were no objections.

He reached the door with the book tucked under his arm. It felt hot, and somehow prickly.

At every step he expected a cry, a protest, and none came. He had to use every ounce of control to stop himself from laughing. It was easier than he could have imagined.

The others were halfway across the claustrophobic dungeon by the time he was through the door, and perhaps they had noticed something in the set of his shoulders, but it was too late because he had crossed the threshold, gripped the handle, slammed the door, turned the key, smiled the smile.

He walked easily back along the corridor, ignoring the enraged screams of the wizards who had just discovered how impossible it is to pass spells in a room built to be impervious to magic.

The Octavo *squirmed*, but Trymon held it tightly. Now he ran, putting out of his mind the horrible sensations under his arm as the book shape-changed into things hairy, skeletal and spiky. His hand went numb. The faint chittering noises he had been hearing grew in volume, and there were other sounds behind them—leering sounds, beckoning sounds, sounds made by the voices of unimaginable horrors that Trymon found it all too easy to imagine. As he ran across the Great Hall and up the main staircase the shadows began to move and re-form and close in around him, and he also became aware that something was following, something with skittery legs moving obscenely fast. Ice formed on the walls. Doorways lunged at him as he barreled past. Underfoot the stairs began to feel just like a tongue . . .

Not for nothing had Trymon spent long hours in the University's curious equivalent of a gymnasium, building up mental muscle. Don't trust the senses, he knew, because they can be deceived. The stairs are there, somewhere—will them to be there, summon them into being as you climb and, boy, you better get good at it. Because this isn't all imagination.

Great A'Tuin slowed.

With flippers the size of continents the skyturtle fought the pull of the star, and waited.

There would not be long to wait . . .

Rincewind sidled into the Great Hall. There were a few torches burning, and it looked as though it had been set up for some sort of magical work. But the ceremonial candlesticks had been overturned, the complex octograms chalked on the floor were scuffed as if something had danced on them, and the air was full of a smell unpleasant even by Ankh-Morpork's broad standards. There was a hint of sulfur to it, but that underlay something worse. It smelled like the bottom of a pond.

There was a distant crash, and a lot of shouting.

"Looks like the gates have gone down," said Rincewind.

"Let's get out of here," said Bethan.

"The cellars are this way," said Rincewind, and set off through an arch.

"Down *there?*"

"Yes. Would you rather stay here?"

He took a torch from its bracket on the wall and started down the steps.

After a few flights the walls stopped being paneled and were bare stone. Here and there heavy doors had been propped open.

"I heard something," said Twoflower.

Rincewind listened. There did seem to be a noise coming from the depths below. It didn't sound frightening. It sounded like a lot of people hammering on a door and shouting "Oi!"

"It's not those Things from the Dungeon Dimensions you were telling us about, is it?" said Bethan.

"They don't swear like that," said Rincewind. "Come on."

They hurried along the dripping passages, following the screamed curses and deep hacking coughs that were somehow reassuring; anything that wheezed like that, the listeners decided, couldn't possibly represent a danger.

At last they came to a door set in an alcove. It looked strong enough to hold back the sea. There was a tiny grille.

"Hey!" shouted Rincewind. It wasn't very useful, but he couldn't think of anything better.

There was a sudden silence. Then a voice from the other side of the door said, very slowly, "Who is out there?"

Rincewind recognized that voice. It had jerked him from daydreams into terror on many a hot classroom afternoon, years before. It was Lemuel Panter, who had once made it his personal business to hammer the rudiments of scrying and summoning into young Rincewind's head. He remembered the eyes like gimlets in a piggy face and the voice saying "And now Mister Rincewind will come out here and draw the relevant symbol on the board" and the million mile walk past the waiting class as he tried desperately to remember what the voice had been droning on about five minutes before. Even now his throat was going dry with terror and randomized guilt. The Dungeon Dimensions just weren't in it.

"Please sir, it's me, sir, Rincewind, sir," he squeaked. He saw Twoflower and Bethan staring at him, and coughed. "Yes," he added, in as deep a voice as he could manage. "That's who it is. Rincewind. Right."

There was a susurration of whispers on the other side of the door.

"Rincewind?"

"Prince who?"

"I remember a boy who wasn't any—"

"The spell, remember?"

"Rincewind?"

There was a pause. Then the voice said, "I suppose the key isn't in the lock, is it?"

"No," said Rincewind.

"What did he say?"

"He said no."

"Typical of the boy."

"Um, who is in there?" said Rincewind.

"The Masters of Wizardry," said the voice, haughtily.

"Why?"

There was another pause, and then a conference of embarrassed whispers.

"We, uh, got locked in," said the voice, reluctantly.

"What, with the Octavo?"

Whisper, whisper.

"The Octavo, in fact, isn't in here, in fact," said the voice slowly.

"Oh. But you are?" said Rincewind, as politely as possible while grinning like a necrophiliac in a morgue.

"That would appear to be the case."

"Is there anything we can get you?" said Two-flower anxiously.

"You could try getting us out."

"Could we pick the lock?" said Bethan.

"No use," said Rincewind. "Totally thief-proof."

"I expect Cohen would have been able to," said Bethan loyally. "Wherever he's got to."

"The Luggage would soon smash it down," agreed Twoflower.

"Well, that's it then," said Bethan. "Let's get out into the fresh air. Fresher air, anyway." She turned to walk away.

"Hang on, hang on," said Rincewind. "That's just typical, isn't it? Old Rincewind won't have any ideas, will he? Oh, no, he's just a makeweight, he is. Kick him as you pass. Don't rely on him, he's—"

"All right," said Bethan. "Let's hear it, then."

"—a nonentity, a failure, just a—what?"

"How are you going to get the door open?" said Bethan.

Rincewind looked at her with his mouth open. Then he looked at the door. It really was very solid, and the lock had a smug air.

But he had gotten in, once, long ago. Rincewind the student had pushed at the door and it had swung open, and then a moment later the Spell had jumped into his mind and ruined his life.

"Look," said a voice from behind the grille, as kindly as it could manage. "Just go and find us a wizard, there's a good fellow."

Rincewind took a deep breath.

"Stand back," he rasped.

"What?"

"Find something to hide behind," he barked, with his voice shaking only slightly. "You too," he said to Bethan and Twoflower.

"But you can't—"

"I mean it!"

"He means it," said Twoflower. "That little vein on the side of his forehead, you know, when it throbs like that, well—"

"Shut up!"

Rincewind raised one arm uncertainly and pointed it at the door.

There was total silence.

Oh gods, he thought, what happens now?

In the blackness at the back of his mind the Spell shifted uneasily.

Rincewind tried to get in tune or whatever with the metal of the lock. If he could sow discord amongst its atoms so that they flew apart—

Nothing happened.

He swallowed hard, and turned his attention to the wood. It was old and nearly fossilized, and probably wouldn't burn even if soaked in oil and dropped into a furnace. He tried anyway, explaining to the ancient molecules that they should try to jump up and down to keep warm—

In the strained silence of his own mind he glared at the Spell, which looked very sheepish.

He considered the air around the door itself, how it might best be twisted into weird shapes so that the door existed in another set of dimensions entirely.

The door sat there, defiantly solid.

Sweating, his mind beginning the endless walk up to the blackboard in front of the grinning class, he turned desperately to the lock again. It must be made of little bits of metal, not very heavy—

From the grille came the faintest of sounds. It was the noise of wizards untensing themselves and shaking their heads.

Someone whispered, *"I told you—"*

There was a tiny grinding noise, and a click.

Rincewind's face was a mask. Perspiration dripped off his chin.

There was another click, and the grinding of reluctant spindles. Trymon had oiled the lock, but the oil had been soaked up by the rust and dust of years, and the only way for a wizard to move something by magic, unless he can harness some external movement, is to use the leverage of his mind itself.

Rincewind was trying very hard to prevent his brain being pushed out of his ears.

The lock rattled. Metal rods flexed in pitted groves, gave in, pushed levers.

Levers clicked, notches engaged. There was a long drawn-out grinding noise that left Rincewind on his knees.

The door swung open on pained hinges. The wizards sidled out cautiously.

Twoflower and Bethan helped Rincewind to his feet. He stood gray-faced and swaying.

"Not bad," said one of the wizards, looking closely at the lock. "A little slow, perhaps."

"Never mind that!" snapped Jiglad Wert. "Did you three see anyone on the way down here?"

"No," said Twoflower.

"Someone has stolen the Octavo."

Rincewind's head jerked up. His eyes focused.

"Who?"

"Trymon—"

Rincewind swallowed. "Tall man?" he said. "Fair hair, looks a bit like a ferret?"

"Now that you mention it—"

"He was in my class," said Rincewind. "They always said he'd go a long way."

"He'll go a lot further if he opens the book," said one of the wizards, who was hastily rolling a cigarette in shaking fingers.

"Why?" said Twoflower. "What will happen?"

The wizards looked at one another.

"It's an ancient secret, handed down from mage to mage, and we can't pass it on to knowlessmen," said Wert.

"Oh, go on," said Twoflower.

"Oh well, it probably doesn't matter anymore. One mind can't hold all the spells. It'll break down, and leave a hole."

"What? In his head?"

"Um. No. In the fabric of the universe," said Wert. "He might think he can control it by himself, but—"

They felt the sound before they heard it. It started off in the stones as a slow vibration, then rose suddenly to a knife-edge whine that bypassed the eardrums and bored straight into the brain. It sounded like a human voice singing, or chanting, or screaming, but there were deeper and more horrible harmonics.

The wizards went pale. Then, as one man, they turned and ran up the steps.

There were crowds outside the building. Some people were holding torches, others had stopped in the act of piling kindling around the walls. But everyone was staring up at the Tower of Art.

The wizards pushed their way through the unheeding bodies, and turned to look up.

The sky was full of moons. Each one was three times bigger than the Disc's own moon, and each was in shadow except for a pink crescent where it caught the light of the star.

But in front of everything the top of the Tower of Art was an incandescent fury. Shapes could be dimly glimpsed within it, but there was nothing reassuring about them. The sound had changed now to the wasp-like buzzing, magnified a million times.

Some of the wizards sank to their knees.

"He's done it," said Wert, shaking his head. "He's opened a pathway."

"Are those things demons?" said Twoflower.

"Oh, demons," said Wert. "Demons would be a picnic compared with what's trying to come through up there."

"They're worse than anything we can possibly imagine," said Panter.

"I can imagine some pretty bad things," said Rincewind.

"These are worse."

"Oh."

"And what do you propose to do about it?" said a clear voice.

They turned. Bethan was glaring at them, arms folded.

"Pardon?" said Wert.

"You're wizards, aren't you?" she said. "Well, get on with it."

"What, tackle that?" said Rincewind.

"Know anyone else?"

Wert pushed forward. "Madam, I don't think you quite understand—"

"The Dungeons Dimensions will empty into our Universe, right?" said Bethan.

"Well, yes—"

"We'll all be eaten by things with tentacles for faces, right?"

"Nothing so pleasant, but—"

"And you're just going to let it happen?"

"Listen," said Rincewind. "It's all over, do you see? You can't put the spells back in the book, you can't unsay what's been said, you can't—"

"You can *try!*"

Rincewind sighed, and turned to Twoflower.

He wasn't there. Rincewind's eyes turned inevitably toward the base of the Tower of Art, and he was just in time to see the tourist's plump figure, sword inexpertly in hand, as it disappeared into a door.

Rincewind's feet made their own decision and, from the point of view of his head, got it entirely wrong.

The other wizards watched him go.

"Well?" said Bethan. "*He's* going."

The wizards tried to avoid one another's eyes.

Eventually Wert said, "We could try, I suppose. It doesn't seem to be spreading."

"But we've got hardly any magic to speak of," said one of the wizards.

"Have you got a better idea, then?"

One by one, their ceremonial robes glittering in the weird light, the wizards turned and trudged toward the tower.

The tower was hollow inside, with the stone treads of its staircase mortared spiral-fashion into the walls. Twoflower was already several turns up by the time Rincewind caught him.

"Hold on," he said, as cheerfully as he could manage. "This sort of thing is a job for the likes of Cohen, not you. No offense."

"Would he do any good?"

Rincewind looked up at the actinic light that lanced down through the distant hole at the top of the staircase.

"No," he admitted.

"Then I'd be as good as him, wouldn't I?" said Twoflower, flourishing his looted sword.

Rincewind hopped after him, keeping as close to the wall as possible.

"You don't understand!" he shouted. "There's unimaginable horrors up there!"

"You always said I didn't have any imagination."

"It's a point, yes," Rincewind conceded, "but—"

Twoflower sat down.

"Look," he said. "I've been looking forward to something like this ever since I came here. I mean, this is an adventure, isn't it? Alone against the gods, that sort of thing?"

Rincewind opened and shut his mouth for a few seconds before the right words managed to come out.

"Can you use a sword?" he said weakly.

"I don't know. I've never tried."

"You're mad!"

Twoflower looked at him with his head on one side. "You're a fine one to talk," he said. "I'm here because I don't know any better, but what about you?" He pointed downward, to where the other wizards were toiling up the stairs. "What about them?"

Blue light speared down the inside of the tower. There was a peal of thunder.

The wizards reached them, coughing horribly and fighting for breath.

"What's the plan?" said Rincewind.

"There isn't one," said Wert.

"Right. Fine," said Rincewind. "I'll leave you to get on with it, then."

"You'll come with us," said Panter.

"But I'm not even a proper wizard. You threw me out, remember?"

"I can't think of any student less able," said the old wizard, "but you're here, and that's the only qualification you need. Come on."

The light flared and went out. The terrible noises died as if strangled.

Silence filled the tower; one of those heavy, pressing silences.

"It's stopped," said Twoflower.

Something moved, high up against the circle of red sky. It fell slowly, turning over and over and drifting from side to side. It hit the stairs a turn above them.

Rincewind was first to it.

It was the Octavo. But it lay on the stone as limp and lifeless as any other book, its pages fluttering in the breeze that blew up the tower.

Twoflower panted up behind Rincewind, and looked down.

"They're blank," he whispered. "Every page is completely blank."

"Then he did it," said Wert. "He's read the spells. Successfully, too. I wouldn't have believed it."

"There was all that noise," said Rincewind doubtfully. "The light, too. Those shapes. That didn't sound so successful to me."

"Oh, you always get a certain amount of extradimensional attention in any great work of magic," said Panter dismissively. "It impresses people, nothing more."

"It looked like monsters up there," said Twoflower, standing closer to Rincewind.

"Monsters? Show me some monsters!" said Wert.

Instinctively they looked up. There was no sound. Nothing moved against the circle of light.

"I think we should go up and, er, congratulate him," said Wert.

"Congratulate?" exploded Rincewind. "He stole the Octavo! He locked you up!"

The wizards exchanged knowing looks.

"Yes, well," said one of them. "When you've advanced in the craft, lad, you'll know that there are times when the important thing is success."

"It's getting there that matters," said Wert bluntly. "Not how you travel."

They set off up the spiral.

Rincewind sat down, scowling at the darkness.

He felt a hand on his shoulder. It was Twoflower, who was holding the Octavo.

"This is no way to treat a book," he said. "Look, he's bent the spine right back. People always do that, they've got no idea of how to treat them."

"Yah," said Rincewind vaguely.

"Don't worry," said Twoflower.

"I'm not worried, I'm just angry," snapped Rincewind. "Give me the bloody thing!"

He snatched the book and snapped it open viciously.

He rummaged around in the back of his mind, where the Spell hung out.

"All right," he snarled. "You've had your fun, you've ruined my life, now get back to where you belong!"

"But I—" protested Twoflower.

"The Spell, I mean the Spell," said Rincewind. "Go on, get back on the page!"

He glared at the ancient parchment until his eyes crossed.

"Then I'll say you!" he shouted, his voice echoing up the tower. "You can join the rest of them and much good may it do you!"

He shoved the book back into Twoflower's arms and staggered off up the steps.

The wizards had reached the top and disappeared from view. Rincewind climbed after them.

"Lad, am I?" he muttered. "When I'm advanced in the craft, eh? I just managed to go around with one of the Great Spells in my head for years without going totally insane, didn't I?" He considered the last question from all angles. "Yes, you did," he reassured himself. "You didn't start talking to trees, even when trees started talking to *you*."

His head emerged into the sultry air at the top of the tower.

He had expected to see fire-blackened stones crisscrossed with talon marks, or perhaps something even worse.

Instead he saw the seven senior wizards standing by Trymon, who seemed totally unscathed. He turned and smiled pleasantly at Rincewind.

"Ah, Rincewind. Come and join us, won't you?"

So this is it, Rincewind thought. All that drama for nothing. Maybe I really am not cut out to be a wizard, maybe—

He looked up and into Trymon's eyes.

Perhaps it was the Spell, in its years of living in Rincewind's head, that had affected his eyes. Perhaps his time with Twoflower, who only saw things as they ought to be, had taught him to see things as they are.

But what was certain was that by far the most difficult thing Rincewind did in his whole life was look at Trymon without running in terror or being very violently sick.

The others didn't seem to have noticed.

They also seemed to be standing very still.

Trymon had tried to contain the seven Spells in

his mind and it had broken, and the Dungeon Dimensions had found their hole, all right. Silly to have imagined that the Things would have come marching out of a sort of rip in the sky, waving mandibles and tentacles. That was old-fashioned stuff, far too risky. Even nameless terrors learned to move with the times. All they really needed to enter was one head.

His eyes were empty holes.

Knowledge speared into Rincewind's mind like a knife of ice. The Dungeon Dimensions would be a playgroup compared to what the Things could do in a universe of order. People were craving order, and order they would get—the order of the turning screw, the immutable law of straight lines and numbers. They would beg for the harrow . . .

Trymon was looking at him. *Something* was looking at him. And still the others hadn't noticed. Could he even explain it? Trymon looked the same as he had always done, except for the eyes, and a slight sheen to his skin.

Rincewind stared, and knew that there were far worse things than Evil. All the demons in Hell would torture your very soul, but that was precisely because they valued souls very highly; evil would always try to steal the universe, but at least it considered the universe worth stealing. But the gray world behind those empty eyes would trample and destroy without even according its victims the dignity of hatred. It wouldn't even notice them.

Trymon held out his hand.

"The eighth spell," he said. "Give it to me."

Rincewind backed away.

"This is disobedience, Rincewind. I am your superior, after all. In fact, I have been voted the supreme head of all the Orders."

"Really?" said Rincewind hoarsely. He looked at the other wizards. They were immobile, like statues.

"Oh yes," said Trymon pleasantly. "Quite without prompting, too. Very democratic."

"I preferred tradition," said Rincewind. "That way even the dead get the vote."

"You will give me the spell voluntarily," said Trymon. "Do I have to show you what I will do otherwise? And in the end you will still yield it. You will scream for the opportunity to give it to me."

If it stops anywhere, it stops here, thought Rincewind.

"You'll have to take it," he said. "I won't give it to you."

"I remember you," said Trymon. "Not much good as a student, as I recall. You never really trusted magic, you kept on saying there should be a better way to run a universe. Well, you'll see. I have plans. We can—"

"Not we," said Rincewind firmly.

"Give me the Spell!"

"Try and take it," said Rincewind, backing away. "I don't think you can."

"Oh?"

Rincewind jumped aside as octarine fire flashed from Trymon's fingers and left a bubbling rock puddle on the stones.

He could sense the Spell lurking in the back of his mind. He could sense its fear.

In the silent caverns of his head he reached out for it. It retreated in astonishment, like a dog faced with a maddened sheep. He followed, stamping angrily through the disused lots and inner-city disaster areas of his subconscious, until he found it cowering behind a heap of condemned memories. It roared silent defiance at him, but Rincewind wasn't having any.

Is this it? he shouted at it. When it's time for the showdown, you go and hide? You're frightened?

The Spell said, that's nonsense, you can't possibly believe that, I'm one of the Eight Spells. But Rincewind advanced on it angrily, shouting, Maybe, but the fact is I do believe it and you'd better remember whose head you're in, right? I can believe anything I like in here!

Rincewind jumped aside again as another bolt of fire lanced through the hot night. Trymon grinned, and made another complicated motion with his hands.

Pressure gripped Rincewind. Every inch of his skin felt as though it was being used as an anvil. He flopped onto his knees.

"There are much worse things," said Trymon pleasantly. "I can make your flesh burn on the bones, or fill your body with ants. I have the power to—"

"I have a sword, you know."

The voice was squeaky with defiance.

Rincewind raised his head. Through a purple

haze of pain he saw Twoflower standing behind Trymon, holding a sword in exactly the wrong way.

Trymon laughed, and flexed his fingers. For a moment his attention was diverted.

Rincewind was angry. He was angry at the Spell, at the world, at the unfairness of everything, at the fact that he hadn't had much sleep lately, at the fact that he wasn't thinking quite straight. But most of all he was angry with Trymon, standing there full of the magic Rincewind had always wanted but had never achieved, and doing nothing worthwhile with it.

He sprang, striking Trymon in the stomach with his head and flinging his arms around him in desperation. Twoflower was knocked aside as they slid along the stones.

Trymon snarled, and got out the first syllable of a spell before Rincewind's wildly flailing elbow caught him in the neck. A blast of randomized magic singed Rincewind's hair.

Rincewind fought as he always fought, without skill or fairness or tactics but with a great deal of whirlwind effort. The strategy was to prevent an opponent getting enough time to realize that in fact Rincewind wasn't a very good or strong fighter, and it often worked.

It was working now, because Trymon had spent rather too much time reading ancient manuscripts and not getting enough healthy exercise and vitamins. He managed to get several blows in, which Rincewind was far too high on rage to notice, but he only used his hands while Rincewind employed knees, feet and teeth as well.

He was, in fact, winning.

This came as a shock.

It came as more of a shock when, as he knelt on Trymon's chest hitting him repeatedly about the head, the other man's face changed. The skin crawled and waved like something seen through a heat haze, and Trymon spoke.

"Help me!"

For a moment his eyes looked up at Rincewind in fear, pain and entreaty. Then they weren't eyes at all, but multifaceted things on a head that could be called a head only by stretching the definition to its limits. Tentacles and saw-edged legs and talons unfolded to rip Rincewind's rather sparse flesh from his body.

Twoflower, the tower and the red sky all vanished. Time ran slowly, and stopped.

Rincewind bit hard on a tentacle that was trying to pull his face off. As it uncoiled in agony he thrust out a hand and felt it break something hot and squishy.

They were watching. He turned his head, and saw that now he was fighting on the floor of an enormous amphitheater. On each side, tier upon tier of creatures stared down at him, creatures with bodies and faces that appeared to have been made by crossbreeding nightmares. He caught a glimpse of even worse things behind him, huge shadows that stretched into the overcast sky, before the Trymonmonster lunged at him with a barbed sting the size of a spear.

Rincewind dodged sideways, and then swung around with both hands clasped together into one fist that caught the thing in the stomach, or possibly the thorax, with a blow that ended in the satisfying crunch of chitin.

He plunged forward, fighting now out of terror of what would happen if he stopped. The ghostly arena was full of the chittering of the Dungeon creatures, a wall of rustling sound that hammered at his ears as he struggled. He imagined that sound filling the Disc, and he flung blow after blow to save the world of men, to preserve the little circle of firelight in the dark night of chaos and to close the gap through which the nightmare was advancing. But mainly he hit it to stop it hitting back.

Claws or talons drew white-hot lines across his back, and something bit his shoulder, but he found a nest of soft tubes among all the hairs and scales and squeezed it hard.

An arm barbed with spikes swept him away, and he rolled over in the gritty black dust.

Instinctively he curled into a ball, but nothing happened. Instead of the onslaught of fury he expected he opened his eyes to see the creature limping away from him, various liquids leaking from it.

It was the first time anything had ever run away from Rincewind.

He dived after it, caught a scaly leg, and wrenched. The creature chittered at him and flailed desperately with such appendages as were still working, but Rincewind's grip was unshakable. He pulled himself up and planted one last satisfying blow into its remaining eye. It screamed, and ran. And there was only one place for it to run to.

The tower and the red sky came back with the click of restored time.

As soon as he felt the press of the flagstones under his feet Rincewind flung his weight to one side and rolled on his back with the frantic creature at arm's length.

"Now!" he yelled.

"Now what?" said Twoflower. "Oh. Yes. Right!"

He swung the sword inexpertly but with some force, missing Rincewind by inches and burying it deeply in the Thing. There was a shrill buzzing, as though he had smashed a wasp's nest, and the melee of arms and legs and tentacles flailed in agony. It rolled again, screaming and thrashing at the flagstones, and then it was thrashing at nothing at all because it had rolled over the edge of the stairway, taking Rincewind with it.

There was a squelching noise as it bounced off a few of the stone steps, and then a distant and disappearing shriek as it tumbled the depth of the tower.

Finally there was a dull explosion and a flash of octarine light.

Then Twoflower was alone on the top of the tower—alone, that is, except for seven wizards who still seemed to be frozen to the spot.

He sat bewildered as seven fireballs rose out of the blackness and plunged into the discarded Octavo, which suddenly looked its old self and far more interesting.

"Oh dear," he said. "I suppose they're the Spells."

"Twoflower." The voice was hollow and echoing, and just recognizable as Rincewind's.

Twoflower stopped with his hand halfway to the book.

"Yes?" he said. "Is that—is that you, Rincewind?"

"Yes," said the voice, resonant with the tones of the grave. "And there is something very important I want you to do for me, Twoflower."

Twoflower looked around. He pulled himself together. So the fate of the Disc would depend on him, after all.

"I'm ready," he said, his voice vibrating with pride. "What is it you want me to do?"

"First, I want you to listen very carefully," said Rincewind's disembodied voice patiently.

"I'm listening."

"It's very important that when I tell you what to do you don't say 'What do you mean?' or argue or anything, understand?"

Twoflower stood to attention. At least, his mind stood to attention, his body really couldn't. He stuck out several of his chins.

"I'm ready," he said.

"Good. Now, what I want you to do is—"

"Yes?"

Rincewind's voice rose from the depths of the stairwell.

"I want you to come and help me up before I lose my grip on this stone," it said.

Twoflower opened his mouth, then shut it quickly. He ran to the square hole and peered down. By the ruddy light of the star he could just make out Rincewind's eyes looking up at him.

Twoflower lay down on his stomach and reached out. Rincewind's hand gripped his wrist in the sort of grip that told Twoflower that if he, Rincewind, wasn't pulled up then there was no possible way in which that grip was going to be relaxed.

"I'm glad you're alive," he said.

"Good. So am I," said Rincewind.

He hung around in the darkness for a bit. After the past few minutes it was almost enjoyable, but only almost.

"Pull me up, then," he hinted.

"I think that might be sort of difficult," grunted Twoflower. "I don't actually think I can do it, in fact."

"What are you holding on to, then?"

"You."

"I mean besides me."

"What do you mean, besides you?" said Twoflower.

Rincewind said a word.

"Well, look," said Twoflower. "The steps go around in a spiral, right? If I sort of swing you and then you let go—"

"If you're going to suggest I try dropping twenty feet down a pitch dark tower in the hope of hitting a couple of greasy little steps which might not even still be there, you can forget it," said Rincewind sharply.

"There is an alternative, then."

"Out with it, man."

"You could drop five hundred feet down a pitch black tower and hit stones which certainly are there," said Twoflower.

Dead silence came from below him. Then Rincewind said, accusingly, "That was sarcasm."

"I thought it was just stating the obvious."

Rincewind grunted.

"I suppose you couldn't do some magic—" Twoflower began.

"No."

"Just a thought."

There was a flare of light far below, and a confused shouting, and then more lights, more shouting, and a line of torches starting up the long spiral.

"There's some people coming up the stairs," said Twoflower, always keen to inform.

"I hope they're running," said Rincewind. "I can't feel my arm."

"You're lucky," said Twoflower. "I can feel mine."

The leading torch stopped its climb and a voice rang out, filling the hollow tower with indecipherable echoes.

"I think," said Twoflower, aware that he was gradually sliding farther over the hole, "that was someone telling us to hold on."

Rincewind said another word.

Then he said, in a lower and more urgent tone, "Actually, I don't think I can hang on any longer."

"Try."

"It's no good, I can feel my hand slipping!"

Twoflower sighed. It was time for harsh measures. "All right, then," he said. "Drop, then. See if I care."

"What?" said Rincewind, so astonished he forgot to let go.

"Go on, die. Take the easy way out."

"*Easy?*"

"All you have to do is plummet screaming through the air and break every bone in your body," said Twoflower. "Anybody can do it. Go on. I wouldn't want you to think that perhaps you ought to stay alive because we need you to say the Spells and save the Disc. Oh, no. Who cares if we all get burned up? Go on, just think of yourself. Drop."

There was a long, embarrassed silence.

"I don't know why it is," said Rincewind eventually, in a voice rather louder than necessary, "but ever since I met you I seem to have spent a lot of time hanging by my fingers over certain depth, have you noticed?"

"Death," corrected Twoflower.

"Death what?" said Rincewind.

"Certain death," said Twoflower helpfully, trying to ignore the slow but inexorable slide of his body across the flagstones. "Hanging over certain death. You don't like heights."

"Heights I don't mind," said Rincewind's voice from the darkness. "Heights I can live with. It's depths that are occupying my attention at the moment. Do you know what I'm going to do when we get out of this?"

"No?" said Twoflower, wedging his toes into a gap in the flagstones and trying to make himself immobile by sheer force of will.

"I'm going to build a house in the flattest country

I can find and it's only going to have a ground floor and I'm not even going to wear sandals with thick soles—"

The leading torch came around the last turn of the spiral and Twoflower looked down on the grinning face of Cohen. Behind him, still hopping awkwardly up the stones, he could make out the reassuring bulk of the Luggage.

"Everything all right?" said Cohen. "Can I do anything?"

Rincewind took a deep breath.

Twoflower recognized the signs. Rincewind was about to say something like, "Yes, I've got this itch on the back of my neck, you couldn't scratch it, could you, on your way past?" or "No, I enjoy hanging over bottomless drops" and he decided he couldn't possibly face that. He spoke very quickly.

"Pull Rincewind back onto the stairs," he snapped. Rincewind deflated in midsnarl.

Cohen caught him around the waist and jerked him unceremoniously onto the stones.

"Nasty mess down on the floor down there," he said conversationally. "Who was it?"

"Did it—" Rincewind swallowed, "did it have—you know—tentacles and things?"

"No," said Cohen. "Just the normal bits. Spread out a bit, of course."

Rincewind looked at Twoflower, who shook his head.

"Just a wizard who let things get on top of him," he said.

Unsteadily, with his arms screaming at him,

Rincewind let himself be helped back onto the roof of the tower.

"How did you get here?" he added.

Cohen pointed to the Luggage, which had trotted over to Twoflower and opened its lid like a dog that knows it's been bad and is hoping that a quick display of affection may avert the rolled-up newspaper of authority.

"Bumpy but fast," he said admiringly. "I'll tell you this, no one tries to stop you."

Rincewind looked up at the sky. It was indeed full of moons, huge cratered discs now ten times bigger than the Disc's tiny satellite. He looked at them without much interest. He felt washed out and stretched well beyond the breaking point, as fragile as ancient elastic.

He noticed that Twoflower was trying to set up his picture box.

Cohen was looking at the seven senior wizards.

"Funny place to put statues," he said. "No one can see them. Mind you, I can't say they're up to much. Very poor work."

Rincewind staggered across and tapped Wert gingerly on the chest. He was solid stone.

This is it, he thought. I just want to go home.

Hang on, I am home. More or less. So I just want a good sleep, and perhaps it will all be better in the morning.

His gaze fell on the Octavo, which was outlined in tiny flashes of octarine fire. Oh yes, he thought.

He picked it up and thumbed idly through its pages. They were thick with complex and swirling script that changed and re-formed even as he looked at it. It seemed undecided as to what it should be; one moment it was an orderly, matter-of-fact printing; the next a series of angular runes. Then it would be curly Kythian spellscript. Then it would be pictograms in some ancient, evil and forgotten writing that seemed to consist exclusively of unpleasant reptilian beings doing complicated and painful things to one another . . .

The last page was empty. Rincewind sighed, and looked in the back of his mind. The Spell looked back.

He had dreamed of this moment, how he would finally evict the Spell and take vacant possession of his own head and learn all those lesser spells which had, up until then, been too frightened to stay in his mind. Somehow he had expected it to be far more exciting.

Instead, in utter exhaustion and in a mood to brook no argument, he stared coldly at the Spell and jerked a metaphorical thumb over his shoulder.

You. Out.

It looked for a moment as though the Spell was going to argue, but it wisely thought better of it.

There was a tingling sensation, a blue flash behind his eyes, and a sudden feeling of emptiness.

When he looked down at the page it was full of words. They were runes again. He was glad about that; the reptilian pictures were not only unspeakable but probably unpronounceable too, and reminded him of things he would have great difficulty in forgetting.

He looked blankly at the book while Twoflower bustled around unheeded and Cohen tried in vain to lever the rings off the stone wizards.

He had to do something, he reminded himself. What was it, now?

He opened the book at the first page and began to read, his lips moving and his forefinger tracing the outline of each letter. As he mumbled each word it appeared soundlessly in the air beside him, in bright colors that streamed away in the night wind.

He turned over the page.

Other people were coming up the steps now—star people, citizens, even some of the Patrician's personal guard. A couple of star people made a halfhearted attempt to approach Rincewind, who was surrounded now by a rainbow swirl of letters and took absolutely no notice of them, but Cohen drew his sword and looked nonchalantly at them and they thought better of it.

Silence spread out from Rincewind's bent form like ripples in a puddle. It cascaded down the tower and spread out through the milling crowds below, flowed over the walls, gushed darkly through the city, and engulfed the lands beyond.

The bulk of the star loomed silently over the Disc. In the sky around it the new moons turned slowly and noiselessly.

The only sound was Rincewind's hoarse whispering as he turned page after page.

"Isn't this exciting!" said Twoflower. Cohen, who was rolling a cigarette from the tarry remnants of its ancestors, looked at him blankly, paper halfway to his lips.

"Isn't *what* exciting?" he said.

"All this magic!"

"It's only lights," said Cohen critically. "He hasn't even produced doves out of his sleeves."

"Yes, but can't you sense the occult potentiality?" said Twoflower.

Cohen produced a big yellow match from somewhere in his tobacco bag, looked at Wert for a moment, and with great deliberation struck the match on his fossilized nose.

"Look," he said to Twoflower, as kindly as he could manage. "What do you expect? I've been around a long time, I've seen the whole magical thing, and I can tell you that if you go around with your jaw dropping all the time people hit it. Anyway, wizards die just like anyone else when you stick a—"

There was a loud snap as Rincewind shut the book. He stood up, and looked around.

What happened next was this:

Nothing.

It took a little while for people to realize it. Everyone had ducked instinctively, waiting for the explosion of white light or scintillating fireball or, in the case of Cohen, who had fairly low expectations, a few white pigeons, possibly a slightly crumpled rabbit.

It wasn't even an interesting nothing. Sometimes things can fail to happen in quite impressive ways, but as far as non-events went this one just couldn't compete.

"Is that it?" said Cohen. There was a general muttering from the crowd, and several of the star people were looking angrily at Rincewind.

The wizard stared blearily at Cohen.

"I suppose so," he said.

"But nothing's happened."

Rincewind looked blankly at the Octavo.

"Maybe it has a subtle effect?" he said hopefully. "After all, we don't know exactly what is supposed to happen."

"We knew it!" shouted one of the star people. "Magic doesn't work! It's all illusion!"

A stone looped over the roof and hit Rincewind on the shoulder.

"Yeah," said another star person. "Let's get him!"

"Let's throw him off the tower!"

"Yeah, let's get him *and* throw him off the tower!"

The crowd surged forward. Twoflower held up his hands.

"I'm sure there's just been a slight mistake—" he began, before his legs were kicked from underneath him.

"Oh bugger," said Cohen, dropping his dogend and grinding it under a sandalled foot. He drew his sword and looked around for the Luggage.

It hadn't rushed to Twoflower's aid. It was standing in front of Rincewind, who was clutching the Octavo to his chest like a hot-water bottle and looking frantic.

A star man lunged at him. The Luggage raised its lid threateningly.

"I know why it hasn't worked," said a voice from the back of the crowd. It was Bethan.

"Oh yeah?" said the nearest citizen. "And why should we listen to you?"

A mere fraction of a second later Cohen's sword was pressed against his neck.

"On the other hand," said the man evenly, "perhaps we should pay attention to what this young lady has got to say."

As Cohen swung around slowly with his sword at the ready Bethan stepped forward and pointed to the swirling shapes of the spells, which still hung in the air around Rincewind.

"That one can't be right," she said, indicating a smudge of dirty brown amidst the pulsing, brightly colored flares. "You must have mispronounced a word. Let's have a look."

Rincewind passed her the Octavo without a word. She opened it and peered at the pages.

"What funny writing," she said. "It keeps changing. What's that crocodile thing doing to the octopus?"

Rincewind looked over her shoulder and, without thinking, told her. She was silent for a moment.

"Oh," she said levelly. "I didn't know crocodiles could do that."

"It's just ancient picture writing," said Rincewind hurriedly. "It'll change if you wait. The Spells can appear in every known language."

"Can you remember what you said when the wrong color appeared?"

Rincewind ran a finger down the page.

"There, I think. Where the two-headed lizard is doing—whatever it's doing."

Twoflower appeared at her other shoulder. The Spell flowed into another script.

"I can't even pronounce it," said Bethan. "Squiggle, squiggle, dot, dash."

"That's Cupumuguk snow runes," said Rincewind. "I think it should be pronounced 'zph.'"

"It didn't work, though. How about 'sph'?"

They looked at the word. It remained resolutely off-color.

"Or 'sff'?" said Bethan.

"It might be 'tsff,'" said Rincewind doubtfully. If anything the color became a dirtier shade of brown.

"How about 'zsff'?" said Twoflower.

"Don't be silly," said Rincewind. "With snow runes the—"

Bethan elbowed him in the stomach and pointed.

The brown shape in the air was now a brilliant red.

The book trembled in her hands. Rincewind grabbed her around the waist, snatched Twoflower by the collar, and jumped backward.

Bethan lost her grip on the Octavo, which tumbled toward the floor. And didn't reach it.

The air around the Octavo glowed. It rose slowly, flapping its pages like wings.

Then there was a plangent, sweet twanging noise

and it seemed to explode in a complicated silent flower of light which rushed outward, faded, and was gone.

But something was happening much farther up in the sky ...

Down in the geological depths of Great A'Tuin's huge brain new thoughts surged along neural pathways the size of arterial roads. It was impossible for a sky turtle to change its expression, but in some indefinable way its scaly, meteor-pocked face looked quite expectant.

It was staring fixedly at the eight spheres endlessly orbiting around the star, on the very beaches of space.

The spheres were cracking.

Huge segments of rock broke away and began the long spiral down to the star. The sky filled with glittering shards.

From the wreakage of one hollow shell a very small sky turtle paddled its way into the red light. It was barely bigger than an asteroid, its shell still shiny with molten yolk.

There were four small world-elephant calves on there, too. And on their backs was a Discworld, tiny as yet, covered in smoke and volcanoes.

Great A'Tuin waited until all eight baby turtles had freed themselves from their shells and were treading space and looking bewildered. Then, carefully, so as not to dislodge anything, the old turtle turned and with considerable relief set out on the long swim to the blessedly cool, bottomless depths of space.

The young turtles followed, orbiting their parent.

Twoflower stared raptly at the display overhead. He probably had the best view of anyone on the Disc.

Then a terrible thought occurred to him.

"Where's the picture box?" he asked urgently.

"What?" said Rincewind, eyes fixed on the sky.

"The picture box," said Twoflower. "I must get a picture of this!"

"Can't you just remember it?" said Bethan, not looking at him.

"I might forget."

"*I* won't ever forget," she said. "It's the most beautiful thing I've ever seen."

"Much better than pigeons and billiard balls," agreed Cohen. "I'll give you that, Rincewind. How's it done?"

"I dunno," said Rincewind.

"The star's getting smaller," said Bethan.

Rincewind was vaguely aware of Twoflower's voice arguing with the demon who lived in the box and painted the pictures. It was quite a technical argument, about field depths and whether or not the demon still had enough red paint.

It should be pointed out that currently Great A'Tuin was very pleased and contented, and feelings like that in a brain the size of several large cities are bound to radiate out. In fact most people on the Disc were currently in a state of mind normally achievable only by a lifetime of dedicated meditation or about thirty seconds of illegal herbage.

That's old Twoflower, Rincewind thought. It's not that he doesn't appreciate beauty, he just appreciates it in his own way. I mean, if a poet sees a daffodil he stares at it and writes a long poem about it, but Twoflower wanders off to find a book on botany. And treads on it. It's right what Cohen said. He just looks at things, but nothing he looks at is ever the same again. Including me, I suspect.

The Disc's own sun rose. The star was already dwindling, and it wasn't quite so much competition. Good reliable Disc light poured across the enraptured landscape, like a sea of gold.

Or, as the more reliable observers generally held, like golden syrup.

That is a nice dramatic ending, but life doesn't work like that and there were other things that had to happen.

There was the Octavo, for example.

As the sunlight hit it the book snapped shut and started to fall back to the tower. And many of the observers realized that dropping toward them was the single most magical thing on the Discworld.

The feeling of bliss and brotherhood evaporated along with the morning dew. Rincewind and Twoflower were elbowed aside as the crowd surged forward, struggling and trying to climb up one another, hands outstretched.

The Octavo dropped into the center of the shouting mass. There was a snap. A decisive snap, the sort of snap made by a lid that doesn't intend to be opening in a hurry.

Rincewind peered between someone's legs at Twoflower.

"Do you know what I think's going to happen?" he said, grinning.

"What?"

"I think that when you open the Luggage there's just going to be your laundry in there, that's what I think."

"Oh dear."

"I think the Octavo knows how to look after itself. Best place for it, really."

"I suppose so. You know, sometimes I get the feeling that the Luggage knows exactly what it's doing."

"I know what you mean."

They crawled to the edge of the milling crowd, stood up, dusted themselves off and headed for the steps. No one paid them any attention.

"What are they doing now?" said Twoflower, trying to see over the heads of the throng.

"It looks as though they're trying to lever it open," said Rincewind.

There was a snap and a scream.

"I think the Luggage rather enjoys the attention," said Twoflower, as they began their cautious descent.

"Yes, it probably does it good to get out and meet people," said Rincewind, "and now I think it'd do me good to go and order a couple of drinks."

"Good idea," said Twoflower. "I'll have a couple of drinks too."

It was nearly noon when Twoflower awoke. He couldn't remember why he was in a hayloft, or why he was wearing someone else's coat, but he did wake up with one idea right in the forefront of his mind.

He decided it was vitally important to tell Rincewind about it.

He fell out of the hay and landed on the Luggage.

"Oh, you're here, are you?" he said. "I hope you're ashamed of yourself."

The Luggage looked bewildered.

"Anyway, I want to comb my hair. Open up," said Twoflower.

The Luggage obligingly flipped its lid. Twoflower rooted around among the bags and boxes inside until he found a comb and mirror and repaired some of the damage of the night. Then he looked hard at the Luggage.

"I suppose you wouldn't like to tell me what you've done with the Octavo?"

The Luggage's expression could only be described as wooden.

"All right. Come on, then."

Twoflower stepped out into the sunlight, which was slightly too bright for his current tastes, and wandered aimlessly along the street. Everything seemed fresh and new, even the smells, but there didn't seem to be many people up yet. It had been a long night.

He found Rincewind at the foot of the Tower of Art, supervising a team of workmen who had rigged up a gantry of sorts on the roof and were lowering the stone wizards to the ground. He seemed to be assisted by a monkey, but Twoflower was in no mood to be surprised at anything.

"Will they be able to be turned back?" he said.

Rincewind looked around. "What? Oh, it's you. No, probably not. I'm afraid they dropped poor old Wert, anyway. Five hundred feet onto cobbles."

"Will you be able to do anything about that?"

"Make a nice rockery." Rincewind turned and waved at the workmen.

"You're very cheerful," said Twoflower, a shade reproachfully. "Didn't you go to bed?"

"Funny thing, I couldn't sleep," said Rincewind. "I came out for a breath of fresh air, and no one seemed to have any idea what to do, so I just sort of got people together," he indicated the librarian, who tried to hold his hand, "and started organizing things. Nice day, isn't it? Air like wine."

"Rincewind, I've decided that—"

"You know, I think I might re-enroll," said Rincewind cheerfully. "I think I could really make a go of things this time. I can really see myself getting to grips with magic and graduating really well. They do say if it's summa cum laude, then the living is easy—"

"Good, because—"

"There's plenty of room at the top, too, now all the big boys will be doing doorstop duty, and—"

"I'm going home."

"—a sharp lad with a bit of experience of the world could—what?"

"Oook?"

"I said I'm going home," repeated Twoflower, making polite little attempts to shake off the librarian, who was trying to pick lice off him.

"What home?" said Rincewind, astonished.

"Home home. My home. Where I live," Twoflower explained sheepishly. "Back across the sea. You know. Where I came from. Will you please stop doing that?"

"Oh."

"Oook?"

There was a pause. Then Twoflower said, "You see, last night it occurred to me, I thought, well, the thing is, all this traveling and seeing things is fine but there's also a lot of fun to be had from having been. You know, sticking all your pictures in a book and remembering things."

"There is?"

"Oook?"

"Oh, yes. The important thing about having lots of things to remember is that you've got to go somewhere afterward where you can remember them, you see? You've got to stop. You haven't really been anywhere until you've got back home. I think that's what I mean."

Rincewind ran the sentence across his mind again. It didn't seem any better second time around.

"Oh," he said again. "Well, good. If that's the way you look at it. When are you going, then?"

"Today, I think. There's bound to be a ship going part of the way."

"I expect so," said Rincewind awkwardly. He looked at his feet. He looked at the sky. He cleared his throat.

"We've been through some times together, eh?" said Twoflower, nudging him in the ribs.

"Yeah," said Rincewind, contorting his face into something like a grin.

"You're not upset, are you?"

"Who, me?" said Rincewind. "Gosh, no. Hundred and one things to do."

"That's all right, then. Listen, let's go and have breakfast and then we can go down to the docks."

Rincewind nodded dismally, turned to his assistant, and took a banana out of his pocket.

"You've got the hang of it now, you take over," he muttered.

"Oook."

In fact there wasn't any ship going anywhere near the Agatean Empire, but that was an academic point because Twoflower simply counted gold pieces into the hand of the first captain with a halfway clean ship until the man suddenly saw the merits of changing his plans.

Rincewind waited on the quayside until Twoflower had finished paying the man about forty times more than his ship was worth.

"That's settled, then," said Twoflower. "He'll drop me at the Brown Islands and I can easily get a ship from there."

"Great," said Rincewind.

Twoflower looked thoughtful for a moment. Then he opened the Luggage and pulled out a bag of gold.

"Have you seen Cohen and Bethan?" he said.

"I think they went off to get married," said Rincewind. "I heard Bethan say it was now or never."

"Well, when you see them give them this," said Twoflower, handing him the bag. "I know it's expensive, setting up home for the first time."

Twoflower had never fully understood the gulf in the exchange rate. The bag could quite easily set Cohen up with a small kingdom.

"I'll hand it over first chance I get," he said, and to his own surprise realized that he meant it.

"Good. I've thought about something to give you, too."

"Oh, there's no—"

Twoflower rummaged in the Luggage and produced a large sack. He began to fill it with clothes and money and the picture box until finally the Luggage was completely empty. The last thing he put in was his souvenir musical cigarette box with the shell-encrusted lid, carefully wrapped in soft paper.

"It's all yours," he said, shutting the Luggage's lid. "I shan't really need it anymore, and it won't fit on my wardrobe anyway."

"What?"

"Don't you want it?"

"Well, I—of course, but—it's yours. It follows you, not me."

"Luggage," said Twoflower, "this is Rincewind. You're his, right?"

The Luggage slowly extended its legs, turned very deliberately and looked at Rincewind.

"I don't think it belongs to anyone but itself, really," said Twoflower.

"Yes," said Rincewind uncertainly.

"Well, that's about it, then," said Twoflower. He held out his hand.

"Goodbye, Rincewind. I'll send you a postcard when I get home. Or something."

"Yes. Anytime you're passing, there's bound to be someone here who knows where I am."

"Yes. Well. That's it, then."

"That's it, right enough."

"Right."

"Yep."

Twoflower walked up the gangplank, which the impatient crew hauled up behind him.

The rowing drum started its beat and the ship was propelled slowly out onto the turbid waters of the Ankh, now back to their old level, where it caught the tide and turned toward the open sea.

Rincewind watched it until it was a dot. Then he looked down at the Luggage. It stared back at him.

"Look," he said. "Go away. I'm giving you to yourself, do you understand?"

He turned his back on it and stalked away. After a few seconds he was aware of the little footsteps behind him. He spun around.

"I said I don't want you!" he snapped, and gave it a kick.

The Luggage sagged. Rincewind stalked away.

After he had gone a few yards he stopped and listened. There was no sound. When he turned the Luggage was where he had left it. It looked sort of huddled. Rincewind thought for a while.

"All right, then," he said. "Come on."

He turned his back and strode off to the University. After a few minutes the Luggage appeared to make up its mind, extended its legs again and padded after him. It didn't see that it had a lot of choice.

They headed along the quay and into the city, two dots on a dwindling landscape which, as the perspective broadened, included a tiny ship starting out across a wide green sea that was but a part of a bright circling ocean on a cloud-swirled Disc on the back of four giant elephants that themselves stood on the shell of an enormous turtle.

Which soon became a glint among the stars, and disappeared.